SoulShares

HARD AS STONE

BOOK ONE

Rory Ni Coileain

For more information contact:
Riverdale Avenue Books
5676 Riverdale Avenue
Riverdale, NY 10471.

www.riverdaleavebooks.com

Design by www.formatting4U.com
Cover by Insatiable Fantasy Designs Inc.

Digital ISBN 9781626011922
Print ISBN 9781626011939

Second Edition May 2015
First Edition, Jan 2013 by Ravenous Romance

Dedication

To my son, who is made of pure awesome.
To my mom, who's always had my back.
And to the memory of my dad, the reason my veins
flow with printer's ink.
I love you, and I hope I've made you proud.

PROLOGUE

The Realm
165 years ago

"The kinslayer's awake."

Tiernan heard the words like the loving caress of a needle blade driven directly into his ear. It was also dark around him and cold. Well, no. Yes, it was cold, but not necessarily dark; whatever covered his head let in just enough light to give his eyes the same sweet attention his ears had already received. He tried to raise a hand to magick off the sack—or whatever the hell it was—but the vicious cramp in his gut told him his hands were chained with truesilver an instant before he felt the cool clasp around his wrists.

His movement, as slight as it was, was greeted by the sound of steel being drawn. A hell of a lot of steel. Tiernan froze, even his lip hidden by his shroud ceasing to curl. He was sick, probably drugged, blinded, and truechained, against at least six. Not odds he liked.

"Wise choice, kinslayer."

If the sound of swords had paralyzed his body, the voice reaching him through the darkness damn near stopped his heart. Ardan Carraig. The Prince Royal of Tiernan's own house, that of Earth. And… *kinslayer*. The word was like ice. *I. Am. SO. Fucked.*

Tiernan drew in a deep, slow breath. The Prince didn't necessarily know anything. And even if Ardan thought he knew, the crime of which he was accusing Tiernan was so unthinkable for a Fae, he might yet be persuaded he *didn't* know, after all.

"Highness." The word didn't so much issue from his throat as crawl out over shards of broken glass; he coughed and tried again. "Highness, are the chains really necessary?" The truesilver, which had been quiescent while he was unconscious, was heating now that he was awake, and feeding off the magick inherent in his nature. If he tried to actively use magick, or had any used on him, he'd be greeted with a twist to his gut like the length of it wrapped round a spiked pole, and more heat as well. He'd end up permanently branded, or worse. Although there was at least the possibility he wouldn't be around to care.

Growls came from several places around wherever he was. From the echoes, it sounded like a stone cell of some kind. Small. And crowded.

"Hands that slew a brother should be severed. Would you prefer that?" Ardan's voice was cold, almost a monotone. "It could be arranged easily enough." Someone muttered, as if in agreement or perhaps it was meant as an offer of help in the arranging.

A muscle jumped in Tiernan's jaw. *He has no proof. There's no fucking **corpse**.* "If those are my choices, Highness, I'll wear the chains. But why?"

A booted foot slammed into his kidneys, and he

shouted as his back spasmed hard, arching like a speared fish. "Do you insult our intelligence, boy? Or our honor?" Tiernan couldn't quite place the voice, especially over his gasps of pain, but somehow it sounded as if the speaker wore the tabard of the Royal Defense. Trimmed with gold, no doubt, And probably stained with the blood of the last luckless son of a bitch who'd pissed him off.

"Is there…" He sucked in a breath. "…any answer… that won't get me another one of those?" Tiernan realized in that moment, something in him had accepted his imminent death, and had apparently chosen this way to embrace it. Well, fuck it. The Prince Royal could get away with using that tone with him. But Tiernan Guaire was of a Noble house and line—albeit a line now shorter by one—and he still had some small shred of pride left to die with.

"Highness, time grows short."

Tiernan cursed under his breath as another piece of what must have happened to him during the last few hours fell into place in his abused brain. This voice he knew; he'd last heard it over cheap *uiscebai* in The Maid's Round Heels. His hands had still been shaking from the committing of murder and the aftermath of the magick that had done away with the evidence, and a shot or two of the amber liquor with his chance-met former lover had seemed just the camouflage for that little problem at the time. But he'd forgotten the dear boy's sister was in the Royal Defense, and he'd also overlooked the peculiar taste of the *uiscebai.*

Shit.

"What did you put in my drink, Niall? *Veissin*, I'm guessing from the headache, and knowing that you're too damned cheap to spring for anything that could have done the job without leaving me with—"

This kick caught him in the throat and left him gagging. "You're lucky the Prince Royal had a sworn warrant for your delivery alive." Niall's usual silken tenor had taken on a hard edge, disgust and anger. "Else you'd be dead by now, and I'd have had much more pleasure by it than dragging your oblivious ass here from the tavern afforded me."

Tiernan shook his head, trying to clear the last of the drugged haze from it. "So sorry my ass seems to have lost its capacity to please you—"

The sack was pulled off Tiernan's head, cutting him off mid-jibe. His head was jerked up, then slammed back down onto a floor of black stone. Bright lights flashed behind his eyelids, and he groaned. And then he groaned again, as he opened his eyes to try for more than a brief glimpse of his surroundings. Torchlight flared, dazzling him until his eyes watered and his skull pounded. Whoever had removed the sack stood before him. Blinking tears out of his eyes, Tiernan recognized the boots. Niall had always been one for leather play, and the boy *did* love his spikes.

He struggled up onto an elbow, awkwardly since his wrists were still chained together, with blisters rising under the truesilver links. The room lurched, swam, and finally came into focus, though the edges of things still seemed to vibrate with the beating of his heart. Niall was nearest, stepping back in the sudden silence to give him a clear view of the pale, raven-haired Prince Royal. In that moment, Ardan could have been sculpted of stone, every inch an embodiment of the element of his Demesne. He was clad all in black, wearing both his circlet of rank and his signet. Tiernan's heart sank. Whether or not there was any evidence against him, the Prince had obviously come prepared to pass sentence, and Tiernan was as good as dead.

Surrounding the Prince Royal stood men who Tiernan knew well, the heads of the four Noble houses of Earth other than his own, likewise arrayed for judgment in their various somber finery, together with a lapdog bodyguard from the Royal Defense, a sandy-haired swordsman with a bored expression but a fine array of weaponry. The round room itself was unremarkable, with walls of ancient stone, the only visible feature being torches fixed in wall brackets..The floor was black stone, smooth and featureless, almost mirrorlike.

Mirrorlike? No. Something in the floor was catching the torchlight. No one spoke or moved as Tiernan studied the elaborate tracing of hair-fine silver wire set into the gleaming black surface. His heart started racing, bile rose in his throat. "You're exiling me." The polished floor showed him his own eyes gone wide with fear, whites clear around the blue of them, before he turned his gaze on the Prince and the four councilors who flanked him with drawn swords. "To the human realm."

The Prince Royal nodded gravely. His gaze flickered from side to side, as if to take in the four Heads of House. "Execution would also have been proper, but there was no one who wished to defile a blade with a kinslayer's blood." Ardan's fingers tightened around the hilt of his own undrawn sword, as if they took issue with the decision. "We could have left you here to await the opening of the portal alone, but your accuser is oathbound, and wished to confront you."

Tiernan's head bowed as he fought to stop the room from spinning. No lawful decision could have been taken in his case, of course, not without a vote from the head of Tiernan's own House, and since that particular piece of shit had bled out his life at Tiernan's hand several hours previously, it wasn't fucking likely. But even that notion faded away to nothing beside the Prince Royal's assertion of someone bringing an accusation against him. There had been *no one* there...no one but himself, his brother, and the one he'd killed the bastard to protect and avenge. "That's... not possible." His voice was thick, unsteady. No one could be oath-bound for him, sworn not to eat or drink or sleep until justice was done against him. No one.

Ardan beckoned, and someone stepped over Tiernan from behind. The face attached to the legs wasn't one the Fae knew, but it undoubtedly belonged to the hard-case who had kicked him in the kidneys. Tiernan tried to rise again, opened his mouth to protest. He'd never laid eyes on the fucker in his life, and he wasn't going to go meekly into exile based on a lie—

He closed his mouth again, this time on a sob, as the Defender extended a hand to help another step over his prone body. Moriath. Still in the mud-stained silk she'd been wearing when he pulled their brother off her, still barefoot, her face bruised, her long fair hair now caught back with a length of cord, but still disheveled and filthy.

The eyes she turned on him were red with

weeping, but her lips curled in a knife-edged snarl. "I assure you it's more than *possible*." She spat the word at him, and looked ready to follow it with teeth, nails, and anything else capable of doing damage. "Did you think I'd let Lorcan go unavenged?"

"But he—" The words stuck in his throat. The naked pain in her eyes rendered him mute. She suffered, not for him, but for the feral creature who dared to defile her. For what he, Tiernan, had done to that animal.

And his own pain was more than a match for hers. By her bearing, and her silence, she told him she refused to have it known what their brother had done to her; she loved her older brother enough to wish to keep his name and his memory clean of his crimes, and had instead chosen to give the younger up to face a kinslayer's fate. That he loved her enough to avenge her honor, even on the body of his own brother, meant nothing to her.

"He will be well avenged, then." Tiernan kept his voice low, kept tight rein over his rage and despair and the hurt, deeper than bone and blood. He looked up at his sister, seeing all at once the beauty even Lorcan's malice and lust hadn't been able to mar, and the coldness all his own love had proved insufficient to touch. Perhaps there was some flaw in his bloodline? Love of kin was the only love that endured, among the Fae; though other loves were not unheard of, no other ever lasted through the centuries of a Fae's life. But love of kin had mattered not to Lorcan Guaire, and if it mattered to Moriath, it was only in some dark and twisted way. And to Tiernan himself? "Do you know what will happen to me, sister mine?"

Her dark blue eyes could have been Fire Fae, for the sparks they shot at him. "I only wish I could watch it happen, watch the Pattern sunder your soul."

Tiernan's gaze involuntarily went to the silver tracing within the gleaming black surface of the floor. His soul would be torn in two... protection of a sort, for a Fae condemned to exile in the human realm abandoned by his kind nearly two thousand years ago. A half-souled Fae, it was said by those of the Realm, could not die; and half-souled he would live, unless he chanced to meet, and love, the human who would someday be born with the part of his soul that was about to be wrenched from him.

And what chance was there of that? When his line was clearly incapable even of the one kind of love the Fae knew? He would be safe. And alone. Forever.

His eyes met hers, held them. "Beware Niall, sister. Whatever you promised him, to persuade him to deliver me up, it won't sate him long." He smiled, just a little, as she tried to cover her shock—had she believed him too stupid to put the pieces together? Or had she assumed he would be too stunned to care? "Nothing ever does—I learned that long ago."

"Lady Moriath." Ardan's deep voice cut in, and her head jerked around... and the heart Tiernan thought scarred past any further pain wrenched once more. His older sister was now the head of House Guaire. And the votes of the heads of all the Houses would have been required, in order for him to have been lawfully condemned to exile.

She shot him one final, cold, triumphant smile before turning her full attention to the waiting Prince. "Highness." Her bare feet glided over the polished floor; she moved to stand beside the Prince Royal, capturing Niall's hand on the way. *Oh, you'll regret that one day, snake.* Something in him cried out, already torn, as he thought of his sister so. But that something fell grimly silent as it watched her go, the tear already beginning to scar over. There was no room for love in the heart he would take to whatever new life awaited him.

The Heads of House, Niall, and their Defender escorts gathered around the Prince Royal. For some reason, Tiernan thought of birds, flocked together for safety and all of them prepared to take flight at once. And perhaps that wasn't such a poor comparison after all, for they looked up as one, at a small round window set high in the wall, giving onto the night sky and more than half filled with the full moon. Looks were exchanged, and nods, and then as one they turned to him.

Tiernan laughed harshly. "Get the hell out of here." He held up his hands, the truesilver deeply blistering the skin around his wrists in advance of the Great Magick already building in the floor beneath his body. "It's not like I'm going to escape justice, and frankly I'd rather have my last sight in this world be fair stone and the face of the moon than any of you." Ah, Moriath at least had the decency to blush at that.

The Prince Royal growled, no doubt less than thrilled about being dismissed, but just the same he was the first to Fade. One by one his companions did likewise, the color fading from their forms until only the hint of them remained. Then even the hint vanished, with a flicker-like motion not quite seen, out of the corner of the eye.

Moriath was the last to go. She watched him, intently, expressionless, not so much as twitching, And he watched her with the same intensity; he told himself he eyed her the way he would a venomous snake, alert for one last deadly strike. But he lied to himself, and the lie was bitter.

"No repentance, even at the end?" The hatred in her voice quivered in the air between them, and his head jerked as if she had slapped him. When his gaze fell on her he saw, not the ancient stone cell, not the beauty that could still take his breath if he let it, but what had been done only hours before.

Lorcan has her by the hair, pulling her head back as she kneels in the mud, beside the base of a waterfall; the water isn't enough to drown out the sounds of her cries as he takes her. Short, sharp thrusts, like a rutting animal. And laughter. You are too late to prevent this. Too late to spare her the pain. But you could end it, if you could do the unspeakable, the unthinkable. Lorcan turns; he laughs, a low, sick, gloating sound, and offers you a turn. A red crystalline haze shrouds your vision, crazing everything you see into shards of blood. You don't even realize you've drawn your stiletto until it's in your hand, and his hair is in your fist. You yank him off her at the last, not wanting to add the defilement his blood will be to what's already been done to her. Your grip on the hilt white-knuckled and trembling with the enormity of what you are going to do; you draw his head back hard, closing your ears to his desperate pleas. You stop the sound of his final scream by nearly severing his head from his body. And when the body slumps to the ground, the panic starts. You sheath your blade and extend your hands, drawing on one of the Noble magicks. Flesh to stone, transforming what once lived to the Element of your House and Demesne. A statue will not do, here, though; you can't leave an eternal witness to your crime. No. Still trembling with rage and terror and reaction, you channel the power and warp the air, watching as your brother's bleeding corpse slowly transmutes to sand and crumbles away under your hand. And you meet Moriath's gaze over what remains, but only for a moment. You can't bear to add to her shame or increase her pain, so you Fade…

"No repentance, *mo dre'fiur*." *Beloved sister*. It was half a taunt, half a truth that would burn them both as long as they clung to it. "I would do it again. Even knowing how little value you place on your honor."

She snarled, lips drawing back from her teeth. "You stole my vengeance." Her fingers flickered, in an insult too vile to be contained in mere words. "Do you think I would have let that pass? All the while he was at me, I was dreaming of the thousand years of revenge that would be mine." Her hands trembled, nearly as much as his when he had wielded the knife. "But you stole that from me, *mo dre'thair*." Her voice could have etched steel, it was so corrosive. "And what you stole from me meant more to me than what Lorcan stole."

Tiernan could not speak. Their line was truly tainted beyond redemption, if brother raped sister, brother killed brother, and sister despised both brothers. Better an eternity alone, untouched, than risk defiling another with the poison that passed for love in House Guaire.

The moonlight was brighter. Almost unbearable. Flooding the cell, the outline of the moon nearly filling the window. "Go," he choked. "You'll be caught here."

Moriath spat, as she began to Fade. The spittle landed beside his hands, as if she refused to let even that much of her touch him. The color leached from her, and then the form, her eyes the last of her to go, hate-filled sapphires to the very last.

"Live, brother. Live and suffer. As I will."

Tiernan wanted to look away. Tried. But he managed to keep from crying out after her, as she Faded. The echoes against the walls were merely her last words to him, and the wind. He would live. He would outlive her. And he would remain untouched by pain, by love. Both were suffering, and neither would have him. Ever.

The moon now perfectly filled the small round window, and Tiernan held his breath. The torches went out. All that remained now was the moonlight, gone suddenly baleful and cold and impossibly bright.

The floor disappeared. The Pattern, beautiful intricate looping of silver wire looking merely decorative, was all that remained beneath him, and he lay atop it, afraid for his very life. Afraid to move, his instincts whispering that the wire would cut with an edge even keener than a sister's hatred. If he just stayed still until the moon passed...

The wind roared to life. A fury of wind. Sucking him down.

Tiernan screamed.

CHAPTER ONE

Washington, D.C.
Present Day

Kevin Almstead leaned his forehead against his clenched fist, where it rested against the floor-to-ceiling window of the corner office, and looked down. The streets of D.C. were choked with cars, and the sleet wasn't helping matters. One pedestrian caught his eye, a woman in a bright yellow coat, like a sunbeam, making her way up the middle of K Street as if she were navigating the sidewalk. A spring in her step and a "fuck you very much" attitude toward the drivers honking at her—just his type—

"Kevin? You okay?"

He started, straightened, and ran his hand thoughtfully over his five-o'clock shadow, the one that always seemed to start by ten in the morning. He slowly turned away from the window, back into the office. "Yeah, Dave. Fine. Couldn't be better."

David Mondrian was a generation older than Kevin, and looked it, paunchy and balding and sporting the bifocals that proclaimed his disdain for laser eye surgery. But the older man was a good

13

friend, as well as his mentor here at Gladtke, Ross, and O'Halloran, and at this moment he was eyeing Kevin over those bifocals with a great deal of don't-give-me-that-shit-buddy. "Well, now, that's odd, because in your position I'd be pissed to the wide and looking for someone to use as a punching bag."

Kevin shrugged, crossing to the chair opposite the enormous mahogany desk and sinking into it with a sigh, leaning back and crossing his legs in more or less unconscious mimicry of the man on the far side of the desk. "What good would that do?"

"Probably none at this point." David shook his head, his gaze keener if anything. "But the fact that it doesn't even occur to you goes a long way toward explaining why you didn't get the offer again."

"Oh, hell, Dave." Kevin pinched the bridge of his nose, willing away the headache he could feel starting. "Don't tell me you buy that shit, too. They drill that into us from day one of law school—you don't make it in this business unless you're cutthroat, ruthless, yadda yadda yadda. Swim with the sharks." He waved dismissively with his free hand. "Those days are over, or they should be."

"Yes and no." David toyed with a pen, staring at it as if it were some kind of magical inspiration wand. "Sure, it's possible to make partner without being an asshole who would screw his own grandmother if it would make a buck for the firm. I'd like to think I'm a case in point." He chuckled softly, and waited for Kevin's responsive smile before continuing. "But there's more. There's drive. Hunger." Gray brows drew together in thought. "A nice guy *can* make partner, Kevin. But he has to want it. He has to *need* it."

"And you're saying I don't?" Despite himself, Kevin was intrigued. No one had said anything like this to him before, and it certainly never would have occurred to him. He wanted to protest, but the older man's words were striking a chord somewhere deep down. He wanted this. Hell, it was the capstone of a life's work; the best schools, head of the class at every one of them, and too many sleepless nights to count, a fair number of them in this very office, working his ass off. Yet… how much of that was because he'd never known what else to do? Because he was filling up his life until something better came along, and was stubborn-ass enough to want to make a good job of it?

David shook his head. "Kevin, don't take this wrong, you're one of my best friends, and there's not a damned thing wrong with you… but sometimes I think the good Lord left that drive out of your soul, when he put you together. And without it…"

"…I'm in the wrong line of work." Kevin tried to make light of it, but the words caught in his throat, insisting on more weight than he'd intended to give them.

"I didn't say that." David winced.

"You didn't have to." Kevin ran a hand through his dark hair, making a fist of it and wincing slightly at the pull. Anything to distract him from his thoughts. "What happens the next time the partners meet to consider candidates?"

After a moment looking from side to side, as if he desperately wished he could be somewhere else, David took a deep breath and sat forward in his chair, elbows on the desk, leaning forward and looking the younger man squarely in the eye. "You can put your name in again, Kevin. Nothing stopping you. But this will be the third time. And if you're turned down three times…"

"Yeah." A sharply raised eyebrow was all the comment Kevin allowed himself. He'd been over this bit of math too many times in his head during the last six months. Three strikes, and you're out. No one would force him to quit, of course. But if the Big Boys told you three times that they didn't want to play with you, no one else would want to, either. And even if he wasn't sufficiently *hungry*, the prospect of spending the rest of his life sharing an office and a secretary with a succession of kids straight out of law school and on their way up a ladder he'd never climb was not part of his plans.

"Think about it, Kevin."

David's voice startled him back from wherever his musings had taken him; he blinked a few times and got to his feet. "I will, Dave. Just… not tonight, okay?" Kevin looked around for his suit jacket, spotted where he'd thrown it over the sofa when he'd come in to David's office to get the bad news. Reaching, he snagged it, slipped it on, and settled it over broad shoulders. Good thing Armani did custom work, or he'd split the shoulders of every jacket he owned. Though how long custom tailoring would continue to be a concern, or even affordable, was anybody's guess. "I'll see you Monday morning, okay?"

The partner's chair creaked as he stood up. He came around the corner of the desk, apparently looking to cut Kevin off as he headed for the door. "You going to be all right?"

Kevin stepped around him, paused with a hand on

the doorknob. "All right?" He spoke softly, with a little laugh underlying the words. Amazing how calm he felt, really. "With any fucking luck at all."

***

God, the music was loud in here. But it matched what he had going on between his ears. And the liquor was good.

Kevin looked around, bemused, sipping a Jack and coke. How many times had he driven past Purgatory on his way home from work? Of all the bars and the clubs in the Adams Morgan neighborhood, this one most often piqued his curiosity. But he'd never gone so far as to stop the car, much less look inside the doors to discover what happened once *in* the doors. A club named Purgatory seemed a natural enough choice tonight, though, given his current situation. If he made a third failed try at partnership, Purgatory would be the rest of his professional career, so the name appealed to his sense of poetic justice. Then he'd walked in the door and seen the leather. And the bare skin. And the poles set up for dancing. And he'd stood in the doorway and taken it all in. And he'd entered. *Informed consent*, his inner barrister muttered, as his inner don't-give-a-shit drained his third Jack.

He growled, involuntarily, as he motioned to the shirtless and tattooed bartender for another round, sliding his empty glass over the glass-topped bar lit from below in shifting patterns of red and yellow and every now and then a painful pulsating lance of blue-white. There seemed to be a little bit of everything imaginable going on in Purgatory. Most of the patrons

17

had more metal sprouting from their visible body parts than he was accustomed to seeing, and come to think of it, they had more visible body parts than he was accustomed to seeing, period. Suit and tie was definitely overdoing it. Although a few more drinks, and it probably wouldn't be an issue. Fuck it, a few more drinks and he'd probably be out there trying his hand, or whatever, at pole dancing. Along with a half dozen or so men of varying ages and physiques. Either Friday night was amateur night, or the floor show started *really* late.

He picked up the fresh drink the bartender had left by his elbow, and downed half of it without noticing. How long had it been since he'd been out to any kind of bar at all, never mind one where the dress code ran to body ink and serious metal? Not that it mattered to him what kind of bar it was. He wasn't looking for a pickup, he was looking to get shit-faced. Seemed like the thing to do when he felt like one of those stupid cartoon characters that runs over a cliff, and then hangs there before it realizes it's supposed to be falling.

Hell, he wasn't fooling himself. He turned on the bar stool to watch an incredibly limber young man wrap himself around a pole in ways that were probably illegal in several jurisdictions, and utterly mesmerizing. He took off his tie and stuck it in a pocket, unbuttoned his collar, all without really being aware of what he was doing. Why was he here? He was here because he was fucking sick of being himself and wanted to be someone different. Just for tonight, maybe, or for the rest of his life. No knowing. No caring. Just let it happen.

"Enjoying the show?"

The voice was right next to his ear, low and rich and carrying a hint of laughter. Kevin straightened, his drink sloshing over his hand. He took a deep breath, and turned.

And stared. Into the bluest eyes he had ever seen. Long blond hair framed a chiseled face, a strong nose, full sensual lips. Odd, he'd never thought of a man's mouth as being particularly sensual before, but this one could be nothing but. More so when smiling, as it was now.

"The show? Remember?" The man chuckled, a wicked sound barely audible over the music. Somehow, the fact he had to strain to hear it made it more wicked. Decadent. "The boy was holding your attention well enough a moment ago. Have you become distracted?"

The blond had an accent, one Kevin struggled to place. Scots? Irish? Not that he could tell the difference between the two, but trying to puzzle it out gave him an excuse for closing his eyes, turning away. Distracted? Hell, yes.

"I'm sorry." The laughter lingering in the voice told him the speaker was anything but sorry. He was enjoying Kevin's reaction. He'd bet anything that when he opened his eyes again, that devastating blue gaze would be locked on his. Anything.

Fuck, I hate being right sometimes.

"You're incredibly sexy when you blush." The blond didn't sport nearly as much metal as most of the patrons of Purgatory, just three gold rings in one ear and one in his eyebrow. Damned if Kevin didn't want to run his tongue over that one to see what it would feel like.

Wait… he wanted to *what*? "You might want to

find a different come-on. It's too dark in here for you to see a blush." Kevin's throat was tight, his heart was hammering loud enough for this guy to hear it.

"You'd be surprised how perceptive I am." Suddenly, there was a hand resting on top of Kevin's on the bar, the hellish light playing over it. And two fingers, sliding under the lapel of his jacket, lifting it slightly. "Armani, isn't it?" When Kevin didn't answer, he leaned closer, nostrils flaring. "The scent, too. Acqua di Gio."

Fingertips stroked the back of his hand, gently, possessively, and Kevin fought to suppress a shiver. Not hard enough, though, because there was that smile again. A lazy, sensual smile that absolutely should not be on the lips of anyone he hadn't spent at least 24 hours having mind-blowing sex with. Which short list did not include anyone of this seductive blond's gender.

Yet.

As if he'd heard Kevin's thought, the man arched that ringed eyebrow; the grip on his hand tightened, a thumb slid around to stroke his palm. "You don't even know why you're here, do you?"

"And I suppose you do?" His voice came out gruff, harsh; the air thrummed around the two of them, tingling with a dark electricity.

The blond chuckled, a sound like warm honey. "You're buttoned down tight, *lanan*. And you came in here because…"

Shit.

"Secretly, you want someone…"

Damn, damn, DAMN…

"Someone like me…"

Long thick blond hair. Black leather jacket,

20

gleaming with a sheen like melted butter in the flickering light from the bar. White muscle shirt. Jeans first painted on and then sliced half off. God *damn*.

"…to unbutton you."

Get up. Walk away. The voice in his head was calm, level, reasonable. *This isn't for you. **He** isn't for you*.

Yeah, the voice was reasonable. And it was the voice of the miserable bastard who'd never dared to want anything for himself in his life.

"I don't even know your name." The hoarse whisper was a surrender, and they both knew it.

The blond leaned in and kissed him gently. "Tiernan Guaire. You don't have to tell me yours if you don't want to. Although I'll own it, I'd like to be able to scream it as I come."

Kevin's eyes closed, almost in pain. Almost. "Kevin. Kevin Almstead." *Esquire*, he nearly added, like an idiot.

Another kiss brought his eyes open, to meet the haunting blue gaze, alive with a promise of pleasure. "Kevin." Tiernan's teeth caught gently at his lower lip, tugged. "Did you drive, *lanan*? Because I didn't. And I'm impatient." A low throaty laugh seemed to hang in the air between them.

As he exited Purgatory with Tiernan, a young woman was passing, a vivacious young woman in a bright yellow coat like sunshine. Kevin blinked as he recognized her, as much from the spring in her step as from her distinctive clothing. The woman he'd seen from Dave's window. A few hours ago. Another life.

"You're too late," he whispered as she passed.

And Tiernan smiled slowly, as if he knew exactly what was meant.

CHAPTER TWO

It was going to be a damned good night.

Tiernan had no idea what had moved him to check out Purgatory tonight. His weekends were usually spent in places far darker, with humans unlikely to expect much in the way of conversation or other pleasantries. Pickups in bars had grown old, oh, half a century ago—and that was back when one still risked a great deal, approaching a male in a bar and interesting him in sex. It was almost too easy now. The thrill was gone from the hunt.

Except for tonight. Tiernan glanced sidewise at his companion, who appeared to be having no small trouble getting a key to fit in the lock of his own townhome door, and a smile of pure anticipation touched his lips. A most satisfying hunt indeed, even factoring in the torment of being enclosed in a car, too much like imprisonment to suit him, or any Fae. And the prey was close, so close to being brought to ground. The Fae's erection was already pleasantly uncomfortable, and the way Kevin's full lower lip was caught between his teeth as he fumbled with his keys was only making it worse. Or better.

The door swung open, and Kevin stepped inside.

When light bloomed from within and the door opened wider, Tiernan took a step forward. His eyebrows arched as the human reached out and took him by the hand, drawing him in before closing and locking the door behind them.

"Touching," he murmured, looking down at the hand Kevin still held, and then back up, in time to catch the blush creeping over the dark-stubbled cheeks. The sight kicked his arousal up another couple of notches. He raised Kevin's hand to his mouth, brushed his lips across the knuckles. "Are you sure you've never done this before?"

"I think I'd remember." The blush still lingered, but the little laugh that accompanied the words was dry. "It just seemed appropriate," he added, his dark gaze flickering briefly, speculatively to Tiernan's brow piercing.

"You were looking at that earlier." Tiernan smiled slowly. "It appeals to you?" Kevin was hardly his first virgin, and the surest way to drive a virgin wild was to make him admit, aloud, to every new feeling, urge and sensation. Or at least as many as possible while he was still capable of speech.

Kevin was no exception to the rule. He swallowed hard, and a thin film of sweat appeared on his upper lip. "Yeah, it does. I don't know why, but it's sexy as hell."

The Fae chuckled softly. He buried the fingers of one hand in Kevin's thick black hair, pretending to ignore the way the human shivered at the touch; he stepped closer, bowing his head slightly and drawing Kevin's mouth toward his brow. The thought of those lips on him was exquisite. He barely stifled a groan,

23

turning it into a low purr. "Try biting it. I like that."

His cock jerked hard as he felt not teeth but tongue, a long, slow hot swipe teasing at the gold ring, then withdrawing to the sound of a gasp. "Oh, God."

"You enjoyed that." Tiernan met Kevin's melting deep brown gaze with his own knowing one. "Your tongue on me. You enjoyed it."

"Fuck, yes." Kevin dropped Tiernan's hand with a groan, but not before Tiernan noticed the human's hand shaking; he turned on his heel and took a few steps away, his stride choppy, urgent.

For the first time, as Kevin moved away from him, the Fae noticed the room. They had come in from a tuck-under garage, into what would likely be described as a "family room" to a prospective buyer, but which Kevin had turned into a man cave. There was a fireplace at one end, faced by a dark leather loveseat, with a companion table piled high with books. A matching sofa and wingback chair faced a plasma screen television only slightly smaller than a billboard, with several gaming consoles and a computer hooked up to it. A freestanding wet bar occupied one corner, a Nautilus machine another.

Kevin's aborted attempt at flight had only gotten him as far as the chair. He slipped his suit jacket off and tossed it over the arm—and from the glimpse Tiernan got of the muscles of the human's back as they shifted under that oh-so-impeccably tailored shirt, he knew he wasn't going to make it as far as the bedroom. Not the first time, anyway.

He reached into the pocket of his leather jacket, palmed the little bottle of oil he always carried—because one never knew when an emergency would arise—and shrugged out of his own jacket, letting it dangle from a finger, over his back. When Kevin turned toward the sound, Tiernan smiled, lobbing the leather jacket over the back of the sofa and working his shoulders subtly. "Do you see anything else you like, *lanan*?"

"I know what you're trying to do." A muscle worked in Kevin's jaw, his hands clenched briefly into fists at his sides. But then the hands relaxed, the jaw likewise, and the eyes that met his were clear and deep and far warmer than any turned on him in a *very* long time. "And I'm letting you do it, because I want you to."

Tiernan's mouth dropped open slightly as Kevin walked back to him. The human hesitated, reached out his hands and then his arms, slipping them around Tiernan's waist. "Is this right?" Now it was the Fae's frame that rippled with a sudden shiver, as the human leaned slightly into him. He was tentative, but his arousal was obvious.

"Right?" Tiernan blinked, words having temporarily deserted him. Definitely not what he expected. "It's fucking perfect."

He reached up, caught Kevin by the back of the neck, groaning as dark hair tickled his palm. He met that dark gaze with his own, and waited for the human's eyes to close in anticipation. Tiernan never closed his eyes when he kissed, that was a level of trust he shared with no one. Besides, watching was delicious. He bent and took the other male's mouth hard, forcing his tongue between those sensual lips before Kevin's breath even had time to catch.

But it was Tiernan's own breath that caught, hard,

as the human groaned softly and gave himself up to the kiss. Kevin's arms tightened around his waist, one hand sliding slightly up his back, splaying over the hard-muscled skin, burning him even through the thin shirt that was far too much to have between them.

Not breaking the kiss—deepening it, if anything—Tiernan worked his hands between the two of them and slowly, teasingly unbuttoned the other male's fine tailored shirt, parting it and running his open palm up what had to be an even finer set of abs than he had dared to let himself imagine, heaving with Kevin's gasping breath. Further up he explored, pecs that jumped and shuddered under his touch, a nipple that pebbled hard just from a brush of his fingertips and puckered to a fine point when he pinched it.

He couldn't resist, he had to taste; he broke the kiss and bent his head, deliberately trailing his pale blond hair over Kevin's smooth, tanned chest before licking the hard nub of flesh with the same broad stroke the other male had used on him minutes before. "Is this good, lover?" Another slow lick, and then a bite—

"God *damn*." The words were strangled. Kevin's breath was hot in his ear and the arms tightened; the Fae's cock ground into the hollow of the human's hip.

Tiernan felt the human tense at the new contact, and laughed softly, his free hand running up the broad back, under the shirt, stroking possessively. "I think I'm going to leave this on you when I fuck you, *lanan*. At least the first time." He bent again to suck the dark hard nipple deeper into his mouth, murmuring approvingly when Kevin responded by inching his other hand lower and hesitantly curved his fingers, digging them into the dish of his ass. "Harder," Tiernan whispered. "I like it harder."

And oh *fuck* it was good when Kevin obeyed. Who knew such a simple thing, a firm grip on his ass pulling him hard against a proudly erect cock, could shock the breath from him and leave him fighting down his own orgasm? Maybe there really *was* magick in virginity.

"Pants. Off." Tiernan straightened, and met the human's wide dark eyes with a predator's smile. He licked his lips as Kevin's strong hands released him and went to the soft and supple leather belt that went so perfectly with the Armani, and was just loose enough to give him a glimpse of the nearly purple erection already trying to force its way out.

His free hand unbuttoned his jeans, started to work them down. His own shaft sprang free as soon as the zipper went down, the head thick and flat and brick red, falling forward under its own weight. He growled with approval at Kevin's faint moan. Collecting a drop of his own clear fluid on his thumb, he forced it abruptly between the male's lips, eyes going heavy-lidded with pleasure as, after a moment's resistance, Kevin sucked it into his mouth and swirled his tongue around it.

Tiernan's whole body jerked then, as Kevin's hand suddenly encircled his cock and stroked it in long, slow pulls. The tongue never left off his thumb, but damned if the dark eyes that looked at him over it weren't a silent challenge. *This is what I like*, they told him. *Do you?*

The Fae's growl started low in his chest, vibrating all the way down to the hand that gripped and twisted.

"I said *off.*" Yanking his thumb from between those soft lips with a wet pop, he grabbed belt and trousers and oh fuck those were silk boxers, all at once, and shoved at them, working them down over well-muscled thighs until a breathless Kevin took over, bending to toe out of his shoes and ease the trousers off.

And the glimpse of ass the movement gave Tiernan very nearly ended matters then and there. It was enough to make a Fae wish there were gods to swear to, or by, or at. "Turn around." His voice was thick, choked—and failed him altogether when Kevin straightened and he got his first good look at what was waiting for him, pushing aside the linen shirt and glistening purple in the light. *I'm spending the night, because I'm not going to be able to fucking **walk**.*

Kevin swallowed hard, color high in his cheeks. "You're going to…" A muscle twitched in his jaw. "Right." Slowly he turned, and leaned forward, bracing his hands on the back of the leather sofa, spread wide apart to take his weight, his feet edging apart.

He thinks I'm going in dry. The realization brought the Fae's brilliant blue eyes open wide. *And he'd let me.* It was obvious in his stance: the bowed head, the hunched shoulders. It was so tempting to let him go on expecting the forcing. The tension in the human's body already brought every muscle out in stark relief, the little shivers chasing themselves over his skin making Tiernan's cock throb.

But Kevin turned, looked back over his shoulder, black hair curling down over his forehead, distress, even fear, in his eyes. And to his astonishment, the Fae gave a damn. His hand uncurled from around the little vial of oil and he held it out until a little nod told him it had been seen, then popped the top with his thumb as he nudged Kevin's feet apart with one of his.

"Tell me what you want." His voice was like silk, now, but rough silk, as he drizzled the warm oil over his turgid shaft and stroked slowly. "Exactly what you want." He poured a thin stream of oil into the dimple at the base of the human's spine, let it spill down the crack of his ass.

"Oh, Christ…" The dark head dropped again, but there was nothing of surrender in it. A gathering of strength, rather, a focusing. "I want you to fuck me… hard… I want to know what you feel like in me." One hand slipped on the back of the sofa, regained its grip. "I need to know what you feel like coming in me—"

Tiernan swore, once, explosively. He gripped one perfect ass cheek, pulled it to the side; fisted himself tight, his hand slipping on the oil, and guided himself to Kevin's tight puckered virgin entrance.

He tried to go slowly. He tried. The attempt lasted until Kevin's tight ring closed hard around his sweet spot and Kevin's shivering passionate moan reached into him and made his blood sing like struck crystal and his eyes go wide with the shock. He gripped the male's hips with a white-knuckled ferocity and slammed himself home, ripping another cry from him. Or was it he himself who sobbed with pleasure? Pulling out as slowly as he could bear, driving in again, unable to stand being outside that hold. Tunneling in, pistoning, sweat stinging his eyes as he stared down at that perfect dimple.

"Fuck, yes." Kevin's words were almost

unrecognizable. His head was thrown back, his arm muscles quivered with the effort of holding himself upright and bracing himself against the pounding Tiernan was administering. "Jesus, Tiernan... so good... I'm so close..." His voice broke as his head snapped forward and down, his body tightened and trembled, almost as if in fear of what was about to happen.

Tiernan's lips drew back from his teeth in a snarl of pleasure. One hand let go of the human's hip and reached around him, gripping Kevin's huge erection and pumping hard, slicked slightly by the oil and more by the stream that wept from the tip. "Come with me." The Fae sucked in one deep breath, then another. A surge of heat shot down his spine, pooled at the base; his balls drew up, his cock curved hard in his lover's tight virgin hold—

Tiernan screamed, his knees nearly buckling under him as the pleasure seared through him like living fire. Molten glass could have been no hotter, shooting from him in thick ropes to coat his human's dark passage. And Kevin clamped down agonizingly tight around him as he, too, exploded, coating Tiernan's hand with his own thick pearly seed, throbbing and pulsing in the Fae's firm grip. Gasping, sobbing, moaning.

It wouldn't stop. Queen's *tits,* it wouldn't stop. Thick glassy streams trickled down the insides of his human's thighs, and *still* it wouldn't stop. The humming, the singing in his blood was louder, dizzying. His body quivered with it like a plucked harp string even as the body-wracking pulses of his climax began to fade away and Kevin's writhing beneath him slowed to a rhythmic rocking.

A sensation he'd never known before. Joy.

Finally, he was aware of himself and his surroundings once more. He was slumped over Kevin's broad back, his cheek laid against the back of his human's neck. Their sweaty bodies rose and fell together as both struggled to catch their breath—

Wait. Wait justafuckingminute. *His* human?

Oh, no. Oh, *no*. Not for one effing *second*. His head shot up. He spotted his jacket, just out of arm's reach on the back of the sofa. A quick lunge, a Fade, and he'd be gone. If he was lucky, the sex-on-a-stick lawyer would go over to the wet bar, get smashed, and wake up with nothing but a hangover and the memory of one hell of a wet dream. *His* human? Shit, no.

And then Kevin turned and looked back over his shoulder, dark eyes aglow. If the angels humans believed in ever had sex, and smiled afterward, surely they looked that way. He reached back blindly, and caught Tiernan's hand. "My turn? After we've rested a little?"

Mutely, Tiernan nodded, drawn into those eyes. Was it already too late?

CHAPTER THREE

"Worried about dropping the soap?"

A corner of Kevin's mouth quirked up at the dryly amused voice that floated over the door of the shower stall.

"Should I be?" He ran his hands over his upper arms, down over his torso, sluicing soapy water off the hard pecs, down over his hard-won six-pack. Sculpting this body had been another chore, one more thing to do right solely for pride in the craftsmanship. But now... damn. Whatever Tiernan had under that muscle T and those ripped jeans was going to be spectacular, he just knew it. And he, himself, hadn't felt this self-conscious since his eighth grade dance. At which he'd been wearing mismatched socks.

Christ, I'm gibbering. Kevin took a deep breath, and wasn't surprised when it had no calming effect whatsoever. *Think about eighth grade. Think about the Nautilus machine. Think about anything other than the most incredible orgasm you've ever had in your life. Or the man who gave it to you. Or the fact that he's on the other side of this frosted glass door, waiting to give you another one.*

"No, it's your turn this time." Yes, there was

laughter in Tiernan's voice, but laughter with an edge, laughter that teased and pushed and dared. Kevin had no illusions at all about the devastating blond he'd brought home with him. He'd felt the tension in the other man. Just when a man would normally be closest to complete physical collapse, Tiernan Guaire had been ready to bolt for the door. Kevin had known it, he'd been ready for it, and yet he'd turned, and asked Tiernan to stay.

And Tiernan had agreed. *Hell.*

Kevin was reaching for the tap to shut off the water when the door clicked softly open behind him, and closed again. Arms slid around his waist from behind, as Tiernan's mouth caressed the back of his neck; one hand skimmed up his torso, long fingers exploring his chest, as the other slid down and encircled his half-erect cock. "Ready for playtime yet, *Ianan*?" A tongue stroked up the back of his neck, somehow a perfect counterpoint to the water still cascading down. Water he felt on every inch of his skin, waking him up, bringing him alive, in a way he'd never been.

"I've been ready since the first time." Why it was so easy to admit Kevin had no clue. Unless it was because it was true. He sucked in a breath between clenched teeth as Tiernan's hand stroked slowly from the base of his shaft out to the tip; looking down, he watched in fascination as his erection lengthened into that expert touch, bit his lip as the hand curved to let the palm play over his head.

"I can feel you looking, you know." Teeth closed gently on the back of his neck. "You are *so* hungry for this."

Momentarily dizzy, Kevin leaned forward, palms splayed out against the tile. It was hard to breathe. Just the steam? "Yeah… damn." Hungry? Hell, yes.

"Turn around."

Definitely not "just" the steam. Kevin's heart was hammering as Tiernan let go of his cock, rested a hand on his hip and urged him to turn. *This doesn't mean anything. To either one of us.*

He turned, and met eyes the bluest he'd ever seen. He buried his fingers in long, silken, wet hair, and drew those eyes, that face, down to his own. And the eyes didn't close.

I am such a fucking liar.

A shiver rippled through Kevin's body, despite the steaming heat of the shower, as he pulled Tiernan into an open-mouthed kiss. Teeth clashed, tongues stroked and danced and dueled; soft, urgent sounds rose over the sound of the water, sounds of need, his own as intense as the other man's.

Kevin gripped Tiernan's hard shoulder with his free hand, pressing his body against him, deeply certain that once he caught a glimpse of the tall, perfectly cut blond's nakedness, he was going to lose what precious little self-control he still possessed. But now there was an erection lying like a bar of hot iron against his stomach, and he could feel Tiernan's ravenous growls from his cock to his nipples… oh, Christ, was that a nipple ring he felt? *Shit.*

Tiernan nipped sharply at Kevin's lower lip, then licked, almost gently. "Sorry, *lanan*," he murmured, in a tone clearly not sorry at all. His hands slid down Kevin's back, locking the two of them together at the hips. And then Kevin groaned, as Tiernan leaned back, opening space between them, exactly what he'd wanted to avoid. "Oh, would you look at that, now." One blond eyebrow quirked up, as hooded blue eyes glanced down.

Kevin swore softly as his eyes swept down Tiernan's gleaming wet body. He'd been right, he'd been more than right. Every muscle stood out in perfect definition, and yes, it *was* a nipple ring, only this one was stainless steel rather than gold. Designed for use. Perfectly contoured abs, and an erection that stood up proudly, pinned between their bodies next to his own, clear fluid already trickling out and down the thick hard length of it.

"You want to touch." Not a question, and purred into his ear in a voice that brought back every moment of their earlier tryst. "Both of them. Don't you?"

"You don't need to do this to me." Kevin's teeth were gritted, his knees locked to keep himself from falling. Though in this small space, the only falling he'd be able to do would be to his knees. Which would put his mouth right at… oh, *fuck*.

"No, I don't, do I? But I want to." Lips and tongue began to work their way from Kevin's ear to his throat, slowly, languidly. "I don't know many virgins, at least not for long. And you're only half deflowered." A soft chuckle preceded a lazy bite, as Tiernan's hand caught at Kevin's and brought it between their bodies, curled it around their cocks and squeezed. "Or have you ever taken a girl that way?"

Kevin was suddenly unable to speak. He shook his head, as much to clear it of images of what he was about to do as to answer Tiernan's question. "No, never. I was… afraid I'd hurt them." Which was true as far as it went, the few women he'd been with would probably have been torn apart by what one of his exes had lightheartedly referred to as his "concealed weapon," if he'd dared to use it on them that way. But he'd never wanted to try. Never known the kind of need he felt right at this moment, as he quivered with eagerness to tunnel his cock into Tiernan's ass.

Teeth grazed along the line of his jaw. "You don't have to worry about the pain, as long as you take your time. I'm sure it'll hurt, even if you do—you're hung like a bull elephant—but that makes it sweeter as far as I'm concerned." Tiernan moved his hand, and Kevin's within it, up and down their shafts, bringing them together, rubbing them against each other, as the water from the shower played over them. "And it's not like I'm new at this."

The sensations—the stroking, the fevered heat he held in his hand and pressed against his cock—drew a strangled sound from Kevin, along with a strange, falling feeling, like vertigo, nearly as intense as he'd experienced when Tiernan had released in him. Unreality. *What the hell am I doing?* Even as he wondered, his head dropped back in response to firmer strokes from Tiernan's skilled hand. *Maybe it's not really happening... nothing real ever felt like this.*

With an effort, he raised his head, and met Tiernan's keen, heated gaze. It felt like a touch, deeper and more intimate than the hand playing over his erection. But that was bullshit, wasn't it? This was a bar pickup, a one-night stand, possibly temporary insanity, nothing more. His world was coming apart and he needed something to help him ignore the coming train wreck for a little while. And his evening's companion? Out for a quick, hot fuck, nothing more.

So why couldn't either one of them look away? "My turn."

Had he actually spoken? He didn't think so. But Tiernan's body went tense against him, and for a second Kevin's heart stopped. It was as it had been the first time; the other man hadn't budged, but he seemed frozen in the act of flight, his muscles quivering with arrested movement. Only the drum of the water on their bodies told Kevin that time was passing at all.

And then the moment, whatever it was, passed. Tiernan released the grip holding Kevin's hand around their erections, and, with a slow, knowing smile, turned around. "Take what you want."

Kevin's heart lurched. He caught at Tiernan's arm with one hand, and reached with the other to turn off the spray. "Let's go to bed—"

Tiernan shook his head, gripping the wrist that stretched past him. "No. I want it here."

Kevin's nostrils flared as the other man's hand closed around his wrist. His dark brows drew together at the imperious tone, but he said nothing, only watched.

And for the space of a breath, the blond was a statue. His inhumanly handsome face could have been carved from marble. Then he let go of Kevin's arm, and the smile was back, touching his lips with something sublimely wicked. "You're every wet dream I've ever had."

"'Every'?" Now it was Kevin's turn to be quietly amused—better that than nervous as fuck. "Why do I doubt that?" This time, when Tiernan turned to the wall, he let him, allowing the gliding of skin under his hand to become a caress. He stroked the flawless sides before him as the other man leaned against the tiled wall and took his weight on his hands.

His erection was still standing up eagerly, resting in the crack of Tiernan's ass. Damn, that felt good. Kevin's hips swayed, back and forth, to savor the feeling of smooth hard muscle gliding over his cock. Then he looked, really *looked*. Christ on a *crutch*, what an ass. And ink, not visible until now, a gorgeous piece of silver-blue Celtic knotwork riding over one hip. His cock jerked hard, the clear drops it scattered across Tiernan's back quickly lost in the spray from the shower. And didn't Tiernan peer around, over his shoulder, at that exact moment, looking ready to laugh? "If you tell me that's the first time anyone's ever had that reaction…" Kevin growled, even as he blushed.

Tiernan shook his head, with a knowing grin, before turning back to the wall and bracing himself once again. "Not many virgins have ever been where you are, boyo."

The words sent a thrill running through Kevin. Almost without being aware of what he did, he took himself in hand, wringing gently, his grip pulsating. Not that he needed more stimulation—hell, he had no idea why he wasn't glazing the shower tiles already— but looking at the magnificent blond man, spread out and waiting for him, quivering slightly with eagerness… erotic stimulation was every bit as natural as breathing.

Slowly, he eased the broad, thick head of his cock to Tiernan's tight, puckered entrance. Stared at it, gone dry-mouthed. *It IS a weapon. How the hell am I ever going to—*

"Losing your nerve?"

His eyebrows shot up. "Like fuck I am."

He had to force the head in. By the time Tiernan's ring clamped down around it, he was dizzy, and would have been sweating if not for the shower. *So good… oh, damn.* A long, low shuddering moan filled the air around them, growing louder with every inch he gained in the other man's dark passage. It was joined by Tiernan's gasps, interspersed with occasional soft curse words Kevin couldn't quite make out over the roar in his own ears.

Two inches in, one inch out, bracing his knees to tunnel deeper. How he knew what to do, he had no idea. But it didn't matter. His body knew what to do. His body had been made for this. Water rolled down over Tiernan's back, limning the muscles of it, gleaming with every harsh breath the other man drew. Beautiful. Like a dream, one he'd never known to have but finally had the balls to reach for.

His pleasure grew more intense every moment. He was fully seated in his lover so deeply all he could do was circle his hips, and take a fierce joy in Tiernan's fevered moans, and the way the other man writhed where they were joined, gripped him tightly and worked his length in long slow waves. "Too big for you?"

"Like fuck you are," Tiernan snapped. His smile as he turned slightly was bright, dangerous; long hair plastered over his forehead and cheeks, framed eyes that were almost desperate, lips drawn back in what could have been a snarl as easily as a smile. "Are you ready to scream? Because you're about to."

Kevin reached around, as Tiernan had done for him, and gripped Tiernan's shaft. His fingers barely met around the base, and his breath caught. *That was in my ass? Holy shit.* He held the other man tightly, working his cock in the way he himself enjoyed, and was rewarded with a strangled cry.

"Bring it…"

Kevin's hips moved faster, in time with his hand, harder, faster… *God… oh, God, oh GOD—*

His first orgasm, in Tiernan's hand, had nearly brought him to his knees. This one, deep in the other man's ass, was a lightning bolt, and he was riding the current. His whole body jerked violently. He screamed Tiernan's name once, then could no longer breathe. He staggered, nearly fell, barely managing to catch himself and brace himself against the shower wall. *This is not fucking normal*, he thought dizzily. *Never… been… like this…* The cock in his hand was pulsing, too, throbbing, spilling warmth over his hand, wave after wave of it. His orgasm was never going to end. Jet after jet, thick ropes of pearly heat coating his lover, slicking that dark passage, easing the way for continued thrusting, gradually slowing, breathless with pleasure. With delight.

There wasn't a moment when he realized he'd stopped coming. Not really. Not until he opened his eyes, water rolling down over his back, where he'd fallen forward onto Tiernan. The water felt different. As if he could feel every drop, stinging but silken. And the air rang like crystal. He almost laughed at himself, but it was a good-natured kind of almost laughing. *Maybe I'm finally alive… hell, was this all it took?*

He was so very aware of the warmth of the body

over which he slumped. So warm, so hard, so firm. Still clasping him tightly within. Chest heaving under him as Tiernan, too, fought for breath. Soft, involuntary moans.

No. Not moans. Whimpers. Sobs. Silence.

Tiernan straightened, so abruptly that Kevin was thrown back into the shower wall. The other man yanked on the glass door. Cold air rushed in, sending eddies of steam swirling. "Don't try to find me," he snarled, without turning.

Kevin stared, open-mouthed, through the shower door. Tiernan reached for the bathroom door, and paused. The hand on the doorknob went white-knuckled, and for an instant, piercing blue eyes met Kevin's through the steam. The unmistakable anguish in those eyes nearly felled him.

The bathroom door opened and slammed closed. The bedroom door beyond it must have done so as well, but that sound was lost to the rush of the water.

CHAPTER FOUR

"How much? Depends on what you want."

Tiernan barely kept a snarl from his lips. The fact he was down here, in a filthy, poorly lit access corridor that reeked of nicotine, disinfectant, and everything disinfectant might be used to mask in a BDSM club, preparing to pay for sex instead of taking advantage of the offers he'd had upstairs just for walking in the door, should have told the pathetic creature in front of him what he wanted. Something that could get a response out of him. Anything.

But it was one of the stranger quirks of his existence in the human world that he had to hear the price before the money would appear. Some Fae magicks were oddly twisted here. "I'm not sure what I'm in the mood for. Why don't we assume I want the works and am willing to pay handsomely for it?" Because he knew this woman, and all her kind; what aroused her was money. And the more aroused she was, the better the chances she'd be able to do something for him.

She sniffed nervously, and wiped at her nose with the back of her hand. Coke? No, she didn't look strung out. Probably just cold. Her costume barely covered

42

her. It was obviously borrowed—if this bedraggled, nailbitten dirty blonde was really a Domme, he, Tiernan, would personally eat his shorts. Which he'd left back at Kevin's in his panic. *Shit*.

"Two hundred?" Her insistence made him realize she'd repeated herself at least once, probably more.

"Yeah, whatever." He reached into the pocket of his jacket, the one that had been empty moments before, and his hand closed around paper money, withdrew just far enough to let the bills show in the dim light from the caged bulb down the hall. "Cash up front—but you don't stop till I'm finished." He let an edge creep into his voice, the barest suggestion of what might happen if she stopped too soon. But he was willing—eager, even—to risk the possibility, because the alternative meant having to talk to her when it was over. Fuck that.

She nodded, her hands held out eagerly. Tiernan grimaced and handed her the money, watching it vanish into some sort of pocket in the hem of her abbreviated skirt. Damn, if his cock got into her anywhere near as fast as his money did, this might actually be over quickly enough to suit him. "Hand job, first, then we'll see."

She smiled—seductively, he was sure she thought, the two C notes were working their magic already—and wound one arm around his neck as her other hand went for his crotch, tiptoeing for a kiss. He stepped back, so quickly he pulled her off balance. "That's not what this is about," he growled. "Just biz."

What this is about, my dear, is turning back the fucking clock six fucking hours. He watched impassively as she unzipped his jeans and slipped a

43

hand inside, coaxing his quiescent cock to come out and play. *Making what happened tonight, not have happened.*

The moment, over one hundred and fifty years ago, he'd been sieved through the Pattern had mercifully been obliterated from his memory. The pain of the moment before it, and of the moment after it, was more than enough to make damned sure he remembered the agony of having his soul torn in half, he didn't need the golden moment itself. It was supposed to be a protection, that's what the Loremasters had said two millennia ago. After going through the Pattern, a Fae would be truly immortal, and would remain untouched by time, and immune to all disease, just as in the Realm. But legend said a Fae in the human world, with the half a soul left by the Pattern, was also, perhaps, uniquely invulnerable; no injury, starvation, nothing that could otherwise bring him to any of the untimely ends a Fae in the Realm might experience was supposed to be able to kill him. Eternally exiled, but eternally safe.

Almost.

"Come on, baby, you know you want this," the woman crooned, working Tiernan's unresponsive shaft with both hands. He stared down at short, nicotine-stained fingers, nails bitten to the quick, and all he could think about was the strong, eager hand that had reached around from behind him in the shower, had gripped and twisted and pumped his cock in time with steady and forceful thrusts from behind. And for that memory, his cock twitched, began to uncurl, to fill out. For Kevin Almstead, not for whoever this was. Shit, he hoped she didn't try to tell him her name.

Safe for eternity, he'd thought. The sundered half of a Fae's soul didn't die, it couldn't. Instead, it was ejected by the Pattern, somewhere into human space-time. Into a host, for a soul could not survive without a body. There was no telling when, or where, that half-soul would emerge from the intricate loops and knots of the Pattern to be born. And the only way for a Fae to lose the protection the Pattern gave him was to find the other half of his soul, to find that host, and to love him.

And that was where he should have been safest of all. Because even if Fae were capable of loving anyone other than kin, he was not any Fae. He was a kinslayer, and of a tainted line incapable even of that most basic kind of love. He'd spent the last century and a half, as humans reckoned time, wandering from one debauchery to the next, from sordid tryst to bacchanalia to momentary assignation. He never broke his word, for he gave no word to keep; relentlessly, he turned his face away from anything and everything that might remind him of the empty place in what was left of his soul. Clinging to the vow he'd made before night and wind claimed him, before the Pattern had been etched into his flesh. Never to be hurt, never to love.

He gasped, and stumbled back. The woman had somehow gone to her knees in front of him without his noticing—how she'd done it in fetish heels, he couldn't imagine—and her mouth had closed greedily around the head of his cock, her tongue lapping at the slit at the tip. Now she looked up at him, an exaggerated expression of hurt puckering her chapped lips in a pout. "I know you liked that, baby, I could tell—"

45

"I'm not your fucking baby." But hell, yeah, he liked it, and he tangled his fingers in her hair and pulled her back on to him. Why hadn't he gotten Kevin to do this? Shit, those full soft lips of his would have been heaven.

Would have been. Why hadn't he seen it coming? No reason on earth he should have been attracted to Kevin. None. Armani? Shit. Lawyer? No fucking way. Virgin? He'd had no interest in amateur hour. Yet he'd slid onto that barstool behind him with one thing on his mind, and knowing he was going to get it…

"I think you're ready for me," the blonde purred. Yeah, two hundred dollars bought a *lot* of turned on. And maybe he *was* ready. He could get harder looking at the Abercrombie and Fitch catalog, but it might do.

He caught at her arm, pulled her to her feet— faster than waiting for her to do the job herself, in those heels—and reached under her skirt, finding the crotchless panties he'd more or less expected, and a cleft that was, to his surprise, actually wet. Her eyelids fluttered, her head dropped back, and he rolled his eyes. "Save it for the Oscars," he growled, pushing her back against the wall and kneeing her thighs apart, gripping her thighs and lifting her, thrusting at her with a low snarl.

Even if the pickup at Purgatory hadn't tipped him off, he sure as shit should have seen there was something badly wrong when he took Kevin, against the back of the sofa. No orgasm in his life had ever felt like that. The room had spun, he'd almost fallen; the pleasure had been so intense it had choked off his throat. And when Kevin had come in his hand, it had been sheer bliss. The force of it had nearly completed what the spinning of the room had started. Though he'd covered it quickly, there had been a brief, incandescent moment of pure joy. He might have wept with it, if he hadn't been so startled by it.

"Shit." He cursed through clenched teeth, tilting her pelvis up, failing to penetrate yet again. "Help me, damn it—" He groaned as her hand closed around him, positioned him, began feeding his semi-erect cock into a cleft that felt imperfectly shaved. Son of a *bitch*.

Why the hell had he stayed? He'd been ready to leave as soon as he caught his breath after that mind-blowing orgasm. It might not have been too late. But then the human turned that deep brown gaze on him, and asked him to stay, and Tiernan had taken leave of his fucking senses. Kevin had wanted a shower, and he could even have left then. But no, he'd gotten into the shower with him. He'd thought he'd been so clever, refusing to go to bed with the human, making damned sure he wouldn't have to look in those devastating eyes as Kevin took him. But all his precautions hadn't been enough. Kevin had taken his first male; and his reaction had been the twin of Tiernan's own from the feel and the sound of it, though of course the human had had no idea what was happening, or what was about to happen. Kevin had released, and had made sure of his partner's pleasure. Blinding, deafening, consuming pleasure, and the joy—it had welled up in him from the inside this time, filling him all the way out to the skin. And then, when it was too late, there had been time for the tears. SoulShared. Bonded. Completed.

Able to die. And still unable to love.

This wasn't working. It wasn't going to work. He

knew what would, though. He dropped the woman's fishnet-sheathed thighs, tearing a few new holes in the stockings in the process, pulled out of her, and turned her to face the wall, shoving her short skirt up and tearing away the sad black panties that barely covered her tight rosette. She looked back over her shoulder at him encouragingly—not that he cared whether she encouraged him or not; she'd been paid to give him what he needed, and he needed this.

He'd had to run. Six hours, and three clubs, one in Stockholm, one in Rio, and now here in Chicago, had passed since he fled Kevin's townhome. No city could be far enough away. And nothing satisfied him. Nothing, no one. No combination of bodies, mouths, genders, willingness or lack thereof. Tiernan knew of no rules for SoulShares, not surprising since none had ever returned to the Realm to tell of their experiences. All he knew was that Kevin had half of his soul, and all the pleasure had gone out of the thought of any other touch.

His moist cock rose to the sensation of her puckered hole at its tip; she eased her cheeks, and he tunneled his way in, working quickly in case this arousal, too, failed him. Once seated, he gritted his teeth, bent his knees, planted his hands against the wall on either side of her head, and started hammering up into her, hard enough to send her up on her toes with each thrust, even in her FMPs. She was crying out, now, but the sound did nothing for him. He wasn't even hearing her, or the bass line pounding through the walls from the dance floor somewhere over their heads. He was hearing a male in ecstasy with the taking of his first cock, the rush of water in the

48

shower, his own name, in a deep baritone breaking with passion.

Tiernan's head fell back as the thick pulses of his release filled the woman he pinned to the wall. He wanted to feel pleasure, needed to know he could feel pleasure. But there was nothing. He was vaguely aware of her cries of gratification, feigned or real, but he was empty. No knees threatening to buckle, no heart hammering like it was trying to escape from his chest, no white lights sparking at the edges of his vision.

No joy.

Maybe once you ran from that, it was gone for good.

She turned to look over her shoulder, breathless, sweating, her lank dirty blonde hair falling in a curtain over her face. "Who's Kevin?"

CHAPTER FIVE

When Kevin's grammar check told him that he'd entered "pubic lands" instead of "public lands" for the sixth time, he finally admitted it was time to pack it in for the night. One of these times, he was going to get pissed and just leave it there, and the client would probably have an infarct.

He pushed back from his desk, running a hand through his hair until it stood up every which way, staring at the computer screen. Whoever said overwork was a sure cure for a broken heart needed a fucking clue, because seven nights' worth of midnight oil hadn't done anything for him except make it increasingly gut-wrenching to go home.

"There is," he muttered to the empty air, "something seriously wrong with me." There was no effing way he was tearing himself apart. Not for this. Not for a one-night stand who hadn't even made it the full night. Not even for the first man he'd ever desired. He wasn't losing it. Hell, he'd made it a whole week, and he was still eating and sleeping and bathing.

Not showering, though. He'd tried that. Fuck, he hated to cry.

Kevin pushed back from the desk, got to his feet.

There was very little room to pace in his tiny office, so he did what he'd been doing a hell of a lot of this last week. Crossing to the window, he stood looking down into the midnight city. The weather had turned genuinely cold in the last week; it had even snowed a couple of times, leaving the streets outlined in dirty gray ridges. From nine floors up, though, it didn't look too bad.

Wonder if he's out there somewhere.

With a forearm against the window, he rested his forehead against the cold glass, looked down at K Street without really seeing it. *"Don't try to find me,"* Tiernan had said. Was he fucking kidding? It was like he'd vanished into thin air or something. What was he going to do, hire a private investigator? Oh, wouldn't *that* be hilarious? *Yeah, I want you to find this guy, blond hair, gorgeous blue eyes, an accent I can't place for the life of me, and a dick that'll make your ass sing in four-part harmony.*

He swore softly and turned away from the window, dropping back into his office chair with a sigh, rolling across the floor until he got it under control with a foot and hitched his way back to the desk. Time to finish, double-check his billables for the week, and get the hell out.

His fingers danced over the keyboard as he called up his bootleg copy of the firm's timesheet management software; he'd stopped feeling guilty about this practice a year ago, the first time he'd been passed over for partnership. They'd given him a lame ass reason the first time, telling him he just hadn't been working hard enough. So he'd done some nosing around, gotten a copy of the tracking software the firm used, and for a while he'd made it a practice to make sure all the hours he reported were getting into the system, to be certain he was getting the credit he was due. He'd stopped doing it after a month or so, back then, when he'd seen everything was checking out; apparently, though, it was time to get back at it. Not hungry for it? Like hell he wasn't.

There he was. *Almstead, Kevin.* He squinted at the figures... frowned. Ninety-eight hours since last Saturday? That didn't look right. He clicked to expand the hours-by-client spreadsheet and studied that.

Ohh... shit. He'd billed ten hours to his current pro bono project, the Urban Wildlife Sanctuary, and somehow the hours had apparently gotten double-billed, because there were also ten hours logged to the Balfour Wild Lands Preservation Trust, an account he wasn't even assigned to. He shook his head as he deleted the improperly billed hours. Double billing was a Bad Thing. Enough of it could get you in trouble with the D.C. Bar, maybe even disbarred, and it made the firm look bad as well. And the client was likely to get extremely pissed, too—and a top-shelf client like the Balfour Trust was *not* one he needed to have writing angry letters to the managing partner.

Like they're going to fire me? He snorted. Well, he might want to be able to get a job somewhere else, down the road, so it was probably best to keep his nose clean. And the extra hours weren't a problem any more; he was back to a much more normal-looking eighty-eight hours for the week, and all was right with the world.

Who the hell am I kidding?

He grimaced and started to shut down the computer, looked around for his coat. He stopped, though, when he realized that he had no idea where he wanted to go or what he wanted to do. Home? Last place in the world. Out? Too late for dinner, too late for a show. Yeah, he could hit a bar, but he could drink himself forgetful a lot faster and cheaper at home. Of course, in order to do that he'd actually have to *go* home.

What about Purgatory? For a moment, the flickering lights of the bar played behind his closed eyelids, and his gut wrenched. *I'm not looking for another pickup. I wasn't even looking for the first one, I sure as hell don't want another one.*

A soft chime announced that his computer was safely asleep for the night; he surged to his feet, grabbed his coat, and hit the office lights on the way out the door. *Home it is.*

***

Kevin sank back into the soft black leather of the loveseat, his fourth Jack and coke firmly in hand. He ignored the smile the bare-assed server flashed him over his shoulder as he walked away, the uneven light from the bar playing randomly over his profile. Part of him was pissed at himself for being here at all, and the part that wasn't, was busy being pissed at the way he kept catching himself looking around for a familiar face.

He tipped his head back, closing his eyes with a deep sigh, letting the E.D.M. from the dance floor wash over him, through him. His skin tingled with it, but nothing was going to make him feel as alive as he'd felt a week ago. At that bar. Not that he was going to sit there tonight; he wasn't interested in advertising, even accidentally. No, this dark recess with its deep leather seats was just right. He opened his eyes and looked up, sighed again as he saw the low ceiling was mirrored.

The face looking down at him from the mirror wasn't exactly a poster child for hard work and clean living. He needed a haircut badly, not to mention a shave, and no amount of expensive tailoring was going to make him look respectable. Not tonight. God, decadence could be lonely.

Sitting up, he took a long slow draw from the glass in his hand, and raised an eyebrow. *Classy joint. The drinks get stronger as you go instead of weaker.* Now if the room would have the decency to start spinning, he'd be fine. He was beginning to suspect, though, that wasn't going to be happening.

Somewhere on the drive here, he'd started coming to terms with the fact he genuinely missed Tiernan Guaire. He ought to feel like a fool for it—he'd known the man for all of a few hours, and they hadn't even been face to face for the most memorable moments—but, strangely, he didn't. He missed him. Ached with it, an ache no amount of Jack was going to touch.

But was it more than that?

Start with the fact he'd never been attracted to a man, and as far as he knew, none had ever been particularly attracted to him. And yet, when his world had started falling apart on him, of all the places he could have gone, he'd ended up here. When he'd heard that softly accented voice in his ear, it had just been right. And what followed after? Better than right. As the man himself had said, fucking perfect.

But you can't be in love with someone who isn't there. Not really. *You can think you are…* not that he thought he was… but ceding the point for the sake of argument—and how fucking lawyerly was that?—*how can it be love if you know the other guy isn't even thinking about you? That's a crush, an infatuation, maybe. But not love.*

Except he'd never had a crush or an infatuation in his life, and he was pretty damned sure he wasn't starting now.

He downed the rest of his drink, and motioned to the server. He didn't have to do much, The guy was watching him like he was one of the pole dancers out there on the floor. Almost on the thought, the music changed. There was a hook to it that drew him in, capturing his attention, making his heart race. Then the lyrics, a male voice full of pain cutting straight through the music and the beat.

I thought you were gone
Knew you were gone
Wanted you gone
Dreamed you were gone
Because I can't get over you until you go away
Let me go
Just go

Was that it? Kevin sat slowly back in his seat, as another drink appeared in front of him. *Is it good that he's gone? Should I just forget? Count my fucking blessings?* The hand that picked up the drink shook slightly. *I can't.*

55

You thought I was weak
You knew I was
You wanted me to be
And for you I was
And I am
I am

Kevin closed his eyes, his free hand clenching into a fist. Turned inside this way, he could feel Tiernan's eyes on him, the way those blue eyes had held him… *yeah, fuck, you knew I was weak.*

You are weak. You are his weakness.

What the hell are they putting in these drinks? Kevin plowed a hand through his hair, destroying whatever was left of the styling it had started the day with.

And now I have found you both.

A chill prickled the skin on Kevin's forearms. But then the chill was gone, along with the soundless dark words, gone utterly as the singer's voice returned. And this time, the words rode the hypnotic music to him with an accent, like music itself, one he still couldn't place.

You needed me to be the one to break
Before you shattered
I did
And you did

He opened his eyes. And his breath caught hard, at sight of the haunted blue eyes, nearly on a level with his own. Tiernan knelt in front of him, sitting back on his heels, barefoot, bare-chested, black leather jacket hanging open and black leather trousers stretched tight over the hard-muscled thighs Kevin hadn't been able to forget no matter how hard he tried.

"Three things you need to know." There was such a weight of pain in Tiernan's voice that Kevin nearly cried out with it. He reached out and caught the other man's hand, and felt him tense, as if he wanted to pull away. But the hand relaxed, and Kevin breathed again.

"First, I can't love you."

Kevin shook his head gently, stroking his thumb over Tiernan's palm. "You don't have to." *I can manage to be in love enough for both of us.*

Tiernan winced. "Second, I need to be with you." His hand tightened around Kevin's, used it to draw him closer. "I need back what we made." The other man groaned softly. His free hand went to the back of Kevin's neck, gripped him hard, and drew him into a kiss. No, not a kiss, a possession. A devouring. Tiernan's tongue forced his mouth, searched it, and the faint sounds from the other man made Kevin's heart pound, because they were pure ecstasy.

That kiss was followed by others, a hot line of them down Kevin's throat, and his head fell back again, too heavy for him to hold up properly. He felt Tiernan rise up from the floor, pin him against the back of the loveseat, kneel astride him. He opened his eyes, and his arousal surged as he looked into the mirror overhead and saw the blond's back, the mouth traveling over his throat. *Oh, fuck.*

"What's the third?" he gasped, like an idiot.

The eyes that met his were clear blue crystal, shadowed with pain and glinting with desire. "I'm not human."

CHAPTER SIX

Slowly, slowly the human's head came up from the seat back. "I beg your pardon?"

Tiernan allowed himself a very small sigh of relief. If he were in Kevin's position—a human with a highly aroused male grinding into his groin while apparently claiming to be some kind of space alien— he would be easing a phone out of his pocket and touch-dialing 911. The fact that neither of Kevin's hands had moved off the space alien's ass was a good sign. Right?

The Fae tried not to grimace. When he tried to be funny with himself, it was a strong indication he should have been asleep a long time ago. And the sleep thing was not going on lately. He ran the backs of his fingers along Kevin's jaw, and caught his breath at the ripples of sensation that shivered up his arm. Fuck, even now he'd hoped he was wrong. But no, Kevin's eyes were as wide and startled as he knew his own to be. And if even a human could feel it, how long was he going to be able to keep persuading himself that he could walk away from this?

"I said, I'm not human." He leaned in to murmur the words into Kevin's ear, doing his best to ignore the male's scent, his body. Like that was going to happen, after the very special hell this last week had been. He could feel zipper teeth in his cock already. His tongue snaked out, without waiting for permission, and rimmed the curve of the ear into which he'd whispered, toyed with the lobe.

Kevin groaned faintly, and his fingers sank more deeply into Tiernan's cheeks, pulling him even closer. "I would be able to think more clearly if you didn't do that."

The dry humor in the warm baritone drew another relieved sigh from the Fae. "Maybe I don't want you thinking clearly?" He nipped at Kevin's earlobe sharply, soothed the spot with his tongue, and only then pulled back far enough to meet the dark brown gaze. "Maybe what I have to tell you is so crazy that if you were *thinking*, you'd have that man-mountain of a bouncer come over here to haul my ass off you." His head tilted toward the door that gave onto the winding staircase leading back up to ground level, where black and red ink covered nearly everything from the top of a shaved head to the soles of two incredibly large feet—everything that wasn't already covered with black leather or steel studs, in any event.

"If I want your ass off me, I think I can handle the job myself." Kevin's voice was soft, and amazingly even. Weight shifted under the Fae, bringing him into better contact with what felt like a very enthusiastic erection. "But at this point… I don't particularly care how fucking crazy you are. You're back."

Now the hands left Tiernan's ass, and slid slowly up his sides, under his jacket, making the Fae groan without even realizing it until Kevin smiled slightly in response. Then those hands cupped his face, a little awkwardly, but more tenderly than Tiernan could remember ever having been held by anyone. An odd contrast to the driving beat of the music, to the fire-shot darkness and the leather all around them, to the scent of sex that clung to the leather like a fine mist. Or, for that matter, to the size and strength of the hands holding him. A muscle twitched in Tiernan's jaw, but he held still, allowed the caress. This time.

"You can say you're from Alpha Centauri, or Middle-Earth… or L.A., for all I care." Kevin chuckled softly. "Maybe I'm the one who's crazy, because I'm so damn happy you're here. For however long you're here," he added, even more softly, the smile dimming a little as he studied Tiernan's face.

Tiernan cleared his throat. Sleepless nights were a lousy preparation for what he was going to do next. "I'm not going anywhere, Kevin. I… don't think I can. We're… you and I are…" How was he going to tell Kevin enough about what he was to enable the human to understand what the two of them were fated— doomed?—to be for one another? Without revealing the emptiness within himself that not even a SoulShare stood the slightest chance of touching? He took a deep breath, tried again. "Maybe Middle-Earth isn't such a bad…" What was he supposed to tell his human, that he was effing Legolas? But with actual functional balls? "Oh, fuck, this isn't working."

Tiernan tried to wrench his head away, but that gentle grip became firm, unyielding. Kevin's eyes held him; puzzled, frustrated, yet patient, in a way the Fae couldn't fathom. Waiting for him to speak, to make sense, and ready to wait as long as it took, from the look of him. Ready to sit in this little island of calm, in the midst of pounding electronic music and writhing bodies, with a male who might yet turn out to be a madman straddling his lap, and wait for him to explain the unexplainable. "*Lanan…*"

"You might start by telling me what that means." One of Kevin's hands strayed, fingertips light and tentative, down his throat, down his bare chest, teasing at his nipple ring.

Tiernan smiled, slowly, and caught Kevin's hand. "It means 'lover', where I come from." He raised the hand to his lips, traced the tip of his tongue over the knuckles. "Which is the part that's hard to explain…" *Just the bare minimum. A child's history. None of the pain.* "My kind left this world of yours almost two thousand years ago, when magick couldn't safely share a reality with the human world any longer."

One dark brow arched, but the human's gaze never faltered; the grip on his hand tightened slightly, the full sensual lips quirked up in a half-smile. "That should sound completely crazy. But the weird thing is, it doesn't. Ever since I was a kid, I've been so sure something like that had to be true. The world just didn't seem worth it, if what I could see was all there was."

"You… *believe* me?"

"I'm still listening." Kevin leaned in and up, and to Tiernan's utter astonishment, kissed him gently.

Tiernan drew a deep breath. For a moment the driving beat from the dance floor filled him, and he wondered whether there might not be such a thing as purely human magick, borne on music. "My kind built walls between the worlds, with only one portal to pass between…"

His voice trailed off, as memory grabbed him and ground him face first into the past he'd walled off as securely as the Fae Loremasters had fashioned the walls between the worlds. Once again he lay on the gleaming black floor, alone, the chains of truesilver burning bone-deep around his wrists. Then the wind, sucking him down, through the Pattern, slicing soul from body, then soul from soul. Never to be whole again. Unless…

"Tiernan! God *damn* it, Tiernan!"

The desperation in the human's voice registered first. And then the arms around him, a tight, trembling embrace. Or was the trembling his? No, not that, never that. And the tears hot against his cheek, those could never be his own. But no more could they be another's, not for him.

"*Lanan*…" He opened his eyes, found his face buried in the hard curve between Kevin's neck and shoulder; raised his head, shook it a little to clear it. "What the hell happened?"

"You tell me." Somehow, Kevin managed to sound calm and profoundly shaken at the same time. "You were talking about portals to… another world, I guess. And then you started shaking, your eyes went blank. I had to get rid of the bouncer, he thought you were O.D.'ing. Christ, I wasn't so sure myself…" Fingertips touched his face, Kevin brushing long sweaty blond hair out of his eyes. "And then you started talking. A mix of English and something else. I couldn't make out most of it. But I remember 'soul share.' You said that a lot." He looked as if he wanted to say something else, but he took a deep breath and sat back, his hands moving to Tiernan's shoulders and resting there, relaxed but ready to grip tightly again if the need arose.

He nodded. "It's what we are, you and I. SoulShares. *Scair-anaim*. The Pattern I passed through to get here tore my soul in two, and sent half of it off. To be embodied… somewhere. In someone. When it happened, I had no way of knowing who, or when, or where." His gut twisted, as if he were again truechained and trying to channel magick. Saying it made it real, made it true. "It was you."

The human didn't look nearly as stunned as Tiernan had expected. Maybe, given that Kevin had been half-souled his whole life, there was something in him waiting for this. Certainly he didn't have any reason to dread it, the way Tiernan did. Kevin had always been human, with no invulnerability to lose. And surely he had no vow to put at risk. Kevin had no one to betray, with a heart that had never known how to love.

"I can't really tell you much more than that." Tiernan coughed, trying to ease the harshness of his voice, turning his head to the side as he did so, to avoid the accusation that had to be in those eyes. "I don't know what it's like to be born half-souled, or what it felt like, to you, when we Shared—"

"Half-souled? Interesting concept." Kevin frowned, pensive, then put up an eyebrow, as if in response to a thought. "Is it going to be that mind-blowing every time we have sex from now on?"

That startled a laugh from Tiernan. "I have no way of knowing. But if sex *with* you is half as good as the sex I've had *without* you for the last week was awful, it's going to be epic."

It was as if every line and plane in Kevin's face turned to stone. *Oh, shit.* Tiernan replayed the other male's last utterance in his mind, and groaned inwardly. *He was letting you know you were welcome back, and you threw your debauchery back in his face.* He struggled not to grimace. *Although it's probably best he knows there's no happily ever after in store. Not with you.*

He started at the touch of Kevin's hand on his cheek. The human's closed expression was gone, replaced by a half-smile. "So, we've established you're not an angel?" A thumb ran along his cheekbone, and if the gaze meeting his was fractionally cooler than it had been, it was also accepting. "I'm not asking you why you ran. The way I was feeling... hell, if it hadn't been my house, I might have been the one heading out the door."

"Bullshit."

Kevin shook his head. Tiernan noticed, *really* noticed for the first time, the dark stubble on the other male's cheeks, the circles under his eyes. As if he, too, had been unable to find any kind of rest or respite. "I don't know what you felt. But I know for damned sure it's never felt that way for me before. Not even in the most erotic dreams I've ever had. It was..." He shook his head again. "'Epic' doesn't begin to do it justice. And if it's going to be like that every time... damn."

There was a low tremor in the human's voice that reached inside Tiernan, stroking like a glove of softest leather, coaxing, demanding. His body responded, surging forward where he straddled those fine woolen trousers and what they concealed. He groaned, his head dropping forward, his hair curtaining the face that turned up to his, closing out the rest of the club. There were only the two of them, gazes locked as the music hammered, mouths close enough to let each breathe the other's breath, taste the soft curses the other whispered as hardness found hardness, rocking together in rhythm.

Tiernan found it hard to breathe, as the waves of pleasure rode up his spine. His mouth came down hard on Kevin's, and that sensation, too, drew a moan from him; there had been no one in this last hellish week he had had the slightest interest in kissing, and his human's kisses alone were better than any of the sex he'd had. He forced his tongue in, caressed Kevin's with it as his hands went around to the small of a well-muscled back and pulled him closer. Shit, this was good. No, better than good. "Fucking perfect," he growled against the other male's lips.

Kevin moaned softly and increased his tempo, and a familiar hot heaviness blossomed at the Fae's groin. Familiar, yet not; he ground down into his lover, groaning with every movement and not knowing or caring who heard, almost afraid of what was bearing down on him. Kevin's thrusts nearly lifted him from the leather surface—

His cry was low and intense and guttural as the hot flood pulsed from him. His fingers hooked into claws in the small of Kevin's back, and his pleasure redoubled as he felt his human's cock throbbing against his own. Pleasure, triumph…

Joy. Pure, fucking, white-light, blissed-out joy.

Shit, this could be habit-forming.

Kevin, he finally noticed, was laughing softly, his head dropped back against the back of the loveseat.

Lustseat. Whatever. "You're definitely not an angel."

"Hell, no." Tiernan grinned. "I'm a Fae."

Kevin's head came up at this, the light in his deep brown eyes dancing with sudden amusement. "This is going to sound incredibly politically incorrect." His downward glance took in his own ruined trousers, as well as Tiernan's stained jeans. "Are you telling me… you're a *fairy*?"

CHAPTER SEVEN

Kevin glanced at his watch as he passed under a street light—only a few blocks to go—4:26 a.m. Not the first time he'd done this walk at this hour, although the circumstances had never been quite like this. Absently he avoided the piles of slush still scattered here and there; not that he cared much about his shoes, but he was going to be in them all day, and that was a much more inviting prospect when they weren't full of gray sludge. He was worried more about the eye that was changing colors.

He turned up the collar of his coat against the sleet as he waited for the light to cross Virginia Avenue. Maybe when he was done chatting with Tanner, he'd go in to work, try to figure out what was starting to look like a bug in the timesheet software before anyone else got in. He'd have to pay extra to take the car back out of the lot to go home for breakfast anyway. And hopefully Tiernan would still be asleep for a while yet, assuming his lover had gotten back to sleep after Kevin left.

Kevin checked the traffic before trotting across Constitution Avenue—the streets of Washington were never entirely empty of cabs and limos full of Very

Important People, even at this hour, even on a Wednesday. His attention was caught, as always, by the Washington Monument, pale against the pre-dawn darkness of the sky, looking, as ever, much better from a distance than up close. Like so much of Washington, when you got right down to it.

His pace slowed as his destination came into view. Even small children tended to slow down in the neighborhood of the Vietnam Veterans Memorial; it was just that kind of place. As he headed onto the Mall, toward the great black gouge in the earth, Kevin gingerly touched his eye. Yeah, that was going to black up nicely. Probably already had.

Memories flooded back at the touch—his feet knew where he was going, they didn't need his brain, it was free to replay the God-awful wrestling match of a few hours ago. Tiernan's screams. Thrashing. The elbow in the eye. The Fae waking, staring into the darkness. Pushing him away.

There was a little bouquet of flowers on the ground at the base of the Wall, near where Kevin liked to stand, one the Park Service hadn't gotten around to clearing away yet. He smiled at it and moved off a little to one side, carefully not touching it. Some people were very picky about where they left things, and one never wanted to get in the way of anyone's memories.

He leaned back against the Wall and looked around, feeling the cold of the stone between his shoulder blades, seeping through his thick wool coat. Off to his left, the Washington Monument reached skyward, looking more phallic than usual, or was that just him? And to the right, past the other black granite arm of the Wall, he could just make out the sad, thoughtful features of Mr. Lincoln.

He tipped his head back. His eyes slowly closed; the adrenalin of Tiernan's nightmare was finally starting to wear off, and he could think about why he'd come here in the first place, after Tiernan snarled at him.

Hey, Tanner, what's doin'?

It had been so long, it was hard to remember what his brother's voice would have sounded like, if he'd been there to answer. But the face, that was always there. A face that would always be five years younger than his own had been, four years ago in August. It was all right, though, Tanner didn't have to answer. It wasn't like he was really here, but there wasn't a memorial for veterans of his war yet, at least not in D.C. And even if there were, Tanner Almstead probably wouldn't be on it, not unless the Defense Department got a whole hell of a lot more open-minded about who it considered casualties of war. But Dad had been in 'Nam, and there were a few guys from his unit here on the Wall, near where Kevin was leaning. So this was good, this was close enough. *I think you'd like Tiernan, little brother. Either that or you'd fight like two tomcats. And even then you'd probably go out for a beer after.*

The image of his kid brother in desert fatigues sitting down with Tiernan at the bar in Purgatory over a couple of tall cold ones made Kevin realize just how very late it was, and how very tired he was. *He screams at night. Just like you did, after you came home. Wish you could talk to him. He won't talk to me. Maybe he can't...*

Perhaps he keeps secrets.

The voice came from beside Kevin, where he sat in the leather loveseat. Startled, he turned, and blinked, bemused, as his eyes refused to focus properly. Loveseat? What was he doing back in Purgatory?

There was a woman in a scarlet gown standing beside the loveseat, looking down at him. No, it was a man, grotesquely erect. No, a scorpion, barbed tail arched over its back.

"Secrets? Bullshit." Tiernan had no reason to hide anything from him.

Are you so sure? That one keeps his own counsel. About many things. The woman's gaze turned to him, infinitely old and infinitely evil. ***Ask him what he hides from you, little human—***

Kevin's phone went off in his pocket, kicking his heart into a wild race. He nearly dropped the damned thing onto the frozen ground beside the Wall before he had it all the way out of his pocket, and seeing the caller I.D. didn't help a hell of a lot. "Tiernan? You okay?"

"I am now." The voice on the other end of the phone was soft, blurred with sleep. "Where are you?"

"I'm at the Vietnam Vets' Memorial."

"What the hell are you doing there? Never mind, are you alone?"

Kevin glanced around. He wasn't sure how long he'd been asleep standing there, but there didn't seem to be any Park Police making rounds just now. Or anyone else, for that matter. "Yeah, I am. Don't know for how much longer, though."

"I'll be right there. Just stay where you are."

"But I took the car."

A soft chuckle. "Not an issue. Incoming."

Kevin frowned, confused. Was he asleep again? The chill of the black granite at his back would seem to indicate otherwise, but… what the *hell*?

Beside him, on the other side of the little bunch of flowers, the air wavered, as if with heat, in an area the size of a human body. Transparent at first, it grew cloudy, luminescent. Then, swiftly, colors filled in, followed by shape, form. Flesh. Tiernan stood beside him, wearing jeans and nothing else, his leather jacket thrown over his shoulder as if he'd snatched it up as an afterthought, before doing whatever it was he'd just done.

"Close your mouth, *lanan,* before something flies—oh, fuck, did I do that?" The smile Tiernan had been wearing when he appeared quickly gave way to a frown; the Fae stepped forward, reached out a hand, tentatively touched Kevin's cheekbone.

"It's all right, you didn't mean to." Kevin's murmur was vague, distracted, given that he was more than a little preoccupied with what he'd seen. Thought he'd seen. "How did you appear like that?"

"It's called Fading. It's how I get where I need to go, when there's no Mercedes on offer." There was a hint of gentle teasing in the tone, but it quickly gave way to concern as the gentle touch continued. "Damn it. And it takes humans so long to heal."

"Don't worry about it." He caught at Tiernan's hand, held it. "I'll just tell the guys at work that I'm involved with a fight club. Might help my image." He squeezed the hand he held, gently. "I'm more worried about you. You were in a bad way when I left. I didn't like leaving you that way."

"I didn't give you much of a choice. I threw you out." Tiernan's face abruptly shut down. He didn't turn away, but he might as well have. "Out of your own fucking house. I should be whipped."

Kevin stared, appalled. "That's not funny."

"It wasn't meant to be." A muscle twitched in the Fae's stubbled jaw. "You've taken me in, and what return have you had for your hospitality? Five nights of sharing a bed with a screaming psychotic."

"Five nights when I was able to be there to hold you when you woke up." Kevin spoke softly, evenly, quietly. "How long has it been since you've had that?"

Tiernan growled softly. "You got the bad end of the bargain, for certain."

"Let me be the judge." Kevin took the jacket his lover carried, draped it gently around his broad shoulders, rested his hands gently on those shoulders, both to hold the leather in place and to give Tiernan some physical contact; he'd learned the Fae always needed touch, eventually, after one of his nightmares. He needed the anchor in some reality, even if it wasn't the reality he'd been forced to leave behind. "Was it the same dream?"

"Hell, yes." A grimace twisted his compelling features. "Falling through the Pattern." He tilted his head, eyed Kevin. "I don't know why I lash out. Maybe we should try separate beds."

"Fuck that noise. I can take it. I'm used to it."

"How?" Tiernan eyed him skeptically. "You never told me you specialized in shacking up with lady wrestlers. Or was it roller derby?"

Kevin couldn't keep back a snort. "Oh, yeah. Definitely my type." He sobered, a little, feeling the chill of the Wall through his coat once again. "My brother went through a lot of the same shit, after he got back from Iraq. You ever hear of PTSD?"

Tiernan's eyes went wide with shock, all out of proportion to what Kevin had just said. "Your brother?"

"Yeah. Tanner. He was five years younger than me. Our dad was a Marine, in Vietnam, and after 9/11, Tanner decided to join up. He was nineteen…" Kevin's voice trailed off. *Too damned young.*

Tiernan's gaze turned to the Wall, behind Kevin's head, when Kevin mentioned his father, searching for an Almstead in the glossy black surface. "What happened to him?" The softly accented voice was gentle, wondering.

"In Iraq?" Kevin brought his own mind back to the present with some difficulty. "He didn't talk much about it, but I know he was in a convoy, just south of Haditha. The Humvee he was riding in tripped an IED, and the—the bottom wasn't armored, the fucker ripped the bottom right out of the Hummer and flipped it. All the other guys in it were killed… Tanner's leg was pinned under the axle. The wreck burned. They managed to save his leg and he got shipped home. That's when the nightmares started."

The crystal-blue gaze burned at him, out of the pre-dawn darkness. "Like mine." It wasn't a question.

"A lot like yours." His hands tightened on Tiernan's shoulders. "He didn't talk about them—any more than you talk about yours—but we were able to figure out, from what he said and from talking with a few of the guys from his unit, afterwards, he was pretty much reliving the explosion. The way you seem

to be reliving what happened to you... that night."
Whatever that night had been. When it came to being
close-mouthed, Tanner had had absolutely nothing on
Tiernan.

"Afterwards?" From the look on his face, there
was something else Tiernan wanted very much to ask,
but was firmly setting it aside. "After what?"

Kevin took a deep breath. Four years and it still
hurt like yesterday. "Tanner died. In a motorcycle
wreck, four years ago in May. The forensics guys said
it looked like he laid the bike down in front of an
oncoming semi. No knowing whether he did it on
purpose or not." He shook his head. "I don't think he
did. I hope he didn't. He loved to ride the edge on that
bike. I've heard a lot of guys with PTSD try to manage
it that way. Look for things that give them the
adrenaline rush."

"You loved your brother." There was a soft,
wondering quality to the Fae's voice. His expression
was far off, as if he only half heard what Kevin was
saying. As if the fact of Tanner's death hadn't touched
him nearly as much as that simple truth, that Kevin
had loved him.

"Of course I did." Kevin frowned slightly. "He
was my brother."

"Very little in this world is 'of course,' *lanan*.
This world, or any other."

Kevin opened his mouth, to ask him what he
meant, but before he could speak, he saw a shiver run
through the Fae's hard-muscled body, bare under
jacket and jeans and barefoot on the frozen ground.
"Damn, come here." His hands encircled Tiernan's
wrists, covering the scars there. He drew his lover in,

74

ignoring wordless protests, guiding the bare arms around his waist, opening his full dark coat and bundling them both in it. "Christ, you *are* insane. You're freezing. Hold on for a little while. Idiot." He laughed softly into long blond hair, closed his eyes as hands opened out across his back, seeking warmth.

And when the voice whispered to him again, he was safe within the circle, and not even the echoes touched him.

That one keeps his own counsel. About many things. Ask him what he hides from you.

CHAPTER EIGHT

Greenwich Village
New York City

Tiernan leaned against the windowsill, looking out into the early evening pedestrian traffic on Bleecker Street. He hadn't really been living in Greenwich Village long enough to get particularly nostalgic about it, only a few years, but it had a pleasant aura to it. A good vibe, he supposed some humans might call it. He'd lived in a lot of places, in more than a century and a half on this side of the Pattern, moving around every few years, before the humans around him started noticing that he didn't age. He'd even lived in D.C. a couple of times, once right after the American Civil War and then again back in the late Forties, for a few years. This place, though, had felt as much like home as anyplace in the human world ever could.

But that was about to change. He shrugged and turned away from the window, his gaze raking the efficiency apartment. The bathroom door stood ajar, revealing the sybaritic tub and shower combination he'd violated pretty much every rule this building had in order to get installed. A shame he couldn't take that with him. He wasn't one to accumulate things, but he'd grown very fond of that bad boy. Sixteen settings on the shower head alone... *damn.*

The coffee maker tugged at what passed for his heartstrings, too, but it at least was a brand name and he could always order another one—should have already, he'd groaned out loud when he'd first discovered that his human drank instant coffee. *Caffeine is caffeine,* Kevin had said with a shrug, their first morning waking up together.

Instant coffee is sacrilege had been his snarled reply.

It had been met with laughter. *You'll have to tell me more about that religion.*

He'd let that one go, since the Fae had no gods. And even if they did, he doubted any would have followed him through the Pattern. What use was a half-souled god? With a congregation of one? So far as he'd ever been able to tell, anyway. Granted, Fae had never exactly lined up in the Realm for the privilege of being torn asunder, but it *had* happened before. There had been stories. But he had yet to meet another of his kind.

The open mouth of his duffel bag beckoned from the California king-sized bed that took up most of the rest of the little space. Most of his clothes were already packed, and his shitkickers stood next to the bed, waiting for him to step into them. Truthfully, he preferred to be barefoot. He didn't like to be encumbered, and he didn't feel the cold. Much.

He had finally felt it, though, in the small hours of this morning, standing on the National Mall with

Kevin. At first, the shivers had been the last fading remnants of nightmare, the same one that had made him lash out. But gradually, the cold had seeped into him, spreading from the soles of his feet up through his body, and when his human had drawn him in, he'd only put up token resistance, leaned in and pressed himself close and sighed, splaying his hands out over that broad strong back.

Come stay with me, Kevin had whispered.

He'd started, and drawn back, and seen chagrin in that dark brown gaze. *I know it's sudden, but if what you've said is true and we really do share a soul...* Kevin's struggle with that concept had been a mighty one, and still was. *Then maybe it's the right thing to do. And maybe I can help you with the dreams.*

Going to let me black the other eye for you? He'd shaken his head, and tried to protest; in the end, though, the lawyer's persuasive powers—and a hot kiss or three, complete with unfair breathless moans -- had carried the argument.

He shook his head, reaching down to pick up the battered leather volume on the small table beside the bed, and the little leather pouch half-full of charcoal sticks. A few leaves had been torn out, and then tucked back in; he ran his fingers idly over the rough edges, then jammed book and bag into the duffel. He stepped into the boots, stomped his feet down into them. Almost done.

A belt hung over one of the bedposts, as if he'd played ring-toss with it; he caught it up, unbuckled it, and slid it through the belt loops of his leathers. The sheath hanging there was empty, but that was easily remedied. His stiletto was stuck in the plaster wall, almost at eye level, over the bed, right where he'd thrown it.

One of the two pages tacked to the wall was his latest attempt to capture in charcoal the intricate knots and loops of the Pattern; no two drawings were ever the same, and none was ever quite right. Even trying to copy his tattoo didn't help, for some reason. Maybe someday he'd get it right, though, and *then* maybe it would quit haunting his fucking nightmares.

Then there was the other. He pulled the stiletto free, slipped it into its sheath, and smoothed the gouge it had left in the thick paper with a fingertip. A breathtakingly beautiful fair-haired woman looked back at him, caught by a few strokes of the charcoal, in the act of looking back over her shoulder. Just as she had when she'd Faded from his cell, a century and a half ago.

If he'd ever had the ability to love, it had died in that cell.

He reached for the torn page… stopped. There was nothing more here he needed. He buckled the duffel shut, hoisted the strap over his shoulder, the truesilver links coiled around the strap jingling softly, and Faded. Without looking back.

***

"Have you ever actually given anyone a heart attack, doing that?" Kevin bent to pick up the bottle of Harp he'd dropped when Tiernan materialized next to the fireplace.

"Not yet." Tiernan smirked. His human was proving to have a talent for improving his darker moods. He let the bag slide from his shoulder to the floor, reached out lazily, and caught Kevin by his expensive silk tie, pulling him over. "There are better ways to do that."

Kevin's breath caught, just a little, a sound that went straight to Tiernan's groin, moved in, and set up housekeeping. His eyes narrowed, his smile became the barest curve of his lips; he took the other male's chin between his thumb and forefinger, and drew him in until their mouths were separated by only a breath. Nothing said this new way of things had to last forever—even a SoulShare's heart could break, surely, and this human's heart would, when it finally faced the void within the Fae. But until then...

"What do you do to me?" Kevin's voice was a husky whisper. His arms slipped around Tiernan's waist, but he resisted the invitation to the kiss. "As unoriginal a question as that is."

Anything I want, came readily to mind. "Anything that gives you pleasure," he found himself whispering back instead, and damn if that wasn't just as good; the other male shivered in his arms and closed the last gap between them, his tongue running around Tiernan's lips in a quick, tentative circle before Tiernan turned the touch into a kiss that meant business.

The Fae moved to loosen Kevin's tie. Something about the caress of the heavy maroon silk against his palm changed his mind, though, and he dropped his hand to the plain silver buckle of his human's belt. Even though his truesilver chains had stopped burning him the moment he passed through the Pattern, becoming nothing more than a quicksilver-gleaming metal that defied all attempts at analysis, it had taken him decades to touch silver with anything other than narrow-eyed suspicion. Now, though, he made short work of the belt, and the fastening behind it, and the zipper, sliding his hand in and growling in approval as it encountered nothing but mostly erect cock. "Did you have a pleasant day, *lanan*?"

"Not the word I'd use." Kevin was slightly breathless, and his hips moved in tight little jerks as he tried to control his response to Tiernan's caresses. Tried, and failed, and tried again, trembling. "Oh, fuck."

"If that was an invitation, I accept." Releasing his grip on the human's strong jaw, he slid his hand around to the back of his neck, gripping firmly, pulling back just enough to get the perfect angle for a searching, demanding kiss. His other hand pushed the trousers off Kevin's hard-muscled hips, to let them pool on the floor around the human's bare feet. "And even if it wasn't, I still accept."

Again that hesitation, sending a thrill rippling up Tiernan's spine. Whether it was something to do with the SoulShare, or simply something buried in Kevin for his whole life without ever finding expression until now, something in his lover hungered for this. Hungered for *him*. Even as everything the human had ever been *until* now looked on and wondered what the fuck was going on.

Kevin stepped out of his trousers, kicked them aside, and pulled Tiernan tightly against him, grinding bare against him and moaning softly. Their mouths met, clashed with each other; Tiernan shifted his weight, nudged at Kevin, and suddenly the two men knelt facing one another on the thick rug in front of the fire. It was a simple enough channeling to kill the light, leave only the firelight, making the human's eyes go wide. Tiernan shook his head and smiled, a smile with an edge. "The ride only gets wilder from here, *lanan*."

"What did you—?"

Tiernan shook his head. He didn't want to talk about magick now. He wanted to make some. A different kind. He leaned forward and bore the other man back to the carpet. He braced his hands on either side of Kevin's head, took his weight on his arms, drove his hips down into the cradle the other male formed for him. Damn, it felt good. It felt right. And it felt even more right when those long strong legs wrapped awkwardly around him and tried to draw him in closer.

Though Kevin sometimes hesitated, though he questioned, the thoughtful pleasure he took in each new discovery was a new experience for the Fae. The joy, the shared joy. Tiernan bit his lip, remembering the wildfire racing through him with every orgasm. His own, or his partner's. Fucking addictive. He circled his hips, his eyes half closing as Kevin groaned.

"Fuck... Tiernan... the leathers..." Kevin's expression was an incredibly arousing combination of wince and plea. His hips jerked up, and he sucked in a breath, the reflexive tightening of his legs telling Tiernan which of the two mattered more to him.

"Like that, do you, *lanan*?" The tight leathers were sweetest torture to him as well, his erection was desperate to be out of them and into Kevin's exquisite hold. He thrust hard, clenching his teeth as the human gasped. "Is there something you'd like more? Tell me."

"You know what I want." Kevin's voice was thick, unsteady; he pushed the leather jacket back off Tiernan's shoulders, enough to let him catch at the bare skin beneath. "You. In me."

Tiernan laughed softly. He shrugged out of his jacket, and tossed it on the floor beside the fire. The heat reached his skin directly, now, licking at it. Licking, ah, now, there was an idea for later. He pulled back far enough to yank one-handed at his belt, the fastening of the leathers. His cock sprang free the moment there was any chance for it to do so, scattering clear drops across Kevin's tight abs and coarse dark curls.

The human cursed, almost inaudibly, and reached for Tiernan's erection, closed his hand around it, his thumb curling up and around to run over the broad flat head. His legs came up; he pushed, urging Tiernan toward his entrance. The Fae groaned and shook his head, his long blond hair falling unheeded into his eyes; he caught at Kevin's shoulder to roll him over, his cock pulsing with need.

"Tiernan, no." Kevin resisted Tiernan's hand. His eyes caught the firelight, a warm dark brown that drew the Fae in despite himself. "Please. Can we try it this way?" A blush was creeping across the human's face, but his jaw was set, his expression determined.

Tiernan felt himself blushing as well, his face giving the fire a run for its money. He ducked his head and growled, his hand closing around Kevin's and pumping harder at himself, needing more lubrication. And needing an excuse not to meet those beautiful eyes, just for a second. Had he really never taken Kevin face to face? Well, no, of course not. Because he never did that. No one got to see him lose control like that.

Not even your SoulShare?

A muscle jumped in Tiernan's jaw as he guided the head of his cock to the tight puckered entrance that drew him like a magnet. *Maybe especially not my SoulShare.* The possibility Kevin might see, so soon, into that void within him, the place where love ought to live, but where in him there was nothing but the echo of Moriath's mocking laughter, was something to be avoided at all costs. He didn't love the human, he couldn't, but he also couldn't stand to hurt him. The thought of the light going out of those eyes was more than he could endure.

"Fuck, yes," Kevin breathed, as Tiernan eased the weeping head of his cock past his tight ring. And the sound brought Tiernan's gaze back to his human's face, as the deep brown eyes went wide in wonder, slowly went heavy-lidded with desire.

The Fae braced his knees and eased himself deeper, releasing his grip on his cock and falling forward once again. He caught his weight on his hands, his hair tumbling to form a curtain around their faces. *Shit, those eyes...* He almost snarled, almost pulled away. But no. He would stay, he would make himself look, because Kevin deserved it. Kevin deserved a hell of a lot more, a partner far better than the one the Pattern compelled him to. But Tiernan would try.

"Christ, Tiernan." The other male's thighs eased wider, the unbearably tight passage relaxed a fraction.

A hand clutched Tiernan's ass, urging him deeper, begging for speed; he resisted, wanting to savor every time the human had to breathe deeply and consciously let go in order to let him penetrate another inch. Then Kevin's other hand came up and fingertips brushed Tiernan's cheek, long strong fingers buried themselves in his hair and drew his head down. Lips grazed his; he felt hot panting breaths against his mouth.

Tiernan growled and took Kevin's mouth hard, his tongue forcing its way into his mouth. There was no need for force, his lover yielded willingly, yet still the Fae took him. His hips pumped hard now. Their bodies slapped together, leather against bare flesh, Tiernan's naked chest and nipple ring feeling the kiss of linen and silk.

Silk. *Aw, fuck.* Tiernan took his weight on one hand, and levered himself up. With the other, he fisted the knot of his lover's so-proper maroon silk tie, and began to twist.

"*Tiernan—*" The beginnings of panic in those beautiful eyes, the face below his going redder.

"Trust me, lover. I'll make it good for you." *Ohh, yeah.* He could do this. He could blow his lover's fucking mind. And never let him see a thing. "Grab yourself—work yourself." He waited until he felt movement, heard a heartfelt groan, and knew that Kevin was complying. Redoubling his own pace, he twisted tighter around his lover's throat. *So fucking good…* harder, faster.

Kevin surged under him, thrashing, demanding. The human's hold clamping down, the heat of him rivaling the flames that played over their bodies. Tiernan's cock went rigid, his balls drew up tight. He gritted his teeth, the timing had to be perfect. Kevin's soft cries, fading, the human's body quivering, stilling, y*es*—

Kevin's dark gaze locked with his, pupils dilated, eyes gone wide with pleasure.

Tiernan was falling. White fire raced down his spine, pooled molten at the base of it, engorged his cock. And he fell. Into Kevin's eyes. Faster. Lost to everything, except the dark gaze seeing straight into him—

Two bodies slammed together, two cries sounded as one. Liquid heat shot from Tiernan's body, pumped into Kevin's tight dark passage; the Fae's body jerked ecstatically, his hand let go the improvised noose around his lover's throat and the human's choked cry sounded in Tiernan's ear as jet after jet coated Kevin's hand and both their bodies.

And the joy. Tiernan nearly wept with it. So much more than pleasure, seizing him, convulsing him. Each time, he nearly forgot what this was like, as if his mind simply couldn't hold it from one sexual collision to the next. All he was left with was the memory of something perfect, and the all-consuming need to know it again.

"Tiernan?" The voice came to him as if from a distance, soft, dazed. "What the hell was that?"

"Nothing." The human couldn't mean the seizure of joy. That happened every time they had sex; they'd talked about it, compared notes, discovered they had been having almost identical experiences, and more or less agreed it had something to do with the SoulShare.

This had to be the other. The falling. And now it was Tiernan's turn to panic, because if Kevin was asking, it meant he'd felt it too. *Shit.* "Maybe I should have let go of the tie a little sooner. Sorry."

Dark eyes met his, puzzled, wary. "I've never heard of that sort of thing happening with erotic asphyxiation before."

His shrug cost him almost everything he had left. "You've never done it with me before, either." *Fuck, tell him the truth—at least tell him that you felt it, too.* "Something to look forward to next time." Tiernan wanted to cry out as Kevin's head fell back. But he clenched his jaw and waited in silence.

"It was incredible." A small smile crept across Kevin's features as he nodded. "Not sure I can take that on a nightly basis."

"Then this tie can be our signal." Tiernan's smile covered so many things—relief, despair, self-hatred. Kevin believed him, and was letting it go. *You should never believe me,* Ianan. *Never.* "When you want this, just wear it."

Kevin chuckled softly, and yawned. "I don't think I want to move."

"Then let's stay right here." Deep breath. "For a while."

CHAPTER NINE

Ask him what he hides from you.

Kevin stared, unseeing, at the monitor on the desk in front of him, trying and failing to will the damned voice from the dream out of his head. He hadn't been sleeping for shit since Tiernan had moved in, what with the Fae's nightmares. Even before those dreams became physical, they'd been spectacular, and when the other man was sleeping soundly, more often than not he himself was lying awake, watching him. Worrying, or just trying to get a grip on what had been a perfectly normal life until a couple of weeks ago.

That one keeps his own counsel. Keeps secrets.

Well, hell, of course he did. He'd only known Tiernan for, what, under two weeks? How much could you tell a person in that amount of time, even if you had the kind of past it was possible to explain and felt like running your mouth? And for a week of *that* time, the Fae had been on the run.

Yeah, fucking his way around at least two continents.

Wearily, Kevin told himself to shut the hell up. The man who had stood his whole life on its head, the man who wasn't really a man at all—his SoulShare—

was deeply wounded. And was covering the best he could, the way Tanner had. Hadn't Tiernan been up front with him about what he'd spent their week apart doing? Not the behavior of a male who was trying to keep deep dark secrets from his lover. What could Tiernan be hiding that was worse than what he'd already told Kevin about?

Stupid fucking dreams.

He shrugged, and tried again to focus on the computer screen. Time to wrap for the day and get the hell out of Dodge. It was early, only 7:00, but it was amazing how knowing you didn't have a future decreased your motivation to burn the old midnight oil. And how a text in your phone instructing you to head straight for the Jacuzzi when you got home and be naked by the time you got there made you anxious to clock out.

Chuckling at himself, he called up the billing software to double-check his time. Yes, another world existed alongside our own. Yes, the inhabitants were beautiful to look upon and possessed powers beyond mortal imagining. But the reality he'd found, or that found him, was *so* not what Tolkien had been on about.

What the hell? Kevin frowned, and leaned closer to the monitor, as if making it bigger might make it go away. "It" being yet another frigging double-bill. From today. And he'd only entered his time half an hour ago. An hour and a half to pro bono, but right next to it on the spreadsheet, an hour and a half to the Balfour Trust. This was the third time it happened, if you counted the times he'd caught a week ago as one time. Once could have been a mistake. Even twice could

89

have been a mistake, especially for someone in the condition he'd been in lately. But three? Not likely.

"Almstead. You're still here?"

The voice from the doorway made Kevin start. Quickly, he minimized the window with the bootleg software plastered across it, then looked up and gave Art O'Halloran a tired smile. "It's not all that late." It was out before he could stop it, pure reflex. One of the basic rules of survival for associates at any law firm— never, *ever* let a senior partner know you don't sleep at your desk and wash your socks in the men's room.

The older man laughed and winked, as if Kevin had told a slightly off-color joke. "You have a life these days, young man. Or so I hear. Best get out there and live it."

"I... what?" No need to feign confusion, not when he was oversupplied with the genuine article. He didn't talk about his personal life with anyone at the firm. Where would O'Halloran have heard anything about his situation? "Vicious rumor, sir. Pay it no mind."

The partner shook his head. He was still smiling, but his broad florid features and his shock of silver hair gave him an aura of gravity at odds with the Irish air of good cheer. "Kevin, I'm on the partnership committee, remember?" He paused, nodding in response to the wince Kevin couldn't help. "I happen to think the vote was completely unfair, but I wouldn't blame you a bit if you started making up for lost time. Nothing can ever give you back the years you sweated blood for this place, but you're entitled to live your life. And if you've found something that makes you want to be somewhere other than within these four walls, enjoy it. That's my advice." Without waiting for a reply, the big man was gone.

Kevin's frown started the moment O'Halloran's back was turned, and it got deeper as he powered down his computer, stood up from the desk, and collected his coat from the brass tree beside the door. He would have expected that soliloquy from a concerned friend like David Mondrian, who actually did give a shit about what happened to him, and whether or not he was happy. But not from a name partner at the firm which rejected him for full membership on the grounds he didn't want it badly enough. And there was something else that didn't sit right, something he couldn't put his finger on. O'Halloran's failure to comment on his shiner? Maybe.

His phone jostled in his pocket, reminding him of the reason he did in fact want to be somewhere other than here; he picked up his pace as he walked down the long corridor to the lobby, passing the offices of younger lawyers, most of them with the lights on, the offices of partners, most of them dark. That was one of the perks of partnership. The partners were the rainmakers, the ones bringing the work into the firm. The associates, like himself, were the ones who *did* the work, until they'd done enough of it to impress the Big Boys and were allowed into the club.

Which brought up another question: what had O'Halloran, one of the Biggest Boys, with his name on the firm, been doing in the office so late? More frowning.

He was standing at the elevator, settling his collar against what was surely going to be the damp miserable cold outside, before the thought lurking unquietly in the back of his mind finally yammered loudly enough to get his full attention.

Art O'Halloran was lead counsel on the Balfour Trust account.

***

"You're home early."

Kevin leaned against the bedroom wall, carefully out of sight of the doorway leading to the master bath, teasing his socks off. The text had been very specific that he was to arrive as naked as the day he was born, and he hadn't quite managed to finish stripping on his way up from the garage. "Wouldn't you be, under the circumstances?" The bed, he noticed, was already turned down, and the lights dimmed; the lights in the bathroom were off, but the flicker of candlelight was visible.

The laugh drifting out of the bathroom was low and wicked, and for some reason made Kevin think of jalapeño honey, the kind his cousin made. Which made him think of drizzling honey all over the body waiting for him in that hot tub. Or, better yet, of being covered in it himself, and letting Tiernan lick him clean. *Was I always this horny, and didn't realize it? Damn.*

Finally naked, and already semi-erect, he pushed off the wall and stepped into the bathroom doorway. And stopped dead, staring. Maybe a dozen pillar candles were scattered around what had been a strictly utilitarian bathroom, giving it an air of mystery, even of decadence, casting everything into deep, flickering shadows. Everything except the Jacuzzi in the far corner, and its occupant. Tiernan reclined in the hot tub, the ends of his long blond hair adrift; one arm was stretched out along the back of it, the other mostly invisible under the water. The water rippled and danced in the candlelight, stirred by the jets under its surface. Little waves lapped at the Fae's chest, now concealing, now revealing the nipple ring that caught the candlelight and winked at him.

"Fuck," Kevin breathed, barely audible even to him.

Tiernan's laugh seemed to snake out and encircle Kevin's wrist, drawing him closer. All right, not his wrist. But something nearly as thick. He knew some of the movement in the water wasn't the work of the jets. It was Tiernan's hand, moving up and down. Stroking.

"Like what you see, *lanan*?" The Fae's voice was soft, but with an edge to it. "I know I do." The barely visible hand stroked upward, and Tiernan's head fell back; those crystal-blue eyes, though, never left Kevin's. "Come here—I want you doing this."

Kevin swallowed hard and climbed into the tub, settling on the seat next to Tiernan. As the Fae's arm came warm and solid around his shoulders, he reached for the other male's cock, curved his hand around it, gripped the thickness of it firmly until he heard the faint groan that told him he had the pressure just right. "B-been waiting long?" He tried to match his lover's casually sensual tone. The slight smile that quirked the Fae's lips told him he was at least a little off the mark. "You're hard as granite."

Tiernan's answering chuckle made Kevin's own cock jerk erect a moment before it, too, was clasped in a warm, demanding hand. "I've been that way most of the day. It's about time I got some relief." His lover's mouth sought his, tongue sweeping across the seam between his lips until they parted to let it in. At the same time, one of Tiernan's legs wrapped around both of his, drawing him even closer in the already close space.

God, the sensation of that tongue caressing his, searching his mouth. Kevin half suspected Tiernan could make him come with just that stimulation alone; the image of the two of them kissing like this in a crowded room flashed through his mind unbidden, and he moaned as his cock twitched hard in his lover's grip. Fuck, yes, he could see it. On a dance floor, or at a restaurant, in the park, at a movie…

Or at work. How many of his co-workers had boasted of late-night office trysts? The thought of being interrupted by Tiernan, tilted back in his office chair, pulled away from the computer, one strong hand taking hold of the knot of his tie—

"What is it, *lanan*?"

Kevin took a deep breath and tried to relax, thanking God the fist he had involuntarily clenched was the one resting on his lover's shoulder and not the one gripping his cock. The image of Tiernan suddenly appearing beside his desk was replaced by Arthur O'Halloran, and even in the steam-swirled heat of the bathroom Kevin's sweat was cold. Did the partner know about the double-billing? Did he suspect Kevin of doing it on purpose? Was that why he'd turned up tonight?

"I—shit, I'm sorry." Kevin's head dropped back; he took one deep, unsteady breath, then another, raised his head, and met the Fae's crystalline gaze. "Work was kind of… well, it sucked." No need to shove his paranoia off onto his lover, especially when it was the kind of thing only lawyers gave a damn about.

"It must have." Tiernan's voice was light, noncommittal, completely unreadable. "Total buzz kill." The Fae's hand moved slightly, releasing Kevin's cock, and Kevin's face went red as he realized its massive length had gone entirely soft.

"Oh, hell," he muttered. "Give me another chance?" He squeezed Tiernan more tightly and grimaced, as he realized his lover, too, was losing his erection.

Tiernan leaned in closer, studying him. Gentle fingertips touched the bruise around his left eye, ran in a semi-circle under his right. The other male shook his head, frowning slightly. "I don't think this is a good time. You're exhausted." The Fae levered himself to a more upright position, water falling away down his body and gleaming in the candlelight.

Kevin couldn't keep back a groan, and at this Tiernan finally smiled. "Come on, *Ianan*. Let's put you to bed." The long, lean, hard-muscled body unfolded. A hand reached down to Kevin and drew him up, pulled him into an embrace and a quick kiss. "Doesn't have to be for the whole night—I'll go downstairs and plug in *Call of Duty* or something, blow shit up for a few hours, and then come back up here and wake you the best way, how does that sound?"

"Like a nursemaid. A really perverted nursemaid." But Kevin's heart wasn't in the grumble, as he let Tiernan towel him off and lead him into the bedroom. The truth was, as soon as the word 'bed' had left the Fae's lips, he'd nearly fallen asleep where he'd been sitting. "Did you just enchant me or something?"

A muscle twitched next to Tiernan's eye as he helped Kevin under the blankets. "No, I promise, the only part I had to play in your not being able to keep your eyes open was supplying the screaming nightmares keeping you up half the night every night since Friday." He straightened as Kevin settled himself, a hand resting lightly on his hair. "I'll wake you later, *lanan*."

Tiernan smiled, in a perfunctory sort of way, turned, and left the room. And the sight of his perfectly muscled ass heading for the bedroom door was almost enough to keep Kevin's eyes open until the Fae switched off the lights by the traditional method and closed the door.

***

"They woke together, hand in hand. Sam was almost fresh, ready for another day; but Frodo sighed. His sleep had been uneasy, full of dreams of fire, and waking brought him no comfort."

Kevin blinked, unsure how long he had been staring at the leather-bound copy of *The Return of the King* in his lap. In fact, he wasn't sure where he'd come by the book at all; he'd never gotten around to buying a leather-bound set. It would most likely be an expensive exercise in futility, given the way he read an entire paperback set of the trilogy to pieces every few years.

And the book rested on a faded pair of green and yellow sweatpants he hadn't seen since his undergraduate wrestling days at William and Mary. *What the hell?*

He looked up, around himself, and a smile slowly spread across his face. He was in a hexagonal room, built mostly of stone. A fireplace was set in one wall, with two wingback chairs in front of it, in one of which he currently lounged, an arrangement he'd tried to duplicate in his townhouse, with moderate success. Nothing could truly duplicate this room, which he'd created for himself during a seminar on self-hypnosis as an undergrad. This was his place of peace, and he didn't need to look around any more to know what he'd find. Two walls of the hexagon were actually floor-to-ceiling windows, looking out over a view that tended to change every time he visited the place, during the seminar and occasionally since then—more often in dreams than on purpose, of late. Like now, apparently. A third wall was the fireplace, and the remaining three walls were bookshelves, full to overflowing.

Kevin stretched, yawning, one hand protectively on Tolkien to keep the precious volume from sliding off his lap. *I'm yawning in a dream. Christ, I really must be out of it.*

Has he driven you away again?

The voice came from the other wingback chair. *That's fucking impossible* was Kevin's first thought. His professor had commented during the seminar that Kevin had an uncanny ability to control his own self-induced hypnotic state, to keep out random and unwanted distractions.

What the hell IS that thing? was the second thought, as he leaned forward and saw the creature, the same one he'd seen as he'd leaned against the Wall just before Tiernan appeared. It looked like a woman, at the moment—no, wait, a man. *Please, God, not the scorpion. Not in my library.*

The man chuckled, a sound like stone dragged over bones. ***As you will. Though I'm not accustomed to holding one form for long.*** As if to prove his point, the scorpion flickered into existence briefly, to be quickly replaced by the cold, elegant woman. ***My apologies.***

"Yeah, right." Kevin's jaw clenched. "You aren't even here to begin with. You can't be."

She laughed softly, running her tongue around very red lips. ***It's not your place, human, to tell me where I can be and where I cannot.*** She sat forward, long scarlet fingernails digging into the leather of the chair. ***And I ask you again, has he driven you away?***

"Tiernan? No, he's letting me sleep." Kevin cursed as the woman's—no, man's—eyes sparkled at his mention of his lover's name. *Probably should have kept that to myself. Shit.* Although whatever it was, it answered his thoughts, so chances were good keeping secrets wasn't going to work very well.

The man smiled. Kevin would have preferred the laughter. ***You can keep nothing from me, human. Though it amuses me when you try. And speaking of secrets…***

Kevin growled. *Fuck off.*

More laughter, of a stomach-churning variety that sounded more like scorpion than like either man or woman. ***No doubt you think he will tell you everything. How touching.*** It was the woman who leaned forward, placed a cold red-clawed hand on his arm. ***Look at his wrists, human. And ask him to explain what you see.*** She was gone, leaving behind only ice-smoke drifting up from where her hand had rested.

Kevin scrubbed at his forearm with his opposite hand, trying to bring warmth back into it. And trying to remember what had chilled it.

CHAPTER TEN

Tiernan looked down at the sleeping human, frowning. Kevin looked peaceful, but dark hair was plastered to his forehead and he was wrapped in sweat-soaked sheets. Whatever sleep he'd managed to get these last few hours probably hadn't done much for him. *Maybe I should let him sleep through till morning.*

He sat down on the edge of the bed, circling his shoulders to get the stiffness out of them, debating. Three hours of blowing shit up, carjacking shit, and fornicating with elves—Queen's *tits*, if he ever played *DragonAge* again, someone come shoot him—had left him entirely unready for sleep. Of course, Kevin might be better off. Maybe he ought to try sleeping during the day, while his human was at work. No more black eyes that way.

The Fae grimaced, bending and studying the bruise. He might be able to heal it; he'd never had occasion to try to find out whether the Noble healing magicks of the Demesne of Earth were among those that had survived his exile. But even if he could work that channeling, no doubt it would cause his human more pain than it eased; that was the way of most Fae healing even in the Realm—only some of the Water Fae could heal painlessly—and there was surely no reason to think it would be any different here.

Still, his hand hovered over the purple and green marks as he growled in frustration. What would it take to get rid of his damned nightmares? They'd been a torment when he first arrived in the human realm. He could remember going without sleep for weeks at a time, fearing what would happen when he closed his eyes. But that had been in Ireland, in 1847, and there were so many other wild-eyed haggard specters wandering that hunger-stricken land no one had paid any mind to another one. In time the dreams faded, became both less intense and less frequent. It was hard to remember the last one he'd had, before the hellish night that had ended with the whore in the basement of that club in Chicago. But since then…

"Penny for them?

He looked down with a start, into dark, amused eyes. "Oh, you're awake."

"No shit, Sherlock." A hand closed gently around his wrist, moved it aside. "Liberty City still standing?"

"Liberty City is still standing, Fallujah has fallen, elf females are easy, and dwarven males are fucking frightening, with or without their pants on." A corner of his mouth quirked up. "Are you feeling any better?"

"Yeah, a little. You should have stuck with GTA for the sex. I have the modified version." Kevin frowned, his expression thoughtful. "Sorry about, um, before." The frown, at least, passed, and he turned his head, kissed the fingers of the hand he held before letting go. Then the frown returned, and he caught again at Tiernan's hand.

Oh, shit. Oh, SHIT. Kevin's fingers were smoothing over the hard ridges in the skin of his wrist. The mark of the chains, the truesilver, burned into his flesh.

"How did you get these?" Kevin's voice sounded odd, its usual clear baritone muzzy, confused. He reached for the Fae's other hand—

Tiernan jerked both hands away. He would have hidden them behind his back, but it would have called more attention to them. Instead, he braced one against the headboard of the bed, behind Kevin's head and out of sight. The other he let fall into his lap, cloaking the movement with a great deal of desperate I-don't-give-a-flying-fuck. "Just an accident."

"Not buying it." The confusion was in Kevin's eyes as well as his voice. He grasped the forearm that lay in the Fae's lap, pulled harder when Tiernan refused to give it up. "The pattern's too regular to be accidental."

Tiernan snorted. "Too regular? You never heard of tire tracks?"

"You're not seriously trying to tell me those are tire marks." Kevin frowned slightly. "What are they?"

How the hell could the human look so calm, when he was so near to panic? "I didn't come up here to talk about my wrists." Tiernan tried to keep his voice light, but nothing could disguise the tension in him. He hummed like a live wire. Better he cut the fucking hands off than tell Kevin what had happened to him. What he had done. What he was. *Kinslayer.* "Come to think of it—"

"Tiernan." The voice was level, now, the confusion gone. "What happened to your wrists?"

"I was chained." The words ripped themselves from him, hung in the air between the two of them, seeming to cast shadows in the light from the bedside table.

Tiernan looked away, unable to bear the human's shocked expression, cursing himself without words, for there were no words in any of the languages he knew capable of bearing the weight of the anger he felt. Not at Kevin, no, at himself. Why couldn't he have lied?

"Chained?" A hand closed once again around his wrist, as gentle as the voice that came with it. "Why?"

The pain in Kevin's tone brought Tiernan's head back around, just as the human softly kissed the hard ridges of the scars. "Why?" he repeated, his eyes meeting Tiernan's, full of outrage, and sympathy, and—

"*Fuck.*" Tiernan ripped his hand from Kevin's, shot to his feet, and was halfway across the room before the human's mouth had time to fall open. "I. Don't. Want. To. Talk. About. It. What part of that don't you fucking *get*?"

"I… Tiernan… "

Kevin's total lack of expression betrayed a hurt so deep it would have broken the Fae's heart if he'd had one. Fortunately for them both, he didn't. He'd donned his leathers for his video game orgy. Now he caught up his studded jacket from where he'd dropped it on the floor before running the bath, hours before. Turning his back on the bed, he settled the leather over his shoulders. He had to get out. Because if Kevin kept asking questions, sooner or later he would answer them.

103

"How long this time?"

Tiernan turned, growling. The temptation to shoot back *who the fuck knows?* was nearly overwhelming. Answer the carefully masked pain in those dark eyes with a slap. Four little words, and the human would know exactly where he stood. And exactly what a bastard the Fae was. Didn't he owe Kevin at least that much? Honesty?

And it would be honest. Wouldn't it?

"I'm going to Purgatory," he snarled. "Go back to sleep."

***

This was going to get him in trouble. Tennessee Honey, the bartender had called it. Jack and honey liqueur. Anything with honey in it hammered a Fae flat faster than a ten-dollar whore could fake an orgasm. But hammered flat was what he needed to be. He had to forget those eyes. The face had been blank, but the eyes... He sipped, and groaned as the sweetness hit him.

One more minute of those eyes, and it would have been over. He would have told Kevin exactly what he had done to his brother, Lorcan. And exactly what had been done to him in return. Because that was what you did to kinslayers. Brother-murderers. Instead of cutting their hands off and leaving them to die, you chained them up like the fucking animals they were, and you banished them.

And then they met gorgeous, brilliant, ripped lawyers hung like fucking bull mammoths and lived happily ever after. So fucking *not*. He sipped again, wishing dully for a synonym for *fucking* that felt as good to beat himself with, because *fucking* was going to get old very quickly tonight.

No way to tell Kevin. None. The human played his video games, he read his fancy-shit stories, and thought he could handle someone like Tiernan. But he'd never lived in a world where pulling your brother off your sister and slitting his throat all the way to the spine was just one of those things you had to do sometimes. Tiernan couldn't even imagine the look on his lover's face.

His SoulShare's face.

Shit.

He took another sip, already feeling the warmth in his hands and feet, pounding as fast and as hard as the beat of the E.D.M. from the dance floor. He couldn't tell Kevin. Because he couldn't bear to see what would be in those eyes then, after the human realized the impossibility of loving a creature such as himself.

Tiernan's laugh was harsh enough to draw a curious gaze from the normally stone-faced bouncer. *Like I'd want him to do that. How fucking unfair would that be? When I can't love him back?*

Fae in the Realm loved, sometimes. Or something like it. For a while. But when life lasted a thousand years or more, barring fatal accidents or your brother's blade giving you a new smile, the only way to live it without going mad was from one moment to the next. Which pretty much ruled out 'happily ever after.' Better to just be… the best human term he'd heard yet was *fuck-buddies*. The only love that really lasted was the love of blood for blood. Unbreakable. Eternal. Unless, of course, you were a Guaire.

So even if there was some kind of weird exception for SoulShares—and who knew? since no SoulShare could cross the Pattern and come back to the Realm to talk about it—he sure as shit wasn't going to be one. Just Kevin's bad luck.

Unthinking, he knocked back the rest of the shot, wiped his mouth with the back of his hand. Pretty fucking selfish of him, when you got right down to it, to be even thinking about wanting his human's love when he couldn't give it in return. Not fair to Kevin, not at all, to be SoulShared with a kinslayer. A spirit like his, spending however long a SoulShared human got to live, chained to a male like him.

And Kevin's soul was a generous one. Unlike his own, which laughed even at the idea of generosity. Generous to a fault, probably, not that it was a fault he himself would ever recognize. Kevin hadn't even asked where he was going, only how long he was going to be gone. Even though he had to have assumed his lover was going off to fuck himself senseless with strangers again. And that *would* be the Fae thing to do in the throes of a fit of pique with a lover.

Except he couldn't. He'd barely been able to get it up with that pathetic drab in the club. And it wasn't just because he preferred men, or because the ambience had sucked. It was because he…

Fuck. No. He didn't. He couldn't.

"Tiernan."

The empty glass clattered to the surface of the bar as nerveless fingers let it go. How the hell had Kevin gotten in here without his noticing? He blinked, tried to focus. *Shit, I am so drunk.* Kevin stood beside him, hands plunged deep into the pockets of a black leather duster he hadn't even known the human owned, wearing a pair of jeans that looked like they'd been airbrushed on him, black cowboy boots, a shiner, and nothing else. "You followed me."

"You have a talent for stating the obvious." There was an edge to Kevin's voice, and a frown on his face. "Did you really think I wouldn't?"

"I wouldn't have, if I were you." Tiernan's eyes narrowed. "I'd have let the asshole go out and get shitfaced."

"Then you're lucky you're not me." A muscle twitched in Kevin's jaw. "Shitfaced, yeah, I can see that. But not laid." The dark, level gaze took in the empty bar stools to either side of the Fae. "That was never part of your intention, was it?"

"Get the fuck out of my head." Tiernan growled and turned back to the bar, motioning to the bartender for another shot.

"Not happening any time soon, or so I hear." Kevin slid onto the barstool next to him, shooting him a sidelong look. An odd one, not so much angry as measuring. And looking up, curiously, as the bartender brought over another shot. "You're doing whiskey shots?"

"Shots, yes. Doing, not so much." Tiernan raised the glass, sipped—feeling like an idiot, but knocking this shit back would fuck him up for fair, and as good as that sounded in principle, having Kevin here, and in this kind of a mood, complicated things. The last thing he wanted was for an irritated human to have to haul his unconscious ass home. "Jack and honey," he growled, as Kevin put up a dark brow. "I told you about the Fae and honey, didn't I?" Yeah, when Kevin

107

had brought home baklava one night. If the Fae had a devil, which strictly speaking they didn't, baklava would be his number one recruiting tool.

Kevin grimaced. Tiernan turned away to nurse his drink, and tried to ignore him, but it did no good. He could feel the human's gaze, like two points of hot light on his skin. Or was that the honey? *I was an ass*, he wanted to blurt. Wanted to, but wasn't going to. Couldn't.

That damn soft kiss on his wrist. No one had ever done that before. Hell, he wasn't sure anyone had ever even noticed the scars before. Not that he made a habit of spending long periods of time naked with anyone. But he was certain no one kissed them before. Tenderness would sure as shit be gone, though, if his human ever found out why those marks were there.

Hell, from the way Kevin was acting, maybe it was gone already. If his lover were Fae, this would be one more night like any number of others. They'd end up either fucking each other senseless or coming to blows, whichever seemed like a better idea. And afterward, either coming around again tomorrow night for another round, or going their separate ways forever—again, with neither really giving a damn. But a human? The rules were different.

No shit, Sherlock, he thought using Kevin's phrase from earlier. Damned shame he'd never spent much time with a human before, because he truly didn't have a clue. Just because you shared a soul with someone didn't mean he had to deal with your shit. Did it?

"I don't think I should have asked you about the scars."

It was not what he was expecting to hear and for a moment he almost didn't hear it at all. "What?" Another swig of the amber liquor. "Just because I didn't want to answer you?" He laughed, the sound bitter even to his own ears. Even the bouncer noticed this time, favoring him with a sneer before returning his attention to the dance floor. Well, if his mouth couldn't get him killed, maybe it could at least manage to lose him half a soul. "Don't go getting all codependent on me, darling. There's no Oprah to get you on anymore."

Kevin's eyes narrowed, his whole body tensed. "No, not because you didn't want to answer." His fists clenched, unclenched. His hands pressed flat against the top of the bar, the embedded lights flickering off them, limning them in faerie fire while the human stared at them. "You think I haven't thought about this before now?" *Asshole*, hung silently in the air between them. Or maybe *bastard*. The lawyer was too classy for *asshole*. "And I think I finally understand."

Tiernan held his breath. He hadn't even seen the abyss coming. And here it was. Maybe he was drunk enough that the fall would feel like flying.

"You're not human."

"My talent for stating the obvious is apparently contagious." The words slurred a little. He made a face and took another sip. He couldn't quite feel his feet, but he assumed they were still there because his boots moved when he moved his legs. *Falling yet?*

Kevin reached out, took the shot glass from Tiernan's nearly nerveless fingers, and set it down firmly on the bar. Then he took Tiernan's chin between thumb and forefinger, and held it there, gaze meeting gaze, holding firm against all of the Fae's attempts to turn his head.

"It finally dawned on me, after you... left." There was still an edge to the soft baritone. But not anger. Not any more. "You look like a man. You talk like a man. You fuck like a man." The human's voice threatened to catch on that last, but he persevered. "But you *aren't* a man. Or anything else I've ever heard of, anything else I think I know. All the reading I've done since I was a kid, I feel like it ought to help me understand, but it doesn't."

The grip on Tiernan's chin tightened; Kevin's dark gaze held him pinned. "I may *think* I know what you want, what you need, but I don't. So when you tell me you can't do something, or won't do something, maybe I'd better listen." His eyes were suddenly shadowed, haunted. "Or I might lose you. And fuck me blind if I know why, but I think that would break me."

It's the SoulShare, stupid, he wanted to shout, something—the honey, it had to be—blurring the intensity of the dark brown gaze transfixing him. *You can't stand to lose me because I have half of what you are. That's all.*

But a voice, too sober to be the honey and too cold to give him any hope it might be wrong, whispered in the depths of his mind. *If you can leave anytime, so can he.* And he could. Fuck, yes, he could. He'd been saying it all along. He'd *known* it all along. So it couldn't be the SoulShare binding Kevin. It could only be...

No.

He reached out, caught Kevin by the back of the

neck, and pulled him into a searing kiss. Lips parted in a gasp, and he drove his tongue between. He had to give the other male's tongue something to do besides talk, had to turn that relentless lawyer's mind to something other than the thought of any kind of lasting attachment to a Fae. Stone cold selfish, he was. Addicted to the human's body, to the sex. Not daring to let himself crave the male himself, his mind, his heart.

Hell, no.

Kevin resisted the kiss, for a split second, but then a shudder ran through his body and he let the Fae draw him in, opened to the demands of his tongue, relaxed into the fiercer demands of his hands. Tiernan's free hand went under the leather duster, caressed the human's hard and heaving abs, slid around to his back, drew him closer, pulling him off the high bar stool and off balance, until he needed the Fae to stay on his feet. Perfect.

Shit, don't love me. Please don't love me.

What he needed was to distract the human, get him off a subject that could destroy them both. There was no loving what he was, and he wasn't about to let the human try.

"I know what I need," he growled. Kevin clutched at the studded jacket, his eyes closing in what might have been desire and might have been a wince. And the absolutely perfect hell of it was, Tiernan did need him. Would kill to be inside him, any way he could get there. And how fucked up was that? Right here, in the middle of the club. Yeah, he was really that sick. Needed his lover that badly.

Somehow, Tiernan managed to get to his feet,

without losing his hold on Kevin. Hell, it was probably his grip on the human making it possible for him to get up at all. And it wasn't far to the corner sanctuary, the maze of leather loveseats and sofas that on busy weekend nights had couples and trios and the occasional orgy hanging around the perimeter for an hour waiting for space to open up, but on a night like tonight gave the two of them their pick of landing sites. Which was a damned good thing, because Tiernan couldn't feel his feet any more, and a long walk or any kind of wait would have been his undoing. He fell back onto a sofa, Kevin on top of him, the human's butter-soft leather duster spreading out to cover them both.

Tiernan's hands were all over Kevin. Skating over his back, his sides, wanting the human to take his weight on his forearms so they could pinch and scrape his nipples until dark eyes closed with pleasure and breath hissed softly between pursed lips. He continued to toy with a nipple with one hand as the other roamed downward, grabbing a handful of ass, his body arching up as his hand pulled down. "You're sweating, *lanan*."

"And this surprises you why? Bastard." Kevin's tongue ran swiftly around parched lips. "Don't think I don't know what you're trying to do. But we'll talk after you're sober."

"I could make that a very long time—"

"Shut up."

For an instant, in the dim and uncertain light, Tiernan looked up into Kevin's dark brown eyes, and felt like he was falling—vertigo, intense, overwhelming. But then the sensation passed. *Maybe it was the honey? Shit.* And then Kevin smiled, almost shyly… and he started mouthing his way down Tiernan's chest, stopping to play with the nipple ring on his slow and torturous track downward, his coat spread out in a careful decorousness, laughable if it weren't so red hot sexual. By the time he got to the waistband of Tiernan's leathers, the broad head of the Fae's cock had come out to meet him, and the rest of the shaft was in exquisite pain in its tight confines.

"Are you…" Tiernan's voice was hoarse, and sweat ran from his forehead to sting in his eyes. "Oh, sweet *fuck*," he breathed, as fingers went to work at the hooks and buttons of the leathers, parted the fly, reached within. He didn't dare look, he'd wanted this too long, if he looked he was going to lose it right now—

He cursed, a long fluid stream of ecstatic Fae obscenities as Kevin's lips sealed around the head of his cock, the hot tongue of his fantasies swirled around and probed the tip. And when the tongue moved on to his sweet spot, his eyes damn near rolled back, and that had never happened to him before. His back arched and twisted, nearly throwing Kevin off the sofa and causing the shielding of the coat to fail for a few breathtaking seconds. "I can't believe… you're doing this."

Kevin released him with a soft wet sound that somehow carried perfectly over the driving music from the dance floor, and smiled his mock-angelic quarter-to-orgasm smile. "I can't, either," he murmured, just before he lollipopped the Fae from balls to tip.

Tiernan's hands fisted in Kevin's thick dark hair, a white-knuckled grip. He bucked up once, twice, just barely easing off enough to let the human avoid choking; his balls drew up, his shaft curved and went granite-hard. The sweet liquid crystalline hum raced down his spine and for one brief perfect instant pooled behind the head before his shaft pulsed hard and he released, like molten glass, shooting down the human's throat.

"Kevin!"

The human was inexperienced, and it showed. He missed nearly as much as he swallowed, glassy streaks painting his face and even disappearing into his hair by the time Tiernan's aching cock finally subsided. Kevin's lips were swollen, his eyes glazed; eyes and lips both smiled, ever so slightly. Smiles the Fae returned. *Everything I dreamed, and then some.*

From that beautiful sight, gradually, his eyes strayed. To meet the gaze of the bouncer, watching from the doorway with a gleam in his eye.

Fuck off, asshole. His lip curled in a snarl. This one's mine.

CHAPTER ELEVEN

Kevin's gaze drifted to the bedside clock. 3:57 a.m. *Christ on a sidecar*. He was going to be a perfect basket case at work. But sleep was out of the question. Between those few hours of sleep he had caught earlier, and what he still couldn't quite make himself believe he'd done at Purgatory, sleep was going to be a long time coming.

He leaned on an elbow, looking down at the Fae. Tiernan could almost pass for innocent, with his long blond hair tumbled over his face and an arm up over his head. Almost. But the little moans kept giving the game away, and the toss of his head every so often, as if he was trying to escape from something. But there was none of the screaming, the thrashing that had marked the last few nights. Maybe that was a side effect of the honey; whatever it was, Kevin hoped Tiernan at least was finding some rest.

He gazed at the arm over his lover's head and the scars around his wrist. He might never know what had caused them. But was that necessarily such a bad thing? He frowned slightly, trying to remember why it seemed so earth-shatteringly important at the time he'd asked the question. Sure, he wanted to know more about this male's past, and Tiernan was, with only a few exceptions, as close-mouthed as the proverbial clam. Why, though, had he pushed?

He shook his head, gently moving a lock of hair from the sleeping Fae's eyes. Even leaving aside the whole my-partner-isn't-human thing, there was so much about his situation any sane, normal person would look at with a jaundiced eye. His sudden attraction to a male, for the first time in a life otherwise spent in choosy but enthusiastic appreciation and pursuit of the female sex. A partner who professed an inability to love. A lover who refused to discuss his past, other than to assure him Fae were incapable of suffering from, or carrying, disease.

But he'd been through all this last night, in his head, after Tiernan left for the club. For one black moment, he'd been certain the Fae was going to return to the demimonde of S&M clubs and anonymous sex he'd originally used to try to forget him. That moment had been devastating, and the relief when Tiernan had snapped he was going to their by-now-familiar haunt had been overwhelming.

And then, after the Fae faded into nonexistence, had come the pile driver question that would have brought him to his knees if he'd been standing. *Why the hell do I put up with this shit?* Why did he give a damn about a male who had picked him up for casual sex in a bar and who had never given him anything except his dick and his attitude?

That had been the anger talking. And the hurt. And once he'd admitted that to himself, the question had been a hell of a lot easier to answer. Maybe Tiernan was right, maybe the Fae couldn't love. But he trusted. The nights of holding him through the nightmares were exhausting, sure. But in those moments when his lover woke, and it dawned on him anew that he wasn't waking alone, Kevin had had to hide tears more than once.

His lover. It wasn't hard to believe he shared a soul with the Fae. Ever since he could remember, he'd felt incomplete. As though he moved through the world without touching it, without taking any of it for himself. But from the moment Tiernan first touched him, just that lightest brush of lips against his ear at the club, the word *mine* had resonated in him like the clear, pure sound of a bell. *This is mine*.

Tiernan stirred, muttered under his breath, the first signs of distress he'd shown since falling asleep. Passing out. Whatever. Kevin sighed, resting a hand lightly on the blond's smooth chest; in short order, he found himself running his fingertips lightly over his lover's chest, tracing the lines of the muscles, and then down, a fingertip traveling along the intricate tattoo over his hip. Tiernan wasn't buff, not like some men were and Kevin himself tried to be. Lean, hard-bodied, almost impossibly fit. And with that long, unruly blond hair, and his crystalline blue eyes, Tiernan would turn heads in rooms full of men or women. And no doubt had.

Mine.

The Fae rolled onto his side, away from Kevin; chuckling softly, Kevin settled himself behind his lover, glancing over the shoulder in front of him at the bedside clock. He could still get almost three hours of sleep if he was lucky. He wrapped an arm around Tiernan, nuzzled into the curve where neck met shoulder, breathed in the scent of wild hair and sated male body and honey, and closed his eyes. *So this is what magic smells like.*

***

He keeps you from me.

Kevin started awake, heart hammering. He was curled up on a stone floor, naked, staring into a cold fireplace, feeling as if he'd been kicked, repeatedly, by someone with steel-toed boots and a major attitude problem.

No. Not a stone floor. The stone hearth of his own place of refuge, inside his own mind. *What the fuck?*

At last you waken. There was a sneer in the woman's voice. But it had been a man's, when he first heard it. **I had hoped you might need more persuasion.**

Fuck. "The management... reserves the right... to refuse service... to anyone—oh, *shit.*" *Don't want the female kicking me.* Damn the heels. Damn this dream.

Did you ask him about the scars? The man again.

"What do you care?"

Another kick, to the kidneys. Maybe the woman was preferable to the man. She didn't kick as hard. **Your place is to answer, human. Did you ask him?**

Great, now I have two people, things, calling me "human". Something tells me this one isn't Fae. "Why would I do anything you tell me to do?"

Because you have no choice. It was as if there was an iron band around his throat, slowly tightening.

And because I think you still prefer to live. The woman, now, coolly mocking.

Kevin clawed at his throat, but his fingers found nothing, only a dent in the skin, as the invisible noose tightened. *I cannot be choking in a dream. No fucking way.*

Do you hear the roar of your heartbeat in your ears? A foot rolled him over, to face the priapic male. He had long, tangled, matted hair, a shade of blond that was not so much dirty as greasy; clawlike, dirty, broken fingernails, and glowing red eyes. Oh, and a dick like a Louisville Slugger. *It will be the last sound you hear, until you answer. Or ever. Your choice.*

This is not worth dying for. Play for time, find out what he wants. The drumbeat of his heart was louder, almost deafening, and spots were starting to appear before his eyes. *Let him think he's won. Christ, I'm thinking like this is real.* "Yes," he gasped. "I asked him."

This laugh was musical. Kevin didn't remember seeing the figure change, but the woman stood before him, coal-black hair, scarlet sheath dress clinging to a figure that was probably illegal in 38 states. One he would possibly appreciate more if he could breathe, and if it didn't belong to something trying to kill him. She waved a finger, stirring the air with a blood-red nail, and the band loosened. *That's a good pet*, she purred, directly into his mind.

And something stirred the pleasure center in his brain. To his total horror, his cock twitched, stirred, started to rise. He gritted his teeth, and sweat came out on his brow as he fought it back down. "Don't do that," he snarled, hands clenched into fists. "Not if you want anything more out of me. I'd rather you kill me."

119

Would you, now? The scorpion's tail lashed out, wrapped around him, burning, biting into him. It lifted him clear of the floor, forced him to look into the oddly beautiful opalescent eyes of the ugliest creature he wished he'd never laid eyes on. All fangs and chitin and greenish yellow ichor and saliva and at least six too many legs. Then, mercifully, the tail lashed, and threw him into one of the armchairs in front of the fireplace. ***Not right now. I have a use for you yet.***

Kevin drew himself up in the chair, and found himself facing the male again, lounging in the other chair, stroking that obscene hard-on. ***I think I like this form***, he mused. ***I will keep it, for a while.*** He turned to face Kevin with a slightly fanged grin. ***Now, what did your male tell you?***

The way he drew out the word 'male' turned it into a vile obscenity. Kevin did his best to ignore it, but he couldn't help the edge to his voice as he replied. "That he'd been chained. Nothing more."

Secrets kept from a SoulShare. The male laughed as Kevin stared. ***Oh, yes, human. I know what you are. And every secret he keeps is a weapon in my hands.*** He glanced down at his erection, which he continued to fondle, almost absent-mindedly. ***As is this. Would you like some?***

"Fuck off and die." Kevin kept his voice carefully even. *Even if this is all in my mind, I'm not giving this thing the satisfaction.*

The male laughed—oh, *shit*, were those bugs in his hair? Crawling out of the mats and the tangles. No, not bugs, miniature versions of the thing that had grabbed him. *I so need to wake up—*

You forget that your thoughts are open to me.

The male chuckled. ***So tell me, SoulShare, why does your male not trust you with his past?*** His mouth gaped in a fanged smile. The eyes, though, were sharp and calculating.

"It's not a question of trust." This was another thing he realized tonight, and it was marginally better to speak it than to have this creature pull it out of his head. His stomach was roiling at the thought of him— it—touching him in any way. "I've heard the tone he uses before, from Tanner, my brother."

You were your brother's lover? One shaggy eyebrow went up.

Kevin closed his eyes until this spasm of rage passed, refusing to give the bastard the satisfaction of a response, opened them again, his face carefully set. "Tanner was nearly killed in Iraq." The story had to be told again, to keep the fucker out of his head, and he told it, but this time he added what the family had learned later, from the medics they'd met in Landstuhl. "His sergeant had been riding next to Tanner in the back of the Humvee. He probably died when the IED ripped out the floor, but Tanner didn't realize it. And when the medics came to pull him out, Tanner kept screaming at them to take the sergeant first. He was still screaming as they evac'ed him. Kept trying to fight them."

And what does this have to do with your male? The glowing red eyes were bright, noticing; the creature leaned forward, its hard-on blessedly forgotten for the time being.

"Tanner could never talk about it. You could ask him, but it would infuriate him. He'd shout that 'they should have taken Sarge first'… and we could never tell him it wouldn't have made sense to take the dead out before the living." Kevin took a deep breath. Somehow, this memory of his brother was restorative. Even the darkest thoughts of someone he loved were better than *this*. "And if we kept asking, he'd explode. He could never get past that one moment. Tiernan sounds the same way when I push him about his past. I don't think he's able to talk about it. And I'm not going to push him." His jaw squared. He looked the filthy obscenity directly in the eyes, and his voice was steady. "You can do what you want to me, you can't make me do that to him."

Is that so? The male reached into his hair, pulled out one of the scorpion-like bugs and idly crushed it between his thumb and forefinger. *Then a change of tactics is called for, because you are my road to him. And he is my path back to your world.*

The soles of Kevin's feet began to burn. The pain, sweet *Jesus,* the pain of it. When he looked down, he could see the flames licking up around the edges, beginning to creep up the sides of his feet, as if they consumed what they burned. The flesh, however, was smooth, pale, unmarked.

It's all in your mind, my lovely boy. The male smiled, once again stroking himself, getting himself off on Kevin's agony. *When it's over, you'll still be whole. Ready for more*. He leaned forward eagerly, watching Kevin trying not to writhe in pain. *Until you beg me to put it out—*

Kevin didn't even think. Not about the pain, not about the fire, not about the threat. Six foot four of college varsity wrestler slammed into the leering obscenity and took him and the chair on which he sat

122

down to the floor. His hands went around the male's throat. Filthy hands clutched at his wrists, the creature choked, coughed.

And then, damn it, it was suddenly standing framed in one of the picture windows, female again. Not a hair out of place. *He is growing in you*. The voice was beautiful, but icy, frost etched on a frozen window. *The balance is shifting, and my time is growing shorter. New tactics…* She raised a perfect eyebrow. *Until the next time, SoulShare*.

She vanished. Kevin collapsed, exhausted, onto the floor of his own mind.

CHAPTER TWELVE

Purgatory was empty. Tiernan stood where he'd Faded in, at the very back of the cock pit, every sense on full alert. The lights were dim, plain white utilitarian track lighting rather than the flickering infernal flames and garish club strobes of business hours. The scents of bleach and other cleansers hung in the air, as yet not overlaid with the sweat, alcohol, smoke, and sex that would make their appearances later in the evening. And the faint whirr of a floor polisher came to him from somewhere in the vicinity of the restrooms, bespeaking a maintenance worker putting the finishing touches on the work of the day shift.

I have a little time. That's well.

The Fae Faded again, not to travel, but Fading of the other sort, the lessened physicality making him translucent to the eye and less substantial than smoke to any living being. It was incredibly fucking dangerous, but used with equally incredible care it was also a useful survival tool in the Realm, with the prevalence of wild beasts as intelligent as their would-be hunters, not to mention jealous lovers, ex-lovers, and would-be lovers. It had been almost as useful in the human world—granted, for most of his century and a half this side of the Pattern he'd been unkillable, but that didn't mean he'd wanted to turn himself into a target. And since Kevin, he needed to get back in the habit of remembering he could bleed out as easily as anyone.

He sank to the sofa. Leaning back, he rested his head against the soft leather, stretched his booted feet out in front of him, crossed his arms over his chest, and reached out with the most capricious of his six senses. For any Fae other than a mage, the magickal sense was subtle, skittish, and easily distracted. With the diversions of loud music and hot males absent, his skin tingled, as if from a shower of infinitesimally small needles.

Something's here. Mos def. He'd suspected as much for a while, which was what he was doing here in the first place. Too much of his life had centered around this place for it to be a coincidence. The site where Purgatory stood had once been a stable, when he first crossed the Atlantic, not long after the American Civil War. He'd stumbled on it by chance, and it had fascinated him. The natural gift of the Fae for dealing with non-magickal animals had made him an accomplished horseman, and he'd thought that was the lure of it. Then it became a brothel, as the horse and carriage trade declined, and small wonder why *that* had drawn him. But then the brothel had burned to the ground, and he'd given in entirely to the lure of other places and other pleasures.

Until he'd returned one day, a strange sentimental journey by a creature utterly devoid of sentimentality, to find the original Purgatory here. It had become a favored haunt immediately, even before the leather boys, the pole dancers, the lap dances. Those were just a latter-day icing on the cake, something to be savored on every return from wherever else in the world he happened to be calling home at the time. The place held him long before he'd met his human here. And he wanted to know why.

He had his suspicions. There was magick here.

Tiernan had learned not all the magick in the human world had disappeared with the Fae into the Realm at the Sundering. He didn't pretend to any deep knowledge of magick, or of the Sundering either, for that matter. The only real experts on those subjects had been the Loremasters. And after they died in the Sundering, the ones most interested were the commoners—those Fae who neither embodied the elements, as the pure-blooded Royals did, nor channeled them, as did he and his fellow Nobles. The ones who gravitated toward one element or another, as their heritage and their inclinations urged them, but who relied mostly on the pure essence of magick.

But even as ignorant as he was perfectly happy to be, he knew what any Fae knew; the Loremasters' act of removing from the human world all those who bore magick within themselves, whether Fae or fauna or flora, had saved both realms. How it had done so, precisely, no Fae living knew. The Loremasters had taken that particular bit of knowledge with them into death.

Yet despite their supreme effort, there was still magick here, in the human realm. Tiernan had been mildly amused the first time he heard of ley lines, lines of power that supposedly ran through the earth. But when he'd visited the small village of Avebury Henge, and felt the surge of power running just out of his reach, thrumming under his hand as it rested on one of the great stones, he had gone from scoffer to believer.

As he continued to study the subject over the years—during those brief periods when he could deal with thoughts and memories of the Realm without immediately breaking and running for the nearest dive bar or leather club—he'd deduced the ley lines had something to do with both living magick and the elemental forces wielded in the Realm by Royals and Nobles. Magick could not be tamed—"wild magick" was a complete redundancy—but it inhabited everything in the Realm. Magick, bound, became a Fae. And something like that magick flowed through the ley lines, combined with and bound to the elemental forces in a way he didn't understand and couldn't imagine separating. It would appear that the Loremasters hadn't been able to work the trick, either, and had been forced to leave the ley lines behind during that ultimate circling of the wagons that was the Sundering.

It would be interesting to see what happened, he mused, glancing around the nearly silent club, if a Royal came into contact with a ley line, given that Royals were, in their way, pure magick that incorporated the embodiment of an element. Interesting in the way of the human curse, or joke, he was never quite sure which, *may you live in interesting times*. Shit blowing up would probably be the mildest of the side effects.

Sitting down with a map and a pencil and a list of possible sites led Tiernan to guess there was a ley line here, in Washington, D.C. And he suspected he knew *exactly* where it was.

What he needed now was a way downstairs. Purgatory was below ground to start with, the ground floor being devoted to a massage parlor, a shop selling club wear, and a tattoo and piercing parlor—but he needed access to the bedrock. Or as close to it as he could get. He got to his feet and went to scout out the bar area.

Bartenders needed a storeroom and he quickly found a door tucked into a recess behind the bar. Locked, of course. Tiernan swore softly and Faded to the other side of it. He didn't need to have been somewhere before he could Fade there, but it sure as hell helped.

He only fell a couple of steps; there was no landing on the other side of the door, but he'd materialized close enough to the door he didn't do more than turn an ankle, and his shitkickers took most of it. Still, he was muttering Fae curses under his breath as he made his way down the stairs.

The tingle grew stronger, the further down he went. By the time he reached the bottom, it felt like being under a constant shower of stinging sleet, and the magick in the air was thick enough his sixth sense actually allowed him to see by it, far more clearly than he could have seen by the little emergency telltale next to the wall switch. In the storeroom there were cases of beer piled around nearly to the low ceiling, crates of bottles stacked on wooden pallets to keep them off the stone floor, and Queen's brats only knew what was sitting on shelves that ran around the walls.

And the floor was glowing.

Only in magickal light, but the light was

unmistakable. Tiernan stared, enraptured. Apart from the one he'd sensed at Avebury, he'd never been this close to an actual line before, and that one had been in broad daylight, with distractions everywhere. They grazed fucking *sheep* at Avebury.

No wonder I was drawn here.

He frowned. This line ran straight through Washington, D.C.—up and down most of the East Coast, if he wasn't completely turned around. What was so special about this particular spot?

Tiernan paced slowly along the eldritch line, starting where it emerged from the base of the stairs. It was as if his feet refused to touch the floor, as if the energy were blasting him upward with only slightly less force than gravity used to pull him down.

"Oh, fuck me," he breathed. "Please."

Another line crossed the line he could feel through his feet. It was fainter to his magickal sense, but definitely there, at right angles to the first, several paces ahead of him, toward the back of the storeroom. He started toward it, but some instinct froze him on the spot. *No, standing on it probably isn't a good idea. But how can I…*

Slowly, he smiled. He got down on one knee and touched his hand to the cold stone floor. This would be a simple enough channeling, not even one of the Noble magicks—those, he hadn't dared to use since transmuting his brother's flesh to stone. This was a far easier thing, for an Earth Fae, changing one form of stone into another. He closed his eyes and concentrated, drawing on his own inherent magick and being careful *not* to tap into the raw power surging below him, trying to get rid of the sudden mental image of a mosquito and a bug zapper. Slowly, in an area spreading outward from where his hand touched the floor, native stone transmuted to nearly flawless clear quartz crystal.

He opened his eyes… and all he could do was stare. The line he'd felt originally bisected the room, its fey light enough to cast magickal shadows on the walls since it was no longer veiled by stone. The power would be white, if it had a color visible to the eye, woven throughout with an intricate web of tracings of what would be green, the combination of pure magick and the barest hint, by comparison, of the elemental force of Earth. Just as he'd suspected. Cutting across it was another line, as potent in its potential energy but not as strong to his ability to detect, white limned with red. Fire, perhaps. He had enough of that bloodline in him to let him see. Diagonal to those, two more crossed lines, visible to him more as waverings in their crystal casing than as magickal light, blue and purest white. Water. Air.

Fuck. Me. Blind. All four.

It's a nexus—

Voices upstairs jolted him out of his reverie. Club staff, arriving for work, from the sound of things. Shit, if they came down here and found this—they wouldn't see the lines, but the whole floor turned to what might as well be glass and him kneeling there in the middle of it, yeah, that would be a fucking picnic to explain.

He needed to hurry. He placed both hands flat on the floor, breathed deeply, and reached within. And swore. He didn't have enough left in him to do this, not anywhere near fast enough. He was going to be caught.

The Earth line pulsed under his hands, as if trying to get his attention.

Oh, shit. A strange excitement started to boil in him, just under the skin. He'd read a book once, some science fiction story about comets falling into the ocean. There had been a surfer, out on a board when the sky caught fire. He'd seen the wall of water, the biggest motherfucking tsunami ever, coming toward him, and gotten up on the board, and ridden it inland.

Yeah, until he smashed into a skyscraper doing a hundred miles an hour, asshole. But it didn't matter; he had to ride this wave. His expression was probably a close match for the face of that beautifully doomed son of a bitch on the board.

He looked down at the line that pulsed under his hands, exquisitely beautiful untameable power, focused on it with his magickal sense rather than his eyes. Reached out toward it, slowly, carefully. Very carefully. Earth Fae were impervious to magick *wielded* from without, but this didn't necessarily mean he was immune to raw, mindless power, power no one wielded. He had to do this right, tap into the line for the bare instant it would take for that much power to undo what he'd done to the floor. And then Fade somewhere safe. Back upstairs?

"Gino, you dick, you should have brought up more olives last night." The faint tones of someone touching the combination to the door drifted down the stairs.

Shit.

White light shot through Tiernan; his body jolted with it. He hoped he wasn't screaming, but fuck all if he could tell. Stone raced away from his fingertips, like some demented fast-forward image of frost forming on glass.

And then he was lying face down on one of the sofas in the cock pit. *If the barrel of a rifle feels anything after it's been fired, I think it feels like this.*

"How the hell did you get here?"

Tiernan surprised himself greatly by being able to turn his head. Judging from what he could see, which was everything from the knees down of a very large man clad all in black leather except for the red soles of his boots, this was the bouncer from last night. "Never left," he croaked.

A hand on his shoulder ungently turned him over. "I remember you." The guy's voice matched his face, which, seen up close, looked like it was regularly used to break down doors. "You're the lawyer's pretty boy. But he carried you out of here not long after he blew you."

A slightly curled lip was all the sneer Tiernan could manage. "I came back. Hadn't had enough."

"You were wasted off your ass. You should have stayed home and let your Daddy take care of you." The gorilla-man chuckled.

"Funny," Tiernan grumbled. "Go the fuck away." He hoped the aftermath of the channeling looked as much like a lethal hangover as it felt like.

"Haul ass out of here when you can." The bouncer walked away, heading for his station at the door.

Tiernan let his head fall back, closing his eyes with a groan he didn't have to fake. *Stupid, stupid, stupid—*

His eyes snapped open. How had that dickhead known that Kevin was a lawyer?

CHAPTER THIRTEEN

Kevin's hooked fingers raked through his hair. He threw himself back in his chair, glaring at the computer screen in front of him as if it would be impressed by his ire. It wasn't, and simply continued to show the impossible. Impossible and highly incriminating.

What the hell? He had made his bootleg copy of the accounting software jump through another hoop, and it was giving him a spreadsheet of his billing for the month. And not only were the phantom hours he'd previously deleted still there, there were more of them. According to this, he'd had his ass right here in this chair for nine hours last Saturday, when he knew perfectly well what his ass had been doing that day, and it had nothing whatsoever to do with the Balfour Trust. *Oh, and look*—first-class round trip airfare to San Francisco, to—he squinted—"advise client on issues related to trust property mineral rights." His specialties were zoning law and alternative dispute resolution, and what he knew about mineral rights could dance very comfortably on the head of a pin. There had to be thirty grand worth of billable time this month alone, not to mention all the perks and extras that went straight to the client to be paid. All neatly locked away under the access code of the partner in charge of the account.

Something is seriously fucked here. This could get him disbarred if he didn't do something about it. He rubbed his eyes with the heels of his hands, sighed, and reached into his trouser pocket and found his key chain, with the flash drive hanging from it. Maybe saving this was a bad idea, the product of too many sleepless nights rather than sober reflection, but he needed to find someone who understood this software and could tell him what was going on. Rolling his chair back from his desk, he reached under it to where he kept his hard drive parked and plugged the little drive in. Save, transfer, and then erased from the hard drive—

His heart missed a couple of beats at the sight of the tiny blinking icon on the task bar. *Oh, shit.* He completed the erasure, reached down, yanked out the thumb drive and pocketed it again, then rested his hands on the desk, palms flat against the surface. One deep breath, followed by another, head bowed; when his heart rate had returned to something closer to normal than to wind sprints, he ventured another look at the monitor. The little icon wasn't blinking any more, but had it been there at all, before he'd saved the spreadsheet? *I need to get home. I need to sleep tonight, damn it, and if that means the sofa, then it means the sofa.*

"You're a bright young man, Mr. Almstead. In all the wrong ways."

Somehow, Kevin managed not to jerk his head around, curse, or do anything else incriminating. Maybe getting whipped with scorpions is good for something after all, it spoils you for any kind of shit mere mortals might try to pull. Assuming any of that was real. "How do you mean, Mr. O'Halloran?" He turned in his chair, regarding the partner in charge of the Balfour Trust account with a fatalistic sort of calm. He even managed to lounge back in his chair and bring up a leg, crossing it over the opposite knee. He didn't bother to reach for the mouse, to minimize or close the spreadsheet still burning there. If he was screwed, he was screwed no matter what he did, and on the remote chance he wasn't, there was no way O'Halloran could read what was on his monitor from the doorway.

The big man laughed. Pushing off the doorframe, he came all the way into the office, closing the door behind himself and lowering his bulk into the conference chair opposite Kevin's desk. "Hacking the Balfour account was smart. Damned smart." He folded his hands over his paunch, his smile seeming to sink into his face, almost unbearably smug. "Saving it wasn't."

"I don't know what you're talking about." *And you can't choke me to death with a wave of your finger, so fuck you and the horse you rode in on.*

O'Halloran shook his head, shaggy silver hair falling over his forehead. "Now, Kevin. I'm giving you credit for intelligence; the least you can do is do the same for me. I've been on to you since the first time you tried to tamper with your hours—"

I am well and truly screwed. "I wasn't tampering with them, I was trying to *fix* them." Kevin's voice trailed off as the other lawyer chuckled and continued to shake his head in an exaggerated, almost comical way. "Wait, you're the one doing this."

"Got it in one, boyo." The enhanced brogue made Kevin feel ill. Tiernan's accent, the one he'd tried so hard to place that first night at Purgatory, was close enough to Irish that hearing it in this context was nearly sacrilege. And coupled with the self-satisfied smirk on O'Halloran's broad features, the package was cringe-worthy.

"Why the hell?" Years of experience at negotiating with bureaucrats of every stripe let Kevin affect an air of disinterest, even as he fought to keep the sweat from coming out on his upper lip. "I mean, what's in it for you?"

"Trying to get me to monologue, Kevin?" The partner was still smiling, but his eyes weren't; they were narrow, and keen, and while there was a hint of laughter in them, it wasn't the kind anyone would want to be on the receiving end of. "The bad guys only do that in the comic books."

"Suit yourself." Kevin shrugged. "I just wanted to know what to tell the managing committee, but I suppose you can do that yourself when they call you in."

O'Halloran leaned forward at this, his grin gone predatory. "You think you're going to tell anyone anything? I assure you, Kevin, all the trails in this little matter lead straight back to you. The associate with a grudge. The passed-over never-been who's trying to feather his own nest while he still has a job."

Kevin hoped he wasn't as pale as he felt, but judging from the tone of the senior lawyer's laugh, he hoped in vain. "You chose me because you knew no one would believe me."

"Mostly." O'Halloran nodded. "Plus, your billing

rate per hour is high enough that I can make a little more than pocket change off the scam. And you're cleared for travel on behalf of clients, which means I can visit my girlfriend in San Francisco without my wife seeing the credit card bills."

This chuckle was reflective, or meant to sound that way, though it put Kevin more in mind of Jabba the Hutt. "And this client will never miss the money. The Balfour Trust doesn't even look at its itemized bill, it just cuts a check every month. So save your indignation for something that warrants it."

"You can't imagine I'm going to go along with this." Now it was Kevin whose eyes narrowed, and there was no trace of a smile anywhere on his features.

"I don't have to imagine what I already know." O'Halloran leaned back in his chair again, studying Kevin with apparent amusement. "I've known you since you started at this firm. You don't make waves. You don't stick your head up. The good little worker drone. And you're always willing to take one for the team." Again the obscene chuckle. "Well, take this one, and who knows? There might even be a little something in it for you."

Kevin growled. The partner was eyeing him almost jovially, and it was grating on him. "Go fuck yourself, Mr. O'Halloran. You're a disgrace to the firm." His leg came down from his knee; he turned, and faced the older man full-on. "And maybe *my* name *isn't* on this firm, and maybe it never will be, but if you think I'm willing to sell it out for a piece of your pathetic action, you don't know me at all."

O'Halloran sighed theatrically. "I know you better than you think, my boy. You're not leaving me with many other options." He reached into the pocket of his suit jacket and took out his cell phone, touched the screen on, and began scrolling, with the air of a man who normally had other people handle mundane chores like that for him.

Kevin's stomach completed the knot it had started tying, and began to tighten it. "What are you—"

"Ah, there it is." O'Halloran grinned and leaned forward in his chair, extending the phone toward Kevin while keeping it firmly in his grip. "Look familiar?"

There was a roaring in Kevin's ears; he clutched the arms of his chair to keep his hands from shaking as he looked at the picture being displayed on the phone's screen, slightly blurred, but easily recognizable. Himself, and Tiernan. At Purgatory, last night. Tiernan's head was thrown back, his expression ecstatic; he himself knelt astride the Fae's legs, his leather duster fallen briefly aside to give the camera a perfect view of him taking his lover's cock down his throat.

"Has your father been doing anything about that heart condition of his, Kevin?" O'Halloran's voice was soft. He waited for a response from Kevin, and appeared satisfied when he got none. "No, I don't think you'll say anything."

The big man got to his feet and pocketed the phone. "I'll just let myself out." The door opened, closed, leaving Kevin staring blindly at the wall.

Now what do I do?

***

Two near-accidents on the drive home were almost enough to convince Kevin his next move had to involve sleep. The third, in which his Mercedes was nearly T-boned on the driver's side when he ran a red light, sealed the deal. He dragged himself up the stairs to the bedroom, loosening his tie as he went, toeing off his shoes outside the bedroom door. There had been no sign of Tiernan downstairs. Hopefully, if the Fae was out, he would let the poor exhausted human sleep when he got home.

Kevin stopped short in the bedroom doorway. Tiernan was already in bed, on his stomach with his face turned away from the door. Only the slow rise and fall of his back betrayed the fact he was still breathing. In the hand Kevin could see, there was a note, and a pen lay on the bedside table. He edged forward and slipped the note from his lover's hand, smoothed it out. In Tiernan's elegant script, it read:

I fucked up big time at Purgatory. But it was incredible. I'll tell you when I wake up. Don't wake me for anything less than the end of the world.

Kevin shook his head, looking from the note to the sleeping Fae. At least he probably wouldn't have to dust off his wrestling moves again tonight. Fighting, but ultimately losing to, a jaw-cracking yawn, he stripped down and climbed into bed beside Tiernan, pulling the sheets up over them both, punching up a pillow and settling onto it with a soft groan. *This isn't quite the end of the world. Hopefully my career won't go down in flames before morning.*

***

This cannot be fucking happening.

The transition from sleep to dream was brutal this time. He had no more than a moment's semblance of normality—if you could call getting dumped naked in a wingback chair normality—before being snatched up by what sure as hell felt like that scorpion whip, then dangled in midair long enough for a chain to come snaking out of nowhere, wrap itself around his wrists, and hang him from the ceiling like a side of beef. *In my own goddamned mind. This is not happening.*

Stubborn. The woman laughed, studying her crimson nails as if she found them far more interesting than the man suspended in front of her. ***Very stubborn. Do you remember your last visit?***

"I'm not the visitor here, bitch." Kevin circled his wrists, trying to grab the chain and raise himself up to take some of the pressure off them, but he needed slack. No good.

Irrelevant. The woman waved her hand, and in mid-wave it went from manicured nails to ragged, the arm from smooth to hairy, and the laugh from quietly amused to leering. ***You remember it. Which means we move on to other methods.***

"And let me guess, I don't want to know what they are." It came out an insolent drawl, and despite his circumstances, Kevin had to work to keep back a pleased smile. In books and movies, his favorite heroes always had the presence of mind to be smartasses under pressure, but he'd always figured he would cave at the first sign of it. *What do you know?*

The male shrugged, scratching his head and freeing a few of the little scorpions. His cock was erect and ready, that obscene Louisville Slugger bobbing over home plate and all set to swing for the bleachers. Kevin bit back a groan, not wanting to give the bastard the satisfaction of the sound. The male grinned, exposing his fangs, reminding Kevin his thoughts were no longer exclusively his own.

Then, without so much of a flicker, it was the scorpion-thing, as if it had been all along. Maybe it had been. It scuttled closer, and instead of fighting a groan, Kevin was struggling not to vomit at the carrion stench clinging to it. It continued closer until its shifting, pearlescent eyes took up almost Kevin's whole field of vision. ***Remember, human. You control what is about to happen. You decide how long this continues. Give me what I want, and it stops. Simple enough***.

Kevin's throat went dry. And then a movement over his head caught his eye; he looked up, grateful for anything to look at other than the gruesome face in front of him.

Spoke too soon. The creature's tail was arched up over its back, the whip-like end dangling down until it was just over his head. This close, he could see the whip was actually made up of hundreds, maybe thousands of tiny creatures, similar to the scorpions in the male's beard, but lacking amenities such as eyes and legs. These were all chitin, ichor, and teeth.

Christ, there was something in his hair.

The creature laughed. Softly, but without a trace of amusement. Things were oozing down Kevin's neck, over his wrenched shoulders, down his chest.

Don't look down. Don't look at them. Don't look—oh, sweet fuck. Four of them clung like slugs to his heaving abs, miniature abominations that would give H.R. Giger screaming nightmares. One of them opened its mouth, revealing a bristling set of razor-sharp needle-like teeth; it probed at his skin with them, as if testing.

And then it bit. Hard.

Kevin's head flew back, his back arched as the thing continued to chew, but damned if he was going to give the scorpion the benefit of a sound. Slowly he forced his head back where it had been. Had to look the monster in the eye. *Jesus, the thing's in my gut…*

His eyes grew wide as he stared at his stomach. His body told him the thing was burrowing into his intestines. The pain was like nothing he'd ever imagined, and the other three on his stomach were leisurely starting to open their jaws as well. But his eyes told him that while the first creature bit him, it shed no blood, left no marks at all on his flesh.

You last longer, this way. Feelers waved around what was probably the scorpion's mouth. It shook its tail again, and Kevin's teeth clenched as he felt more soft landings in his hair.

"How long?" He was starting to shiver, now, both with pain and the anticipation of more. "What do you want?"

You. Your body. The vessel that will capture Tiernan Guaire.

CHAPTER FOURTEEN

"Kevin, what the fuck are you doing?"

A low, throaty purr was all the answer Tiernan got, as his human's hand continued what it started, twisting itself into his long blond hair and drawing his head back. Hell of a way to wake up, and the Fae groaned as Kevin's other hand improved on it by gliding down his chest until it found his nipple ring, and twisting, not quite gently. "Say the word and I'll stop." His breath was hot in Tiernan's ear, his tongue hotter.

"Is the word 'fuck you'?" Tiernan tried to turn his head, managed to catch a glimpse of dark eyes, sleep-tousled black hair, and a sexy smirk before his head was wrenched back around. Tiernan sucked in a breath as Kevin flicked the nipple ring with a fingertip. His head was still buzzing, his ears ringing from the almost literally mind-blowing jolt of energy he'd gotten from the ley line, and this on top of it? This was *not* like Kevin. Not that his cock had any objections; it was begging for someone to get a grip on it. He reached down, curled his own hand around the rigid length, and started a slow stroking, rolling his palm over the head on the upstrokes.

"It kills me to watch you do that." The hard tip of a tongue traced around Tiernan's ear. "That's why you do it, isn't it?" His laughter was low and rich; on the rare occasions when the Fae heard it, it reminded him of dark chocolate. And possibly honey. Though at the moment that particular thought made his head hurt more.

"No, that's a bonus, it's really all about the orgasms." Tiernan's mouth curved up in a smirk of his own, one that became a gasp as Kevin twisted the ring again, harder this time. What the fuck *was* going on?

"Let me take care of that part." The human bent his head, tongued the nipple ring, looking up with an eyebrow raised, as if gauging Tiernan's reaction to each hot stroke.

"Well, fuck me blind." Kevin was rolling Tiernan onto his back, kneeing his legs apart, with a grin suggesting the Fae was going to need serious recovery time in the hot tub. "Are you a mind-reader?" Kevin smiled.

And for the barest instant, there was something else in those dark eyes. A plea, wild, desperate—

But it was gone as quickly as it had come. And Kevin's warm hand wrapped firmly around his shaft, his mouth had moved up and was busy at his throat, and the smooth hot head of his human's cock was making preliminary inquiries between his ass cheeks. "Shit," he breathed, his head falling back. Unusual as his lover's behavior might be, damned if it wasn't perfectly suited to his mood. Ley lines could fucking wait for later.

"That's it, *lanan*, let me in," Kevin crooned. "Let me in."

Tiernan relaxed—as best he could when his whole body was tensed in anticipation of pleasure— then hissed as the thick head of Kevin's cock forced its way past his ring, dry except for a few of his own warm drops. His eyes tried to roll back in his head, but instead he looked up, meeting his lover's dark eyes.

Too dark. Black. Flat, sullen black. And he was falling into them. Losing himself.

***

Tiernan was… someplace else. A sense of near infinity, and yet a prison cell.

Before a Fae's instinctive reaction to imprisonment—blind panic—could take over, he heard a soft sobbing. *Kevin. What the hell?*

Now he could see. And it was obvious where he was. If he had given any thought to what the inside of Kevin's mind would look like, he might have conjured something like this. A comfortable study, half the walls lined with bookshelves, law books and the elves-and-dwarves fantasy shit his lover was hoping to get him hooked on. He took note of the large fireplace with two wingback chairs standing near it.

But there was an air of pain and decay hanging over everything. As if the fabric of the place was rotting, and any minute now a shelf or a chair or the floor would split apart and reveal the corruption underlying the façade. Tiernan's skin crawled. What was this doing inside his lover's mind? He looked around, looked up, looked for a way out. Tried to Fade, and swore when nothing happened. He looked around again, and this time his stomach roiled and twisted as he saw a long chain hanging from the ceiling, on the far side of one of the chairs. He couldn't look at chains. He couldn't bear even the sight of them. He only kept the truesilver chains that had bound him because they, and the knife that had killed his brother, were the last remnants of his past.

The sound came again, chilling him bone-deep, from the far side of the chair, under the chain. Tiernan crossed to the spot, and froze, a fury kindling deep within him. Kevin lay in a fetal position on the floor, his hands clasped behind his head drawing him even more tightly into a ball. His sobs were low and soft, as if he were trying not to be heard. He trembled from head to foot, and on his wrists were the bloody marks of the chains.

The last time Tiernan had known a rage like this, it ended with his brother's corpse turned to sand and crumbled at his feet. Someone was going to die; someone would beg for death, long before it was granted to him.

A laugh came from behind him, a cold dead laugh. ***Your toy is brave, Tiernan Guaire. He thought he could fight the* Marfach.** Tiernan froze. Even before he turned, he knew what he would see; or, rather, what he wouldn't. The *Marfach*, the Slow Death. It couldn't be seen, it repelled the eyes, the heart, the soul of a Fae. One of his kind forced to look on it for long would go mad, would die, eaten away from within.

But it couldn't possibly be here. The *Marfach* was locked away, wherever it had been sent in the Sundering, contained, if never destroyed. It couldn't be here. Not inside Kevin's mind. Not his human. His fists clenched.

Though madness waited, still he tried to look. How could he possibly wrest Kevin away from what he couldn't even look at? His hand came up by reflex to shield his eyes, as his gaze flinched away from the sight-devouring nothingness. "Let him go, damn you, he's nothing to you." His voice was rough, and caught hard at a glimpse of the tortured male huddled on the floor. If only the Slow Death could die.

Perhaps he is nothing to you. But he is everything to me. There was thick gloating in the *Marfach*'s voice. *He is my gateway to this realm. How else to hunt down an exiled kinslayer in the human lands, save through his SoulShare?*

Tiernan cursed as Kevin's eyes went wide, and the *Marfach* laughed. *Oh, your Grace, you never told the boy how you came to be here?*

As if he could. As if he could bear to have Kevin know the truth. "Shut the *fuck* up—"

You've glamoured him, that's obvious. The poor bastard's totally besotted. The nothingness drifted closer to the figure on the floor, and Kevin flinched back. *Have you used any of your other magicks on your toy, your Grace? That would explain his attachment.*

Kevin's head jerked up, as if he were being held by the hair, then fell as if tossed aside, and Tiernan snarled. *Mine, damn you. Mine.*

Or were you stripped of those before your exile? The voice was almost female, now, trickling over him like rancid oil. *That would be such a pity. I'm sure the Noble magicks of Earth would afford you all sorts of decadent pleasures.*

Kevin turned, not to the *Marfach,* but to Tiernan,

slowly raising his head. The Fae's fists clenched tighter, nails biting into his palms, as his lover looked at him with eyes that spoke of a pain Tiernan dared not imagine. A pain Kevin had suffered for him, without even knowing who or what he was.

The voice continued to croon behind him. *And it's evident you've told him nothing of what you truly are and where you come from, or he would have known enough to save himself by surrendering.* Another thick, clotted chuckle. *Hours of his time it took me to break him, hours of being devoured alive. For you, kinslayer.*

Not for me. It can't be. Fuck... don't love me, lanan. *Don't pay that price. Not for me.* Tiernan stared at the tormented figure on the floor, as if he could drive his words into his lover by thought alone. *Don't let it think I mean anything to you.*

Too late, your Grace. His screams were more than enough evidence. The laughter was definitely male now. *At least, until I destroyed the source of his pain, burned it out at the root. But I have you, now, so he can be discarded. You won't mind, will you?*

Tiernan's nostrils flared, his jaw muscles bunched. "Come to me, you syphilitic son of a prolapsed whore, and I'll show you how much I mind."

I have already come to you, your Grace. Even control at this superficial level of your plaything's mind allowed me those few brief moments' dalliance, that taste of intimacy.

Tiernan's skin went clammy and pale, and for one hideous moment he was sure he was going to be sick. "That was never you."

Believe what you like. The voice was female now, cool and almost disinterested. It no longer matters. ***Your toy is broken, and cannot stop me from taking that which I need***.

Fuck. His gaze went to Kevin again. The human raised his head, and his gaze was almost as hard to meet as the *Marfach*'s. He'd been through hell, and every minute of it written plainly in that dark brown gaze. *I'm so sorry,* Ianan…*damn, you deserve better*.

Touching. Derisive laughter. ***Anything at all would be 'better' than the nothing you have given him, your Grace. He is your SoulShare, yet you have given him nothing of yourself save the half soul you have had no use for since you slit your brother's throat.***

At the disembodied words, Kevin's eyes closed, his head turned away, the lines of his face set as impassively as any statue, but his throat worked, and his cheeks were wet.

Tiernan snarled, his hand flashing to the hilt of the knife his dream-self wore. There were legends claiming it was death to attack the *Marfach*. But there were also legends hinting it wasn't, and he was more than ready to throw the dice.

And if he lost, his life would be well spent, making his race's bitter foe pay for those tears. The knife slid easily into his hand, the silk-wrapped hilt warm and familiar, the sweet promise of violence. "Let us both ignore him, then, *Marfach*." He beckoned with the knife, trying to draw the mind-destroying distortion in the air away from his human. "Come dance with me, *bodlag*." The word in the Fae tongue implying so much more than *limp dick*, surely even immortal evil couldn't ignore it.

Oh, fuck me senseless. Kevin staggered to his feet, and was bracing himself against the leather armchair, gasping for breath. For only a moment he stood, precariously balanced, not even time for Tiernan to shout a warning before he flung himself headlong and weaponless at what the Fae could not bear even the sight of, hands outstretched to throttle it. As if it had a throat, as if it were vulnerable at all—

***

As his eyes opened, truly opened, back in their bed, Tiernan rolled, taking Kevin with him, wrapping his body around the human's, covering him, snarling defiance at the creature that had wounded him. He felt his lover shivering against him, and caught him close. "*Lanan*, it's all right, I have you." The words stuck in his throat, the falsity of them gagging him.

Kevin did not seem to notice, either the words or the comforting falsehoods they offered. He held tightly until his shivering subsided, then pulled back far enough to meet the Fae's eyes. The torment Tiernan had seen was still there, and something more, a sadness so utter, so profound, it went straight to his heart.

Or what passed for his heart. The *Marfach* had been right about that much. "Are you all right?" He couldn't tear his gaze away from Kevin's, but his hands skimmed quickly over the body pressed tightly to his own. If anything done to his lover in the dream state had carried over into the waking world, it was already too late. The *Marfach*'s presence on such a deep level of his mind would be impossible to reverse.

"I've… been better." Kevin coughed. His voice

rasped in his throat, as if his body remembered the screams of his mind. But he slowly started to relax, his grip loosening just a little, the trembling easing. "What the fuck *is* that? And how does it know you?" *Better than I do*. The human's eyes spoke the words, or perhaps it was the Fae's stunted conscience that left the razor-edged words hanging in the air between them.

Whether the accusations in those eyes were real or imagined, Tiernan could not face them. He closed his eyes, grimacing. "It's called the *Marfach*. And it's… I suppose you could call it an evil distortion of magickal force." *Yeah, the same way you could call a tornado a stiff breeze*. "Supposedly, it can only live in magick, living things with a magickal essence. And when the ancient Loremasters withdrew magick from this world and sealed it off in ours, they sealed the *Marfach* out. They all died doing it, but they sealed it away from what it needed to survive. Or so the ones left behind thought. But it's surviving, here, somehow." *Obviously. Moron*. "And there have always been legends it watches the Realm, trying to force a way back through the Pattern. More than just legends, apparently."

The words felt stiff and stupid as they passed his lips. They were what Kevin asked to hear, but they were so far from what Tiernan wanted, needed to say. And no words at all could do what he needed to do, which was to make it so those broken sobs he had heard, and everything that had gone into the making of them, had never happened. His fingers laced into the human's dark hair, drew his head into his shoulder. As always, there was a moment of hesitation, almost resistance, before Kevin allowed himself to be drawn in, and this time the sensation that shot through

Tiernan was not the delight his lover's shyness always gave him, but rather a cold feeling of dread.

"So that's how it knew who you were. It's been watching you." Kevin's voice was muffled by the Fae's shoulder, but even allowing for that, he sounded exhausted.

Let it be exhaustion and nothing more. How many times had he begged this male not to love him? Nothing had changed. Loving him was still the most idiotic thing his human could ever do, and now it could get him killed as well. Yet Tiernan felt hollow, empty at the thought his pleas might finally have been answered. "Yeah. I'm guessing it knows pretty much everything that happens in the Realm."

The length of the silence that followed was like a physical weight. Now Tiernan understood why *Mhionbhrú*, the Crushing, was one of the names the Earth Fae had for the *Marfach*. "Talk to me, *lanan*." His fingers clutched in Kevin's hair, his other hand tightened where it rested on the human's thigh. "Please." A peril worse than death was waiting for them both, but this mattered more. This had to come first.

He felt the human's sigh against his shoulder. "Damn."

Kevin drew back enough to let him meet Tiernan's gaze again. He'd never realized how expressive his human's eyes were. *Animal eyes*, the Fae called eyes as dark as these, but Kevin's eyes were lively and intelligent and fucking beautiful. And so full of pain and sadness right now that both overflowed to etch themselves on his face.

"Why did you kill your brother?"

CHAPTER FIFTEEN

Tiernan stiffened against him, and Kevin closed his eyes, bracing himself for what was to come, even as he wondered why that had been the first thing out of his mouth, ahead of so many other competing questions.

He knew why he'd had to ask, though. Because of the sheer pain in Tiernan's eyes, when the creature, the *Marfach*, had exposed that secret. The *Marfach* had only dropped dark hints about what his lover concealed from him, hints Tiernan tried to ignore, to deflect, to ridicule. But *kinslayer,* the thing had called him, and the Fae hadn't denied, had only closed his eyes against the pain of it, clenched his fists as if against the memory of his brother's blood on his hands.

And now Kevin waited, a cold clawed fist clutching at his gut and his own dead brother's restless shade seeming to wait for the answer. How could the male who shared his soul have murdered a brother?

"I killed Lorcan because I caught him raping Moriath. Our sister."

Jesus fucking Christ. Kevin shook his head slightly, barely noticing the hand still cupping the back of his head. "They exiled you for that? They should have given you a fucking medal!"

A bitter laugh escaped Tiernan. "Not likely. Ties of blood are everything to the Fae. Murder's done all the time—that and accident are pretty much the only ways a Fae in the Realm can die, short of beating the odds and making it to old age—but never against kin. Never. They'd almost forgotten what to do with an animal like me."

Animal. The word jolted Kevin to his core. "Fuck that shit. He raped his own sister, and *you're* the animal?" All the ways he'd played this out in his head, during the *Marfach*'s perverted mind games, none of his guesses had even come close to this.

Tiernan looked at him, in what Kevin was stunned to recognize as genuine confusion. A whole world of hurt as well, and even after the *Marfach*'s tortures, the Fae's pain still sliced into him as deep and as hot as a rusty razor, but his lover's pain was shot through with real bewilderment. "I was the one who killed."

No wonder he's kept secrets, if he really believes he's no better than an animal, for what he did. Even with his body throbbing like an infected wound from the aftermath of believing himself eaten alive, and his soul still breathless from the pain of the creature's final gambit, when it tired of playing with its human toy and simply hammered its way into his mind with a single brutal truth... hell, even knowing any minute the son of a bitch was going to be scrabbling around in the sub-basement of his mind looking for a way upstairs, he ached for his lover. "Trust the lawyer next to you. Here it would have been considered totally justifiable homicide."

Tiernan shook his head. "I don't see it that way. I can't." His beautiful face was a thin porcelain mask over something raw. "Love of kin is in the blood of the Fae. So my very blood is poisoned."

Oh, dear God. It was one of those moments of utter, awful clarity, frozen in time like the moment the M.E. had pulled the sheet back from Tanner's face in the morgue. *This is why he believes he can't love.* Because the bastard he'd sent to hell had also happened to be his blood kin.

But you loved your sister—

Kevin would have cried it out, but Tiernan cut him off with a fierce shake of his head. "Enough of the emo shit. We have to get the *Marfach* out of you."

Kevin cursed softly. Tiernan was right. But he wasn't. *Damn.* "I know, but… fuck." Time for that other important question. "What *is* it?" He shuddered at the memory of the scorpion's tail extending toward Tiernan, changing as it elongated into that obscene set of male genitalia. "I mean, I know what it looks like, but what *is* it?"

One blond eyebrow went up. "You know what it looks like? We have stories, but a Fae can't bear to look at it." He shook his head before Kevin could answer. "Hell, no. I don't need to know if the stories are true. I don't *want* to know. And as for what it is…" Tiernan rolled onto his back, staring at the ceiling, one arm still coiled loosely around Kevin's back. "It's a distortion of magick. As if magick itself was being unstoppably drawn toward evil. It's why the Fae took living magick out of your world. To protect your world, and ours. If it has nothing to warp, to pervert, it can't exist."

155

For a moment, Kevin was almost hypnotized by the light from the bedside table glinting in Tiernan's nipple ring. "Then what was it doing in my head? I'm sure as hell not magical."

"Your soul is." Tiernan's eyes narrowed, as if this was something occurring to him as he spoke. "Your soul is Fae—*our* soul is Fae." He propped up on an elbow, his eyes oddly unfocused yet intense. "A Fae soul in a human body... shit, the human half of a SoulShare has to act like a magnet to it."

"Magnet, punching bag, boy toy—" Kevin would have given almost anything to have those words back, when he saw their effect on his lover. "Tiernan..."

"What did it do to you?"

The Fae's voice was low, and lethal, and Kevin remembered what he'd seen, back in the prison his mind had become. Tiernan gripping a knife of gleaming silver, like someone who knew fuck-all well how to use it, and ready to hurl himself at what had been a seething mass of scorpions. He would have been killed, there wasn't the slightest doubt in Kevin's mind. Or whatever happened to the body, when a person's mind was killed. Kevin shuddered. The fires of Mordor would be a vast improvement over this shit. *At least Frodo and Sam had eagles.*

"I said, *what did it do to you*?" There was an edge to Tiernan's voice, his indefinable accent more pronounced.

Kevin tried to shrug. "None of it was real—"

"Do I look like I give a shit? I want to know what it tried to do to my SoulShare." The words came flashing and sharp-edged like shuriken, and it almost surprised Kevin none of them drew blood.

156

"I'd rather not get you killed." He sighed. "One of its forms looks like a scorpion with too many legs, extra mouths, and a tail made of smaller versions of itself. It dropped those and let them crawl on me, made me think they were eating me. Then, it has human-like forms, or Fae-like, I don't know. One male, one female. They both… played with me, a while. And then—"

A soft, almost subliminal growl started when he described what the *Marfach*-scorpion had done, and had grown louder as he described the other two forms. Now Tiernan cut him off with a gesture. "When you say 'played with you,' is that an unnecessarily polite way of saying they fucked you?"

Sweat prickled along Kevin's brow. If he thought he could get away with lying, he'd do it. Even though the icy anger in those crystal-blue eyes hinted to him the creature *might* have been wrong, or even lying, about the Fae's ability to love, Kevin considered the lie, because he had no desire to write his lover's death warrant. But those eyes were as merciless as those of any hanging judge, and lying was not an option. "She just blew me." With serrated fangs, but no fucking way was he spilling *that* little detail. Or describing any of the other things she'd showed him, without using them. "But him… yeah. He did." Against his will, he shuddered at the memory.

"While you were chained."

Oh, Christ. He'd almost forgotten the raw, bloody welts around his wrists, they'd seemed the very least of his problems. But the marks he'd borne for a short time had been the twins of Tiernan's own. "Yes."

Slowly, the Fae's eyes closed. For a moment, there was silence, even the growl went quiet. Then, behind Kevin, something exploded. Startled, he whipped his head around. His hand came up instinctively to shield his face as shards of crystal from a shattered Waterford vase whizzed past, some of them striking an invisible barrier inches from Kevin's face and sliding to the floor.

"Jesus," Kevin breathed.

Tiernan's eyes opened as slowly as they'd closed. "Sorry." His tone belied the word, his eyes flashing as sharp and hard as any of the crystal fragments. "And what came after that?"

"I… what?" Kevin tried to remember what he'd said, before getting sidetracked onto thoughts of razor-fanged slugs and Louisville Sluggers, and grimaced. "It got tired of torturing me, I guess, and went straight into my head. Or whatever, considering this was all in my mind to begin with." *And please be content with that. Please. Just in case it was right after all.*

Tiernan's eyes narrowed. The hand cupping the back of Kevin's head tightened its grip on his hair, and he could feel it trembling slightly. "You held out for hours, against the worst the *Marfach* could do to you physically. Then it found something that broke you. Enough so it could use you to trap me."

Shit. "Tiernan, please… I *can't*."

"Kevin."

He started on hearing his name. Tiernan hardly ever used it, preferring *lanan*, or 'lover.' In fact, the only other time he could remember hearing his name had been in Purgatory, the precise moment captured on O'Halloran's cell phone. *He doesn't even use my name.* "Don't."

"I have to know." The hand in Kevin's hair

relaxed, came down to cup the line of his jaw. A thumb ran along his cheekbone. But as gentle as the hand was, the Fae's eyes still glittered with a cold wrath, a fury that looked straight to the deepest part of Kevin's soul—and past it, to glare defiantly at the creature lurking on the other side. "I need to know what weapon it has against you, or I can't fight it."

"Why do you have to make sense of this?" Kevin whispered, through a throat closed so tightly it would let no other sound pass.

"We don't have any more time, *Ianan*. Tell me."

He has allowed you to pretend, because it costs him nothing to let you do so, the *Marfach* had murmured, her lips coldly caressing his ear as she held his head up by the hair. **But speak the words, shatter the illusion, and it will be gone forever**.

"God *damn* it." But his lover was right, they had no time. "It got into my head, somehow. And it told me… showed me… made me know… you would never love me." He could feel his face flaming, but kept his gaze locked on Tiernan's.

And something in him broke all over again as those ice-blue eyes closed.

"Don't love me." Tiernan's lips moved almost soundlessly. "You don't deserve that."

What the hell? "It doesn't matter, lover." And it didn't. He'd known even as he'd broken the first time. That obscenity wanted Tiernan, and its only path to him was through Kevin's mind. And that was not happening. When it came to what he would do to stop the *Marfach*, it didn't matter if the Fae ever loved him.

Ever loved him back.

"What do you mean?" Tiernan's hand fell away

from Kevin's cheek as he propped himself up on an elbow, looking everywhere but at his face.

"Whether I love you or not is my own damned business." *Now* the Fae looked him in the eyes, and his eyes were wide at what he saw there. "Either way, it won't stop me from doing whatever I have to, to keep that thing away from you."

Tiernan looked at him forever, hair falling in unreadable eyes. "I'm sorry, lanan, but if losing that dream is the price of keeping you alive, it's mine to pay, and I choose to pay it."

The Fae leaned in, abruptly, catching Kevin at the back of the neck and pulling him into a searing kiss. "Get dressed, lover. Club wear. I know what we have to do… and where we have to be to do it. I'll explain on the way there."

Kevin began to roll, to get out of the bed, but Tiernan's hand tangled in his hair again and stopped him short, pulled him in until their lips nearly met. "And we're going to talk when this is over. The *Marfach* does *not* get the last word in this conversation."

***

The reflections of traffic lights, streetlights and headlights all glared at Kevin as he drummed his fingers on the steering wheel, waiting with poor grace for the light to change. What a night for a fucking sleet storm. At least it gave Tiernan a few extra minutes to explain. Not that it was anywhere near enough.

"Ley lines I get. A nexus under Purgatory I get. You being attracted to it I get."

"So what *don't* you get?" Tiernan slouched against the Mercedes' passenger door, looking as uncomfortable as a male could in a luxury car. *When I want to go somewhere, I Fade*, he'd grumbled, and the drive had been highlighted by many of the classic symptoms of claustrophobia. But he'd insisted on coming along. He hadn't wanted to leave his human to make the trip to Adams Morgan alone, not with the *Marfach* lurking under the radar.

"How you can use the energy in the lines." Cautiously, Kevin hit the gas and felt the tires slip a little before they found purchase. "You told me the whole point of sealing off your world was to pull the magick out of ours. That way the *Marfach* wouldn't have anything here to corrupt. So, Occam's Razor—if you left it behind, it must not be magick. And if it's not magick, how can you use it?"

"Splendid, Holmes." The Fae drew himself up a little, ran a hand through his hair, and wiped the sweat from his forehead, from the look of him glad to have an excuse to keep talking. "You're right, to a point." He cleared his throat and looked out the car window, flinching as a taxi went sliding past. "Shit, does everyone drive like that?"

"First ice storm of the season? We're lucky we haven't been hit." Kevin spared a glance sideways, and regretted his choice of words immediately. "We'll be fine, it's only a few more minutes. You going to answer my question?"

"Oh, Yeah." Tiernan shook his head. "Bear in mind, a lot of this is guesswork on my part, and some of it I've only put together in the last few days. The Loremasters didn't leave behind much in the way of end-user instructions." He pulled himself up, glanced in the side mirror, and went a little paler. "The lines have something to do with magick. Pure, unbound energy that becomes living magick in a Fae's body. But that energy is combined with the essence of the elements in a way that can't be undone. Nobles and Royals use the elemental aspects, more than the pure magick, though we can tap into the pure stuff for extra—shit, I'm babbling, aren't I?"

Kevin nodded tightly, flicking a cautious glance sideways. "And you're a little green, too. But keep talking, I think it's good for you."

"Getting out of this death trap would be good for me. Not that I'm picky." Tiernan cleared his throat. "Think of magickal energy, the living stuff, like electricity. One basic force, but if you run it through a fan, you get wind. Run it through an oven, you get heat. Run magickal energy through an Air Fae, you get instant comprehension of languages. Run it through an Earth Fae, you get shielding from magickal attack. And then there's the elemental energy that only Nobles and Royals have—sweet fuck, look out for the motherfucking traffic light!"

Kevin eased the car to a stop, or his best approximation of one, as Tiernan clung white-knuckled to the door handle. "Wait—you're shielded from magickal attack? It shouldn't be able to hurt you, then."

The Fae shook his head, pulling himself up from where he'd slumped down again. "I'm shielded against attack from without. Not from within. And I'm sure it's realized once it has you, it'll have me."

"Because of the SoulShare." Kevin's voice was

dull, as he slowly entered the intersection, then put on careful speed. "I'm your weakness."

"Fuck, no." Kevin was startled by the words, and even more by the hand resting briefly on his thigh.

Kevin shivered slightly, shirtless under his leather duster. The Mercedes' heater was handling the cold perfectly. The chill was one no external heat could touch. "Okay. I get it. I think. So we have to get down into the storeroom somehow."

He sucked in a breath, his shivers stronger, sharper. Everything was blackness, and a thick, gloating, echoing laughter. He clutched at the wheel, sending the Mercedes into a skid. ***Soon, toy. Very soon***.

A hand gripped his arm, hard. Lost in the darkness, as if from under water, or a great distance, he heard someone calling his name. No, not "someone". Tiernan, calling his name.

The sound drove back the darkness, drowned out the laughter, and he was in possession of his own mind and senses once again. It had only been moments, and the car was still at the beginning of its skid and he managed to wrestle it back under control. "Holy shit," he panted, as the car slid to a stop at the next light. He rested his forehead on the steering wheel, trying to bring his heart rate back under control, acutely aware of the hand on his arm.

"Was that the *Marfach*?" Tiernan's voice was tense.

Kevin nodded. "I'm not sure how much longer we have." Each time he'd forced the creature out of his mind, the respite became shorter. Granted, the other times it hadn't been trying to get at what Tiernan had claimed was the deepest level of his mind, the level that actually cooperated in creating his reality. But that wasn't a whole hell of a lot of comfort at the moment, given he hadn't been broken the other times.

He looked up, as Tiernan did the same, his gaze traveling down the block, toward the familiar door with its barely noticeable sign, writhing dark red neon flames. "Valet parking sounds like a good idea." He tried to keep his voice light, but when his lover turned to him and pinned him with that crystal blue gaze, he knew he'd failed. "We'll make it, *lanan*."

"I'm not letting it have you." The Fae's voice was tightly controlled, a silken sheath over steel.

And I'll die before I let it go through me to get to you. Kevin's knuckles went white on the steering wheel. *Even if I have to make you kill me.*

CHAPTER SIXTEEN

There were still seats empty in the cock pit, and Tiernan chose the one that gave him the best view of the door leading to the basement, the safety pins on the back pockets of his jeans catching on the leather as he slid onto the loveseat. "Here, straddle me and open that coat." He grabbed Kevin's hips and pulled him down, managing a laugh despite himself at the look on his human's face. "That way, when I vanish, maybe no one will notice."

"I was going to ask how you were planning on getting us downstairs." Kevin swung a leg over and settled on top of him, and damn if the Fae didn't respond. Even with a fight to the death—Tiernan's own, if anyone's—minutes away, Kevin could still make his heart race and his cock rise.

And the Marfach taking away his hope I might love him someday broke him. Carefully, Tiernan kept everything but the lust appropriate to the situation from his face. *Fuck, I want to make that bastard suffer.* "Lean in a little and open the coat."

His voice was hoarse, and his breathing quickened as his human complied. "Yeah, that's it… oh, shit." Kevin was teasing at Tiernan's cheeks with his own unshaven ones; the Fae, being blond, tended toward smooth cheeks, while the human usually had a five-o'clock shadow by 10:30 or so, and damn, it felt good.

"Too much?" Kevin drew back slightly.

"Hell, no." Tiernan gripped Kevin's thighs, tightly enough that his knuckles went white. "Once we're down there—I haven't tried to channel the true Noble magicks since I was exiled, I'm not even sure I still can." He grimaced. "Magick is always easier when I'm aroused, that's true for any Fae. And if I'm going to boost what magick I can use by channeling the raw power in those ley lines"—*without burning out my brain*—"I'm going to need you to bring me right to the edge. Like last time." He felt his cheeks going red, remembering that the last time, it hadn't been his lover who had been in control. "And I think I need that kind of push to get into your mind, too. So no, it's not too much."

Kevin nodded, rolling his hips slightly, his eyes going briefly heavy-lidded. He, too, seemed keen to seize what pleasure could be found in the moment. And it was pleasure he sought, nothing more. It had to be. The *Marfach* had done the human a good turn, all unknowing, if it had cured him of his ill-advised desire for the love of a Fae.

Over Kevin's broad shoulder, Tiernan caught a glimpse of the seemingly omnipresent bouncer, and his lip curled in a snarl. The fucker had winked at him as the two of them arrived. His SoulShare had been fighting off another attack by the *Marfach*, and needed an arm around his waist to get safely down the stairs. The male-mountain had tossed off a snide comment the Fae had only half caught, something about the price of good help. But that half had been enough; sooner or later, the son of a bitch was going to bleed, and it was going to be Tiernan's great pleasure to cause it.

Assuming he survived the next few minutes.

Kevin stopped his gentle caresses, and was eyeing him curiously. "What's wrong?" A dry, unamused chuckle. "Apart from the obvious, that is."

"You stopped." Tiernan reached around, out of sight under the duster, and gripped Kevin's ass cheeks tightly, pulling him in close. Fuck it, he was entitled to steal a little pleasure before everything became life and death. His eyes drifted nearly closed, as his lover's hips pulsed against his; his lips parted in a soft groan, one almost immediately stolen by a hungry kiss. *So good...*

A shiver ran through Kevin's body, where it was pressed against Tiernan's. "It's down there, damn it. I can feel it. Not as bad as the last one, when we were coming in, but it feels like it's looking for the way in." The human's expression was stoic, his jaw set. But the terror in his dark eyes—oh, sweet fuck, the *Marfach* was going to pay. Somehow.

"We have to get downstairs. I can't tap the ley lines from here." Tiernan glanced over at the bar. The door to the storeroom was behind one end of the bar. "See the way to the door? It's just around that corner, at this end of the bar. "

Kevin's head turned, ever so slightly, and he nodded. "Got it. What do we do if it's locked?"

"It *is* locked, there's a keypad with a combination. But I've been down there before, so I can Fade to the other side." One of Tiernan's hands

167

wandered up Kevin's bare back, stroking, feeling some of the tension ease out of the hard muscles. "When it looks like you'll have a clear shot, I'll Fade to the far side of the door. You walk back there, and I'll let you in from the inside."

A tight nod was the only answer Kevin gave—that, and another one of those stubble-cheeked caresses. "Damn, who knew this felt so good?" Kevin's voice was rough, and caught randomly.

"Save some for after." Tiernan forced the words past a lump in his own throat, unsure which of them needed the reassurance more. Kevin was the one who had been invaded, but he was the one who knew exactly what the invader was and what it was capable of. The sundering of two worlds and the sacrifice of the lives of almost an entire generation of the Fae had been required to contain the entity now seeking a way into the deepest, reality-controlling level of his lover's mind. And if it got what it wanted, it would have Tiernan next. Once it had possession of a magickal being in the human realm, all the sacrifice would have been for naught.

And all that counted for far less with Tiernan than the sudden hungry kiss his human gave him. The pus-dripping son of a whore was fucking with his SoulShare, and it was going to pay.

Kevin started, and nodded toward the bar. The bartender was glancing at his watch, and reaching down a leather jacket from a hook behind the bar. "Think he's going on break?" he murmured in Tiernan's ear as if it were an endearment.

"Looks that way." A muscle in Tiernan's jaw rippled. *Time to party.*

He waited until the bartender stepped out from behind the bar, then turned back to Kevin, about to tell him… oh, fuck what he'd been about to tell him. He took the human's face between his palms and looked straight into his frightened eyes. "We're going to beat it, *lanan*. I promise you."

Kevin shook his head gently. "No promises. But it won't have you." He nipped gently at Tiernan's earlobe, then spread his coat and redistributed his weight so he wouldn't fall when Tiernan suddenly vanished from underneath him. "Go."

The bite drew a soft growl from the Fae, even as he Faded, one that was still rumbling as he materialized behind the door. The door latch was cool under his fingers, and he held on tight for a moment, trying to calm himself.

But every moment he delayed was a moment the *Marfach* could be trying again; the growl changed to anger, and he eased the door open and peered out. From here, there was no seeing the loveseat he and Kevin had been occupying, and he caught himself holding his breath. *Come on,* lanan, *come ON*.

A dark figure loomed, filling his field of vision. He caught Kevin's scent before he could make out his features, and stepped back to let him in, then closed the door with a quiet click, flipping on the lights for the human's benefit. "This way."

Tiernan led the way down the stairs, the soles of his feet already vibrating with the energy of the lines beneath the floor. Once again the sensation grew more intense the further down he went. By the time he reached the bottom of the stairs, he could swear he felt little rivulets of pure energy running up his legs. He did his best not to shiver, not wanting Kevin to see his nervousness. How he'd managed to channel this power even for an instant was beyond his ken, and how he was going to tame it to his needs now, he had no idea.

Once he was sure he was standing over the right spot, he turned back, surprised to see Kevin looking bemusedly at his own feet. "I'm probably just imagining I feel something, right?"

"Hell if I know." Tiernan caught at the human's hand, and drew him down to sit beside him on the floor. "I was never much of a student of magickal theory. I suppose you'd say it was a geek subject. Who knew it would actually turn out to be worth something someday?" It was a poor jest, but it made Kevin smile, so well enough. And maybe he *was* feeling something. His soul, after all, was Fae, and that might suffice.

Tiernan took a deep breath and lay back on the cold concrete, urging Kevin to lie on top of him. The denim of his jacket did little to keep out the chill, and nothing at all to stop or even slow the flow of power coming up through the floor. The power of the lines was seductive as all hell. It was easy to imagine reaching out, gathering all of it into himself, losing himself in it. But that would, in all probability, be suicide, in which he had not the slightest fucking interest.

Kevin settled over him, his forearms braced against the floor, his leather coat falling open around them both. "What do you need me to do?" A hand tangled in his long blond hair, tugged gently.

Tiernan tried to reply, but his voice had deserted him. He swallowed hard and tried again. "You know what excites me." He turned his head, placed a kiss on the inside of the thick wrist which had been marred and bloodied such a short time before. "You always have."

The human seemed about to speak, but then his eyes closed, and he took all his weight on one arm; his freed hand slid open-palmed down Tiernan's chest, two fingers tweaking his nipple ring through his thin muscle T-shirt. Fingers skimmed over the hard ridges of Tiernan's abs. Kevin's mouth covered his just as those fingers found the button of his jeans. The human's tongue parted the Fae's lips as the button gave way and the purpled and weeping head of Tiernan's cock emerged.

Tiernan hissed as Kevin's palm passed over his head. His hips arched up involuntarily, and he groaned into his lover's hungry mouth at the sensation of what could only be the power of the ley lines, teasing at the base of his spine, where the pleasure Kevin was already drawing from him was beginning to pool. "Shit," he breathed, almost like a prayer, his cock twitching as Kevin slowly worked the zipper down to free it.

"Was that a good 'shit' or a bad 'shit'?" Kevin's hot tongue flickered along the line of Tiernan's jaw, its progress punctuated by sharp little bites, making the Fae's breath catch hard in his throat. The touch of teasing humor the human managed, even now, made Tiernan wish they were anywhere but here. And made him wish the *Marfach* had actual physical balls he could tear off and feed to it.

"Take a guess." He laid a hand along his human's cheek, his eyes going heavy-lidded with pleasure at the feel of the muscles working, the delicious harsh stubble against his palm as the licks and the nips continued. The heat was building, invisible tendrils of power lacing up his spine, spiraling to coil around the base of his sac. His whole body trembled with the effort of restraining the power—restraining *himself*, from embracing it, taking everything it teased him with.

And it only got worse. Kevin shifted his weight, braced his knees against the concrete to grind his tight, hard hips into the cradle of the Fae's thighs, as his palm wrapped firmly around the erection that strained against the vee of his open zipper.

"*Lanan.*" Kevin's tongue was hot in Tiernan's ear. The human's hand gripped, squeezed. The Fae groaned softly, and then not so softly, as his lover's thumb passed over the head of his cock and played in the trickle there. "So good—I'm going to—"

Kevin choked. His body stiffened. "Oh, God—it's *here*."

Tiernan's eyes flew open, to look deep into Kevin's, dark brown soul-wells. And as he looked, those wells went flat, lifeless black, a darkness that reached out to him and took hold of him, drawing him in. For an instant he fought, instinctively, as a drowning man would fight for air. But this battle, this first one, he had to lose. He surrendered, began to fall. With his last conscious thought, he reached out for the power of the ley lines and allowed the eldritch lightning to course through him, arching hard into his lover's body.

Showtime, motherfucker.

***

Tiernan came to himself on his knees, on a cold stone floor. For the space of several precious breaths, he knelt, breathed, hands on his thighs, gathering himself, fighting for control.

The power resonated in him, almost a living thing; every breath he drew shivered with it, every beat of his heart slammed against the wall of his chest as if trying to smash down that wall and escape. Untameable. It filled him, buffeted him—he no more controlled it than a kite controlled the gale it rode. Gale, hell. Hurricane. Typhoon. The powers of a Noble drew on the magick of the elements, and while there was elemental energy in the lines, he was being buffeted by a torrent of proto-magick, raw power untamed to the needs of a Fae until his body did the taming. His head whirled. Instinctively, he hunched in on himself to keep from falling over.

Gradually, a dull, throbbing sound, which wasn't quite a sound, pierced through the power-storm, and Tiernan looked dazedly up. He'd give anything to be able to anchor himself. Something to hold on to in this storm only he could sense. He knelt in the center of a small, roughly circular stone cell, to which a massive wooden door gave the only access. Kevin stood against this door, arms and legs splayed out to brace himself, bare back against the rough wood, head down, shoulders hunched, his body shining with sweat and vibrating to that sinister Lambeg rhythm.

"Kevin?"

The human's head came up. Deep brown eyes wide and unmistakably startled. *Do I say his name so seldom?* And what had he been meaning to ask? His face flamed, as he realized he had been about to ask

173

for help. His lover was spending himself, second by hard second, to buy Tiernan a few moments, and he'd been about to ask him for more, for some kind of help with a task for a Fae alone.

You stone-hard thoughtless bastard. It was as if someone had spoken it aloud—but the only sounds in the cell were Kevin's labored breathing and the ominous pounding. No, the accuser's voice was Tiernan's own. *You let him give to you. You let him love you. And you don't even have the common decency to tell him—*

—that I can't love him? I told him—

No, asshole. That you DO love him.

And while Tiernan knelt, mouth agape, Kevin gasped, lurched as something struck the door from behind. "Shit—Tiernan, that was too damn close."

Do I really love him? CAN I?

Tiernan knew the answer—he knew what the answer *had* to be, what Fae nature and the nature of magick and his own tainted bloodline demanded. But the pain of that knowledge was a very real physical ache. Maybe it would be some small consolation for him, someday, in whatever hell he ultimately found himself in, that his heart at least had the decency to ache for what it wasn't able to give.

And yet the power had an answer of its own, caring nothing for his. And it spoke that answer between one breath and the next, as a deep brown gaze locked with crystal blue in the middle of the invisible storm. The answer was the joy. The joy he'd fled, the joy that was his *scair-anam*'s gift to him, shared every time one pleasured the other. It poured into him, filled him, buoyed him up and set him on the crest of the wave. The power was still the biggest motherfucking tsunami ever. More than any one male could tame. But he was not one male.

And if there were gods, let them have mercy on the *Marfach*, because Tiernan wasn't going to spare the breath for it.

"Come away from the door, *lanan*." His voice was hoarse. He coughed, tried again. "It's going to get interesting over there."

As Kevin staggered away from the massive door, Tiernan got a good look at what the deepest layer of his human's mind conjured for their battleground, and a grim smile touched his lips. *This could be a hell of a lot worse*. The cell reminded the Fae of the one in which he'd been abandoned to await exile, only this one had a floor of ordinary stone and no window to let in the betraying moonlight. And stone was his, whether in the waking world or in deep dream. Even the lesser magicks of the Earth Fae would hold these walls against anything.

The door was going to be more difficult. Not impossible, though. He hoped. Ordinary stone to living Stone, not a problem. That was a lesser channeling, not all that different from the concrete-to-crystal he had managed earlier. But the transmutation of what had once been living to Stone was a Noble magick, one he hadn't dared to touch in over a hundred and fifty years. He'd feared it might drain him—though small chance of that, now, with the power of the ley lines coursing through him—but worse, he'd been afraid he might find the Noble magicks had been stripped from him a century and a half ago by the Pattern's wire-sharp blades. Better not to know.

Moving the pawn away, to avoid a sacrifice? The *Marfach*'s voice was slightly muffled, but the sound of its laughter still managed to be obscene. ***No matter, I'll have it soon enough. And then, mate in two, I think.***

Tiernan was about to snarl, but was forestalled by Kevin's still-breathless murmur in his ear. "Is it a good thing or a bad thing I don't know fuck all about chess?"

The snarl aborted, became a kind of choked laugh. "It's going to be pissed as hell once it realizes you aren't quaking in your boots." Tiernan turned, reached up, buried his fingers in Kevin's thick dark hair and pulled his head down for a quick hard kiss. If there wasn't time for this, there wasn't time for anything.

"I knew there was a reason I'm naked."

The eyes didn't match the dry humor of the voice, and Tiernan's free hand clenched into a fist. Still, he kept his tone light—as light as he could, at least. "Damn, and here I was hoping it was because you can't keep your clothes on around me." *Smile,* lanan, *I need to see you smiling.*

The whole room shook around them. Shivered, like the inside of a bell. *Fuck.* "Stay behind me—it's not a hell of a lot safer than anywhere else but—"

Kevin's hand fell warm on Tiernan's shoulder and squeezed gently. "Got your back." Shit, his human was smiling.

"I know you do."

Tiernan took a deep breath, and focused… rested one hand on top of Kevin's, and bent forward and touched the tips of two fingers of the other hand to the floor. Instantly, the stone began to change, its nature staying the same but acquiring a crystalline transparency, in a circle spreading outward from that careful, deliberate touch. It spread quickly, driven by the power of the lines, but not quickly enough. The Fae cursed under his breath, in every language he knew and a few he guessed at. He could feel the *Marfach* fighting him.

It laughed, on the other side of the door. ***So good of you to feed me again, your Grace. Shall I play with your toy a while, before I take you?***

The pressure against Tiernan's magick increased, making his head pound in time with the throbbing that echoed through the cell, until he snarled and shot the energy of his anger out through the spreading Stone. "Are you going to tell me how to make you bleed, you syphilitic spawn of an incestuous boil, or do I get to have the pleasure of guessing?"

Something slammed hard against the door, hard enough to make it rock. "Temper," Tiernan muttered, pushing more magick through the stone, finally feeling the wood of the door shuddering in a cradle of living Stone.

The easy part's done. Of course, the "stone" he'd changed was actually living—his lover's mind—but the construct Kevin had instinctively chosen made the change much easier for him. Reality was a slippery thing on this level of the mind. This was where magick was channeled by the Fae, and even a human could bend and shape reality if he could find his way here.

But now Tiernan had to deal with wood, something once living, and the shit could very easily hit the magickal fan. Wood would fight the Stone—

was already fighting it, although no doubt it had help. The *Marfach* had broken Kevin—and the thought brought the snarl back to Tiernan's throat—and this door, the gap in the stone, was the sign and the seal of the breaking.

Kevin made a sound behind him, something somewhere between a gasp and a groan. Tiernan started to turn, then his attention was wrenched back, riveted, horrified, on the door. It moved. Crawled. The wood was wood, and yet it was as if it was trying to become flesh. *No. Hell, no.* The Noble magicks would let him change once-living matter to Stone, as he had changed his brother's corpse. But truly living matter? That was a Royal magick, and even a Royal had to pay in blood to wield it. "Kevin... shit, can you fight it? Long enough for me to change it?"

He felt a tight nod near his ear, scented sweat, heard soft gasping breaths. "On it. I hope." The human leaned into him, and Tiernan braced himself to take the extra weight. "Just... hurry."

His free hand snaked out, went around Kevin's waist, drew him in even closer. "Lean on me, *lanan*, I've got you." He dared not take his attention from the door, but Kevin's breathing eased, a little of the tension left his body. New strength surged through the Fae, and he was smiling grimly as he turned his full attention to the obscenity the door was trying to become.

Drawing on the lines anew, he sent tendrils of magick into the substance of the door. Immediately, the ugly not-movement stopped, but Kevin stiffened. "Shit. That's..." His voice trailed off. He squeezed Tiernan's shoulder gently. "That's incredibly weird. But it's good. Keep going."

So good of you to strengthen me, your Grace.
Tiernan sensed steam rising from the far side of the door, a growing heat. A faint groan next to his ear confirmed the reality of the sensation—if "reality" was a word applicable at this point. "I'd tell you to go fuck yourself, but there's a slight chance you might enjoy it if you did." Steeling himself against the burning, he pushed more power into the magick. It felt like trying to push water uphill, but slowly, slowly the door began to take on that crystalline overlay, from the edges inward.

I live in the lines, amad'n—when you use their power, you strengthen me. The laughter Tiernan sensed was somehow very female, and the essence of evil. *And yet you need that power to defeat me. Shall we race, warrior? With the swiftest to enjoy the delights of your plaything?*

In the fucking lines? Tiernan's jaw clenched, and his arm tightened around Kevin; he gave the *Marfach* no answer, though, other than the redoubling of his efforts. The Stone crept inward. The heat increased. Surely he imagined the smell of smoke? Kevin groaned softly, his head falling forward. Out of the corner of his eye, the Fae saw the human's face bathed in sweat. *Fuck.* Maybe he wasn't imagining it.

"Tiernan…"

"Almost there." The door was Stone, save for a circle maybe half a yard across, and growing smaller. "Almost… oh, fuck me *blind*." The wood within the circle was glowing. Like a coal. And Kevin's whole body stiffened, in the circle of his arms, a low keening sound welling up in him.

A red haze settled over Tiernan's vision. "Just another minute, *lanan*—"

"Tiernan." The whisper was soft, yet there was steel behind it.

Startled, Tiernan turned, and had time to catch a glimpse of his lover's face, pale and drawn and framed with hair plastered to his temples by sweat, before Kevin shook his head. "No—the door—fight it—but if you can't hold it…"

Tiernan growled, blasting more power through the conduit his body had become, shrinking the circle to the size of a head. But that circle was glowing, a sinister flickering orange-red. "I'll hold it."

"If you can't… you have to kill me."

"You are out of your fucking mind." Tiernan's gut clenched. He'd been half expecting this, but it didn't make the words any easier to hear.

"Actually, we're both *in* my fucking mind." The thin skein of quiet humor gleaming through the pain in Kevin's soft voice staggered the Fae. "But if you can't stop this thing, then you have to get out of it. And you have to kill me." The words were coming between gasps, now, as the glow from the door brightened, heat at war with Stone. "I took your knife, as we were leaving—it's in the pocket of my duster. Thought it might come to this."

"No fucking way. Not negotiable." More power. Tiernan's body started to hum again, and he embraced the sensation as the undercurrent of obscene laughter swelled around them.

"It's you that it wants. And it can't have you." Tiernan felt Kevin's head come to rest on his shoulder, whether deliberately or because the human could no longer hold it up, he had no idea. "I'm not letting it have you. I… love you."

180

Everything stopped. Breath, heart, thought. Even the *Marfach*'s laughter couldn't reach him, wherever in himself it was those three words had taken him. "You what?"

"I love you. You idiot." Just a hint of breathless laughter, a brush of parched and chapped lips against the Fae's ear. "I think I always have. And it doesn't matter whether you ever love me in return. I can feel whatever the fuck I want."

Say it. Tell him the truth.

"I'll never love you in return." Tiernan brushed his lips across Kevin's unshaven cheek, held him against the trembling that started despite the human's brave words. "Never 'in return.'" Deep, unsteady breath. "I just love you." The second kiss was a real one, all too brief. "And that thing will have you over my three-days-cold ashes."

"You—"

The cell was filled with a blinding light. Or at least, that's what Tiernan had to assume it was, because he couldn't bear to look at it. Coming from the door.

"We are so fucked," Kevin breathed.

"What is it?"

"There's a hole. In the damned door."

Now the laughter was unmuted, and there was a stench in the air threatening to turn Tiernan's stomach inside out. ***You make matters difficult, your Grace, but not impossible***.

Shielding his eyes with one hand, Tiernan tried to peer at the door between his fingers. The whole door was formed of living Stone, wood like crystal, or crystal like wood. But in the center was a hole, not even two inches across. There the Stone stopped, for there was no magick of Earth that would form Stone out of air. And try as he might, he could not make himself look through it.

"Oh, sweet bleeding Christ." Kevin's voice was nearly inaudible. "Not them. Kill me. Right fucking *now*."

"Them?" Even as he asked, Tiernan knew, with a sickening certainty, what his lover meant. "You don't have to say it—"

He was cut off by a burst of laughter that made the walls shake around them. *Say it, or not, it doesn't matter, your Grace. My little pets are real enough, on this level of your beloved's mind. You cannot keep them out forever. And long before they have finished eating him, enough of my substance will be within him to begin on you. And then I will take you. From within.*

"Tiernan. You *have* to—"

"No." Tiernan turned to face Kevin squarely. As if he had all the time in the world, he took the other male's face in his hands, looked into his dark, haunted eyes. "There's another way." Gently, he kissed his human, stroked his cheek.

He staggered a little as he got to his feet, his legs not anxious to obey him after kneeling so long on stone, and on Stone. He oriented himself, letting his gaze creep up the door, until it was just short of the hole. He drew a deep breath, letting himself feel the power welling up from beneath his feet. Ignoring the laughter in front of him. Ignoring everything but his awareness of the male who knelt on the floor behind him.

Blood for blood? A small enough price. Calmly, he reached out and placed his hand over the hole in the stone.

"*NO!*" Kevin lurched to his feet.

Softly, Tiernan spoke the forbidden word that turned his hand to living Stone. And then the second word, that shattered it at the wrist.

The cell quaked around him, pitching him to the floor. Somehow, he was in Kevin's arms, doubled over, his left forearm clutched against his stomach, and his lover wrapped around him. "Jesus, Tiernan… oh, Jesus. No. *No*." He was being rocked, held. There were… damn. There were tears falling in his hair, he could feel them trickling over his temple, down his cheek. How strange, to feel tears. Earth Fae wept diamonds.

When they wept. Which they didn't do.

"Stop, Kevin. Please… stop." The pain left him breathless, but it would pass. And Kevin was safe. "I'll be all right. And it can't get at you any more. A small enough price."

"Your opinion." Kevin continued to rock him, stroking his sweat-soaked golden hair, comforting the Fae as if he were a small child.

And as if it were the most natural and normal thing in the world, Tiernan closed his eyes, and let himself be held. "Fuck, yeah, it is," he murmured.

Soft, incredulous laughter seemed to surround him. "You're completely incorrigi…"

Kevin vanished.

CHAPTER SEVENTEEN

"What the *fuck*?"

Kevin's bare chest was being shoved into the concrete floor, by what sure as hell felt like a knee in the small of his back. There was a hand tangled in his hair, pulling back and up. Out of the corner of his eye, he caught a glimpse of the side of Tiernan's denim-clad leg. Trying to move his head to see more didn't seem like a good idea, though, given the cold blade that was being held at his throat and the slow warm trickle that was painting a trail down his neck. The cell, and everything in it, was gone as if none of it had ever existed. Which it hadn't. Except…

"Jesus Christ, what kind of weird-ass shit have you and your toyboy been smoking down here?" The knife at his throat wavered slightly, bit deeper. "It's hitting me too."

"No clue what you're talking about." His voice was a croak, but best to keep talking. *Keep him interested, keep him talking, keep him distracted.* He wasn't sure where he'd read that. Or maybe it wasn't a book, maybe it was a video game. Whatever. Sounded like good advice. That and *wake up the Fae, God damn it*, which he was pretty sure he'd managed to come up with on his own.

The hand in his hair rammed his face into the concrete. "Smart-ass." Then his head was wrenched around, and he was forced to stare at Tiernan.

Fuck. Me. Senseless. The Fae lay on his back, more or less as he'd been minutes—hours? days?—before, when Kevin readied him to wield the power of the ley lines, in a plain white muscle T and ragged jeans—still open at the crotch, *shit*. His right hand was curled at his side; his left forearm lay across his hard abdomen, rising and falling with his uneven breathing.

Jesus. His hand, splayed out over his six-pack. Clearer than crystal.

Normal flesh stopped just below the ring of scars around his lover's wrist, right where Tiernan had shattered it to leave his hand behind, affixed to the door. But the hand was still there, seemingly made of the same brilliant transparency that had suffused the stone of the cell and the wood of the door.

"Wake the freak up, cocksucker." The hand holding his hair gave his head a shake. "We need to talk."

"Cocksucker? Really?" Why he was wising off, when he *knew* it was going to earn him a knee in the kidney, he had no idea. He didn't seem to be able to help it, though. "Three syllables. I think we have a new record."

All the breath left him in a grunt, as the knee pressed down—

—and Tiernan's eyes snapped open. The Fae sat bolt upright, then cursed and winced, a hand going to his head. It was his left hand, the crystal one, moving exactly as if it were flesh and blood. Tiernan stared at it, in apparent shock, the pain in his head taking a back seat to whatever the hell this was; slowly, he curled the fingers in toward the palm, wiggled them.

Kevin's captor's hand jerked, and another fresh spill of blood trickled down Kevin's neck. "Hey, dickwad." The words were obviously directed at Tiernan. "Your sugar Daddy needs you to do him some favors."

Whoever this asshole was, he obviously had no clue how deep the hole was he'd just dug for himself. Frigid blue eyes looked up through tumbled hair. For an instant, they locked with Kevin's, and the crystal fist clenched hard. Then the gaze moved up, and back, and the Fae's lip curled in a sneer. "I should have guessed."

What the hell? "You know him?"

"Fuck, yes. And so do you." Tiernan moved as if to get up, but Kevin's captor tensed, the knife sliced a little deeper, and the Fae fell back, his eyes going back to Kevin's again, thin rings of ice-blue around pupils gone wide and wild. Still, his voice was mostly level, only a slight roughness betraying the rage within. "Tall, bald, and nasally overcompensated. The bouncer from upstairs."

Kevin started—and swore under his breath, as the movement made him aware of the fist in his hair, the knee in his back and the blade at his throat all over again. "You know, the law frowns on the use of deadly force to deal with a simple trespass."

"Fucking lawyers." The hand in his hair tightened. "You sound just like my asshole Uncle Art, you two should be fuck buddies instead of him trying to take you down."

Kevin felt his face go white. "Your Uncle Art." *Christ on a crutch.* "It all makes sense now."

"Maybe to you, it does." Kevin could barely hear Tiernan over the roaring in his ears. "Who's Uncle Art? Other than an asshole, which obviously runs in the family."

"Arthur O'Halloran. Marquee partner at my law firm." Kevin spoke quickly, and as carefully as he could given that his head was still being hauled back by the hair. "He's running a billing scam, and has me set up to take the fall if it gets found out. He had Chuckles here take a picture of that sweet BJ I gave you the other night, to hold over my head so I won't blow the whistle."

Tiernan's eyes narrowed dangerously, but before the Fae could speak, the bouncer laughed. "Old news, dickhead. Uncle Art's tired of the game, he's giving you up." The hand in Kevin's hair tightened, the knife blade turned to caress his throat with the flat. "He didn't pay me shit for that picture. But I figure, if you've got something *he* wants, then you've got something that can make *me* happy. And I want it, while you can still give it to me." The point of the knife jabbed, broke skin in a new spot. "And your freak can help you give it to me, if he wants to keep you alive."

Kevin choked, coughed. "Were you born this stupid, or did you have to study? What he wants is for me to keep my mouth shut—what the hell do you plan to do with that?"

Too late, he caught the frantic warning look Tiernan was giving him, at almost the same moment, in fact, his whole upper body was pulled off the concrete by the hair. The knife arm came around and placed the blade point first under his jaw. *Never tell the desperate idiot with nothing to lose that he's fucked up.*

"Then I don't have any reason to keep you alive."

Everything happened at once. The point of the knife dug in sharp and cold. Kevin wrenched his head up, trying to avoid it. Tiernan shouted, in no language Kevin recognized. The air seemed to bend around the Fae, warping his appearance. He glowed. No, not glowed, it wasn't light around him. Some kind of energy, though. Tiernan's back arched, his breath sounded like something tearing. The crystal hand reached out.

And... *shit*. A thin rod, maybe half an inch thick, made of that same crystal, shot from Tiernan's hand like a beam of solid light. Grew from it. Shot right past Kevin's face, so close he felt the air sizzle around it. Something... crunched. His captor screamed, a sound that made Kevin's stomach lurch.

The hand in Kevin's hair let go, the knife clattered to the floor. Behind him, what had been his captor was now dead weight, and slumped to the concrete, head hitting the floor with a strangely hollow sound. Kevin scrambled out from underneath, staring at what was left of the man's face. The rod had gone in through his right eye, and all the way through his head... and where it passed, nearly half the bastard's head had turned to glass.

"*Lanan...*"

Kevin lunged awkwardly for Tiernan as the Fae fell backward, barely keeping him from hitting his head on the floor. His lover's body was jerking, spasming. Instinctively Kevin held him close, barely noticing his own blood running from the wounds on his neck to stain Tiernan's hair. "Tiernan—damn it— what's wrong? What can I do?"

"The ley lines—the power—I wasn't ready—"

Kevin could barely understand him, and his gut wrenched as the Fae's body... *flickered*, was the only word for it, it was there and then it wasn't, and then it was again. And that light, that wasn't really light, bathed them both. "God *damn* it, Tiernan, what the hell do I *do*?" He had never seen panic in his lover's eyes before, and he growled at seeing it now. "Don't let go."

He folded the other male even closer—

—shouted, with the last breath left in his lungs, as Fae and human both Faded.

***

Pure evil emerged from its millennia-old hiding place into the reality of Purgatory's storeroom.

I can live only in living magick. Existence in the lines in the earth to which the Pattern condemned me is not life. It is torture. I require the Fae. His bound and living magick. His essence.

But now, I am free. This human, this Janek O'Halloran, he will do, as a mask. His mortal soul is all but spent, he cannot fight me, and his struggles serve only to amuse; his pathetic scattered thoughts will be my entertainment, and the living magick in the Stone my dwelling place. Carefully rationed, until I find the Fae again, and then I will feast.

Unless someone, somehow, connects this shell of a human to Tiernan Guaire, or to his human plaything.

CHAPTER EIGHTEEN

It felt like it took forever for the two of them to form fully, By the time Tiernan was sure he could feel a solid surface under them, he had already convinced himself half a dozen times they weren't going to make it. They were going to spend the rest of eternity suspended between existence and the utter emptiness that engulfed him each time he Faded. *My fault. Why the hell did I tell him to hold me? I should have pushed him away. Fuck. I Faded a human.* My *human.* And it didn't help matters that his own skin still shuddered, his limbs still twitched, with the dissipation of the energy from the ley nexus.

At least he'd managed to land them in bed. Kevin lay beside him, sprawled out on his back, eyes closed, his chest heaving sporadically as he struggled to breathe. No doubt he'd tried to breathe in that place between. Tiernan cursed under his breath, rolled to prop himself up on his elbow, and reached out to place a hand lightly on his lover's chest.

A hand formed of living Stone, a hand that moved and touched and felt the smooth skin that rose and fell under it. How the fuck had he brought that out of Kevin's mind with him?

"Where are we?" Kevin's voice was barely audible. He coughed, and tried to struggle up onto his elbows, but fell back with a gasp.

"We're home, we made it—shit, you're still bleeding." The cuts the knife—Tiernan's own knife, damn it—had made weren't deep, but they were long, and red ran down Kevin's throat, onto his chest, and now onto the sheets. Which weren't showing it much, but black silk wasn't worth shit for bandages, either. Swearing, Tiernan managed to sit up long enough to haul off his muscle T and press it to the wounds with an unsteady hand.

"You look like hell." Kevin's eyes were open now, and his gaze was locked on Tiernan's face. The faint smile lines touching the corners of the dark eyes made Tiernan's throat feel tight. "But I don't mind."

What the hell do I say to him? Tiernan winced as another jolt of ley energy shot through him, a sensation combining all the best parts of an electric shock and what he imagined a raging infection must feel like. *I've been using him since the moment I met him, the most evil creature in two worlds fucking ate him alive because of me, I couldn't stop a petty thug from cutting him up, and here I've just risked his life by dragging him with me through something a human body has never done before. What do I say?*

"That's good." His voice came out a growl. He brushed his lips across Kevin's, traced his tongue around them, breathed in the human's gasps, and groaned softly as they gave way to a rapid, shallow panting. "Oh, fuck…"

"Talk about a one-track mind." Kevin's arm went around him, drawing him close—and closer still, when

Tiernan's body shuddered with another spasm. "Just hold on," he whispered against the Fae's lips, and there was a touch of pain, of fear in the depths of the human's eyes. "I need something to be real right now."

"I'm real."

He took Kevin's mouth in what was intended to be a quick kiss, but became something more between one blink and the next. The other male's tongue stroked between his lips, seeking access; he gave it, and as tongues met and twined and Kevin's hand tangled itself in his long hair, Tiernan's eyes drifted closed. *I'm real.* His lover tasted of honey, and smelled of musk and leather and arousal. The body pressed against his was warm and hard, the arm around him strong. And the sounds that their mouths made as they enjoyed each other were fucking incredible. *Shit, could all our kisses have been this good? All I had to do was close my eyes?* He moaned softly, sucking Kevin's tongue deeper into his mouth. *I am a fucking moron.*

Kevin rolled him onto his back, one knee went between his legs, a thigh pressed warm and hard and insistent against his groin. He reluctantly opened his eyes and brought his crystal hand to Kevin's face, cupping his jaw. He could feel every whisker; his thumb stroked along his *lanan*'s full lower lip, and he felt the warmth and the softness as he watched Kevin's tongue curl out and lick it.

"That's…" Kevin caught at Tiernan's hand, drew it away from his face for a better look. "The *Marfach* did say I made what happened on that level of my mind real." Uncertainty touched his voice. Hesitantly, he kissed the backs of Tiernan's fingers.

"You did this?" Even as the words left his mouth, Tiernan realized the foolishness of the question. "Of course you did. I wasn't in any shape to. Even if I knew how." His fingers tightened around Kevin's, as he shivered again with another twinge. "Damn it."

Kevin frowned. "What's wrong? You said something about not being prepared to use the ley lines?" He pushed himself up on one arm, enough to let him look down Tiernan's body, as if he expected to see some outward sign of whatever was amiss.

"Yeah." Tiernan grimaced. "Earth magicks can't jump through air. And I wasn't sure if the magick that I have, that I *am*, could be pushed hard enough to take that son of a bitch out as fast as he needed to be taken out. So I had to channel the energy from the lines. But I wasn't aroused, and it was too much for me to handle."

"Shit. You got supercharged." Letting go of Tiernan's hand and raising himself up on his elbows, Kevin looked up and down Tiernan's torso, incidentally showing Tiernan the flow of blood from his own wounds had almost stopped. "Is it going to get better?"

Tiernan nodded, knowing that if he tried to speak, what was going to come out was a growl of pure black rage at the chancrous tip of a dick responsible for the blood drying on his lover's throat and chest. It would be good to have the bastard back, just to kill him again, more interestingly.

Kevin must have followed the direction of his gaze, because the human's hand went to the stains on his skin. "Oh, fuck. This reminds me, there's an incredibly bizarre corpse in the basement at

Purgatory."

"And not much we can do about it, *lanan*." Awkwardly—unused to being the partner on the bottom—Tiernan curled a leg around one of Kevin's. "Even if I could Fade back there—and I don't trust myself to Fade across the room right now—I couldn't get him out of there by Fading, and it's not as if I could bring the body up through the club and tell people he'd had a little too much to drink. Not with a hole through his head."

"Point taken." All things considered, Kevin looked remarkably at ease with the notion that his lover had forced a crowbar formed from his own flesh through the eye and the brain of a would-be Mick the Knife.

"They'll find him, by morning if not earlier, but they're not going to know what to make of him." Tiernan frowned. "Something's going to have to be done about the storeroom. If the *Marfach* lives in the lines, a nexus like that is an incredibly dangerous place—"

His breath caught, his back arched, stiffened. Slowly, he lowered himself back to the bed. "That one sucked," he gritted through clenched teeth.

"I thought you said it was getting better?" Kevin grimaced.

"It is." Tiernan drew a slow, experimental breath, and let it out in a sigh. "There's just a hell of a lot that needs to work its way out."

"Let me help you."

Before Tiernan could open his mouth to ask Kevin what he meant, the human buried both hands in Tiernan's hair, lowered his body to cover the Fae's,

194

and locked their lips with a growl more possessive than anything Tiernan had ever heard from him before.

Tiernan's eyes opened wide—then quickly closed, a soft chuckle quickly turning to a groan as Kevin's hips bucked into his. *Damn…* For a moment, he remembered his lover's odd intensity when the *Marfach* had been driving him. But this was nothing like that. This was all Kevin, the body grinding against his, the hands running all over him, the mouth claiming him.

Seized by the identical impulse, both males shucked out of their remaining clothes with an enthusiasm that sent garments flying and a speed that left Tiernan disoriented. Kevin laughed softly, but the sound changed as a tremor passed through the Fae's body. "Damn it."

One large hand splayed over Tiernan's chest, gliding slowly downward, soothing and arousing at the same time. Tiernan tried to sit up, wanting to watch, but Kevin shook his head. "You're going to lie down, and you're going to let me take care of you." One dark eyebrow shot up. "Are we clear?"

The laughter that welled up in him was one of the sweetest things Tiernan had ever known. And he recognized it; it was the forerunner of the joy that coupling with his SoulShare, his *scair-anam*, always gave him. Gave them both. The joy that tamed magick. "Is that an order?"

"Damn straight." Kevin flashed him a wicked grin, then bent and placed a heated, lingering kiss in the hollow at the base of Tiernan's throat. Tiernan's head dropped back with a sigh, and his back slowly arched as Kevin's mouth started to follow the path his hand had taken.

By the time the human's hot tongue was tracing the lines of his abs, Kevin's hand had curled around the base of his cock and was squeezing in the deliberate wringing motion that was the slowest, most torturous path to orgasm. "Fuck, you're trying to kill me."

"Haven't even started yet, *lanan*." Soft lips moved over the sensitive skin just above Tiernan's tight dark-blond curls. Kevin's palm whispered against the silk-over-stone his shaft was fast becoming.

Kevin's mouth started working its way up his cock, barely pausing when Tiernan's back stiffened again. He shifted to lie between the Fae's spread thighs, his free hand going under one leg to hook it over his shoulder. "Just relax. Let it happen." Kevin's tongue teased at the sensitive spot under the rim of the head, stroking it insistently until he was rewarded with a clear spill of fluid. "Oh, shit, yes, that's perfect."

Tiernan's head fell back. He groaned, feeling Kevin's flattened tongue dragging all the way up from the base of his balls to his weeping tip. And then the firm twisting began again; Tiernan's leg tensed over the human's broad shoulder, holding him tightly, a shiver running down his spine. "Kevin…"

Kevin's hand stopped. His lips, his tongue stilled. Tiernan heard a sharp intake of breath, and his head came up. His lover was staring at him, motionless save for his soft panting breaths, his eyes wide.

"What is it? What did I do?" Tiernan was astonished to feel his heart racing. He reached down, flinched back when he realized he'd extended his crystalline hand. But slowly his fingers uncurled, brushed Kevin's rough cheek.

196

"It's stupid." Kevin's dark baritone was thick, husky, his gaze soft. "You said my name."

Tiernan stared, stunned. Kevin met his eyes for a moment. Then his gaze dropped. His hand continued to stroke, gently. Lovingly. *Oh, shit*.

"You realize—"Tiernan's voice caught. He cleared his throat, tried again. "You realize you have the poor judgment to love a complete dick."

A smile spread across Kevin's face. "I don't mind if you don't." Lips caressed the inside of Tiernan's thigh. One dark eyebrow quirked up, indicating the statement was actually a question, and the question wasn't entirely hypothetical.

"Mind?" It was a fair enough question. More than fair, considering how long it had taken him to acknowledge the simple truth staring him in the face, ever since this human had trusted him enough to follow him into what had been utter mystery. "Hell. If humans or non-Royals did *ceangal*…" His throat closed around the word, *binding*. For a kinslayer to even be thinking of such a thing was an outrage.

Kevin's arms wrapped warm around Tiernan's lean hips. "*Ceangal*?" The human's tongue ran languidly over the top of Tiernan's thigh, not demanding, just unwilling to lose contact.

"It's… something Royals do. To prove the legitimacy of a succession." *Fuck*. Of all the times to be explaining the blood politics of a realm he'd never see again. "A ruling pair is a mother and a son, or a father and a daughter. And if the Royals didn't bond with their mates somehow, there would be no way to be sure of the lineage of the Prince or Princess Royal. Oh, like I give a shit any more." Crystal fingers wound through dark hair. "But it's all I've got to offer." As if there was a way to make right what he'd already made so very wrong.

Suddenly, Kevin moved. Letting go of Tiernan's cock, he moved up his body, taking his weight on his elbows, his legs to either side of the Fae's thighs. Pinning Tiernan carefully, he held him through another, fainter round of shivers before working the fingers of both hands into his unruly, slightly bloodstained blond waves. "Let me be very clear about this, please." A kiss fell on Tiernan's forehead. "You would offer me this... *ceangal*? Except that it's not a human thing?"

Tiernan nodded, almost imperceptibly, feeling his cheeks go red. "I would. I know it's not enough to make up for—"

"Shut up." Kevin's head dropped. He kissed Tiernan, quick and hard, with a faint growl and a gentle bite to the lower lip. "Maybe we should just get married instead?"

"We..." Tiernan's voice snagged hard in his throat. Kevin's head tilted quizzically, and the Fae cleared his throat, trying to look and behave as if that's what he'd meant to do all along.

He's gone mad. Completely.

And you got there before he did. Who would have guessed?

"Kevin... *lanan*... are you serious?" The human didn't have to answer, and he didn't, or at least not aloud. The light in his dark eyes was all the reply needed. After everything those eyes had seen, because of him, they still shone, quietly, deeply, lovingly at the thought of marrying him. He should be shocked. He

198

should be appalled. He should be calling the human every kind of fool, *amad'n*, there was, and himself the same thrice over.

But he wasn't. Not any of it. Which made no fucking sense whatsoever. But, sense or no… he wasn't. All there was in him was an incredible lightness. And joy. He brushed a crystal thumb across Kevin's lips, sucked in a breath as it was caught gently between his lover's teeth.

"Yes," he whispered.

And everything changed, just that fast, as Kevin's smile blossomed. It was the portal all over again, a hundred years and more gone, the same sensation of a whole world giving way under Tiernan's feet, then re-forming in a way that would never be the same again.

"Thank you," Kevin whispered, cutting off any further conversation with a kiss, one that started out gentle, almost chaste, but rapidly heated. Soft murmurs and other intimate sounds hung in the air like smoke clinging to skin, breathed in along with the air.

Tiernan ran a hand down Kevin's well-muscled back, feeling the faint dew of sweat forming, groaning when his hand reached and cupped a firm ass cheek, felt it flex against his palm. The slight movement of his lover's hips over his was enough to make his cock jerk back to life—not that his arousal had abated much during the mutual proposal—and his back arched, this time with pleasure, not with a spasm of ley energy.

Hot kisses trailed slowly down Tiernan's throat, and he lifted his neck, offering more of himself. Kevin's tongue traced a path down to the hollow at the base of his throat, playing there long enough to make the Fae gasp. "Damn, you taste good," Kevin whispered, mixing the words with tiny licks and bites. "I could do this all night."

"You can try." Tiernan's crystal fingers worked their way into Kevin's hair, applying a firm, gentle pressure, urging his head down, toward the nipples that were aching to be messed with.

Kevin's head came up. His dark gaze pinned Tiernan. "Lover, have you ever in your life let yourself enjoy foreplay?"

Tiernan opened his mouth… then very sensibly closed it again when nothing came out.

"I thought not." Kevin shook his head. "Finally, something *I* can teach *you*."

"You've taught me much already, *lanan*." Tiernan made himself relax, let himself enjoy the sensation of the thick soft hair under his strange fingertips. "I had no fucking clue how to love, until you made me do it."

"Not true." Kevin leaned into the caress, apparently unconsciously, eyes half closing. "I'd meant to call you on that before. You loved your sister, yes? Why else do what you did to your brother?"

Tiernan frowned. Something was nagging at him, an unwanted distraction from the things Kevin's body was doing to his own, an unscratched itch that, like most itches, was only going to get worse the more resolutely he tried to ignore it.

"I did, yes. But by the time I passed through the Pattern…" Tiernan grimaced at the remembered pain. "She was the only other one who knew what I'd done, *lanan*. She swore out the warrant against me, she went oathbound against my capture—sworn not to eat or drink or sleep until justice was done on me."

The confusion that briefly touched his lover's eyes was slowly replaced by a cold anger, and Tiernan nodded. "You see what I mean. By the time I passed through the Pattern—by the time she'd done berating me for stealing her vengeance—I had nothing left in me for her but the need to know she'd be done unto as she did unto me. And of course, I'll never know for certain, since there's no going back through the Pattern to find out, but I clung to that thought for very life."

Kevin turned his head, and Tiernan caught his breath as his lover gently kissed the scars circling his wrist, just above the broken place. Had anyone ever done that before? Treated the marks of his shame so tenderly? Yes, his human, once before. And he'd returned nothing but anger for that gentleness. He'd do better this time. He opened his palm against Kevin's cheek, stroking lightly with the fingertips he wouldn't even have if not for this male's ferocious insistence.

"I wonder…" Kevin's eyes drifted slowly closed, and a smile touched his lips as Tiernan ran a fingertip around the shell of his ear. "When you… passed through. You were rejecting love. And hanging on to… I don't know. Need, drive. Anger. What if…" He blew out a frustrated breath. "Shit, I don't understand any of this… but when you passed through, and your soul was divided, what if I got what you rejected, and I didn't get what you held on to?"

Tiernan sat up—or tried to, the combination of Kevin's weight and another spasm of misfiring ley energy knocked him back flat to the bed. "Damn. No, no, I'm all right." He waved off Kevin's hovering hand, then thought better of waving him off, and held the hand instead. "That could be. No one really knows how SoulShare works; the generation of Loremasters who devised it all died in the Sundering, and it was information they chose not to leave behind."

Kevin snorted. "Thoughtful of them."

"I doubt you're the first to think so." Tiernan ran a finger along Kevin's cheekbone, watching the light glinting off crystal, captivated by the beauty of what had been forced on him by the need to keep his lover safe. "Did you feel like you were missing something, too -- the way I was?"

"Hell, yes." Kevin laughed, a short, explosive sound. "The night I met you... I'd just come from a meeting, where I was told that I was never going to make partner. Because I didn't want it badly enough. Didn't have the ambition, the drive, whatever you want to call it. Whatever it is that makes you want something badly enough that the rest of the world *has* to take notice." Lips brushed Tiernan's forehead. "I spent my whole career, maybe my whole life, doing all the right things, for all the right reasons. And it got me nowhere. Then the very first time I did the unquestionably wrong thing... for *all* the wrong reasons..."

Kevin's voice had been getting softer as he spoke. By the time he whispered the last words, there was no voice behind them at all, just the brush of one pair of lips against another. "I ended up in the arms of a Fae."

And then not even the brushing, only a kiss. A kiss that became touches, gentle touches at first, and then not gentle. Tiernan moaned as Kevin's fevered mouth found his nipples, tonguing the silver ring as fingertips flicked at the other nipple. He clenched his teeth, fisted handfuls of the bedsheets. Sweat trickled down his temples, darkened his hair, ran down his neck. And when Kevin shifted his weight, and the fingertips teasing his nipple started making their way down his chest and stomach, and the licks at the nipple ring turned to bites, he began to wonder if his *lanan*— now his fiancé—might not have found an entirely new way to kill a Fae.

A knee nudged Tiernan's thighs apart. He yielded willingly, if awkwardly, raising himself on one elbow so he could reach Kevin's cock. His was standing straight up, weeping and purple-red, and it twitched hard as his hand encircled the impossibly thick base of Kevin's monstrous shaft, scattering clear drops over them both.

"Fuck, yes." Kevin caught at Tiernan's cock, gripping tightly, teasing the sweet spot on the underside with the pad of his thumb until he was rewarded with another trickle of fluid. He pumped up into Tiernan's hand, soft skin gliding easily over a shaft hard enough to quarry stone. "I'll teach you about foreplay next time. *Damn.*"

Tiernan laughed, curling up, his abs going rock-hard as he reached up to pull Kevin down into a kiss that was as hot as he could make it. Strange how the laughter, the joy, didn't make things one bit less erotic. In fact, the air was practically quivering between the two of them. Tongues danced, stroked, wrestled, caressed; hands worked cocks in nearly perfect tandem.

Kevin sucked in a breath. His cock throbbed in Tiernan's grip, and hardened even more. "God *damn*, how do you do this?"

"It's a secret." Tiernan smirked. "Ask me nicely

and I'll—oh, shit, yes." Kevin was moving, arranging himself between his thighs, drawing one of his legs up, as awkward about topping as Tiernan was about bottoming, but the awkwardness was arousing as hell. He watched intently as Kevin gripped himself tightly and positioned himself. He spread his legs wide, feeling the smooth huge head like a live coal at his entrance, with just enough wetness there to ease the way. "Do it," he rasped—and his body twisted, his back arched—as his lover did.

So damned good. He groaned and corkscrewed up on Kevin's cock, trying to take him all the way in despite the human's mind-blowing size. And a shudder ran through him as he managed it, as the sac so perfectly proportionate to the cock fell heavy and hot against his ass. But it wasn't going to last long, that sac was already drawing up, and a strong hand was working his own cock hard. He tried to hold it off, desperately thought of blizzards and icebergs and sleet, but it was no fucking good. Kevin gripped and twisted, thrust relentlessly, and cursed softly as his body stiffened.

And then dark eyes went wide with utter astonishment, and Tiernan cried out as Kevin released. His body was electric with his SoulShare's pleasure, as it received one thick, hot jet after another. Kevin's grip around the base of his cock tightened, and Tiernan groaned raggedly with the white-hot pleasure that ripped along every nerve ending, burning out the last of the fevered ley energy as he joined his lover in climax, spurts of glassy heat covering Kevin's hand and spilling out onto his own heaving abs.

But what rolled the Fae's eyes back into his head

and robbed him of breath was the joy. Absolutely pure undiluted bliss. *What an idiot I've been, to fight this for this long.* But thinking was too damned much trouble. He just allowed his head to fall back and let himself feel.

Gradually, he noticed that Kevin had rolled him onto his side and was kissing him again. And even more gradually, he managed to kiss him back. His *scair-anam* chuckled softly, reaching across him to switch off the bedside light, and then again to draw the duvet up over them both. "Damn," Kevin murmured into the warm darkness. "I'll propose to you every day, if that's what it gets me."

"No argument here." The burning out of the ley energy left Tiernan feeling groggy, slow. "Though I think we both did that." He couldn't keep his eyes open. *Fuck, I hope I don't have nightmares.* The mental image of Kevin waking up with a matching shiner on the other side of his face made him cringe.

"Sleep, *lanan*." Kevin lightly stroked his blond waves. "You need it."

And you don't? Tiernan wanted to argue, but his body was being annoyingly obedient tonight. His eyes closed, his breathing slowed, but he still waited until Kevin's solicitous hand fell back to his side before allowing himself to sleep.

And just before sleep claimed him, there came to him the image of Janek O'Halloran's corpse, lying on a concrete floor, a perfect hole drilled through his skull and half his head turned to crystal. *Oh, for fuck's sake…*

CHAPTER NINETEEN

Kevin shifted his weight carefully, so as not to disturb the Fae who slept with his head pillowed on his human's arm. He had yet to sleep as much as a minute and the sky was already graying with what looked like a dreary winter's dawn. His eyes felt as though someone had poured ground glass into them, and his brain seemed to have something fuzzy growing in it. *Coffee. Must. Have.* For a moment, he pictured himself opening the jar of instant he kept in the cupboard over the stove and just tipping it down his throat. The thought seemed to help.

He shook his head, settling his body once more against Tiernan's. He'd started the hours of darkness getting past the stunned feeling that apparently came along with having a marriage proposal accepted. From there, he'd moved on to trying *not* to relive every hellish moment spent inside his own head in the preceding hours. Then came an attempt to not drive himself crazy over the problem that couldn't be helped, the matter of the well-ventilated corpse in the storeroom under Purgatory. After that? Sheer amazement, as it dawned on him Tiernan hadn't stirred, was sleeping free of nightmares for the first time since they'd begun sharing a bed.

And then, as he'd started to think he might be able to snatch an hour or two of sleep, he'd remembered some of the last words of Janek O'Halloran. *Uncle Art's tired of the game, he's giving you up*. Son of a bitch.

What was he going to do? If Arthur O'Halloran was tired of playing and released the rigged billing records, the least he could expect would be to be disbarred, and probably jailed. The spreadsheet showed theft on a fairly impressive scale.

How ridiculous it was, to be thinking of shit like this after everything that happened tonight. A life and death battle with the most evil creature on two planes of existence made Art O'Halloran's petty machinations laughable. But then Tiernan murmured in his sleep and worked back against him, and without thinking Kevin curved an arm around him, kissed his shoulder. No fucking way was he going to prison over this shit. But what was he going to do?

Call David Mondrian. Dave was on the Managing Committee. If Kevin could get him to take his word over O'Halloran's, somehow. Carefully he eased his arm out from under Tiernan's head, swung his legs out of bed, and headed for the closet, grabbing the first suit that came to hand. No, he couldn't call, and he wasn't going to take a chance on e-mail, either. No trusting the firm's phones or its computers, which meant he was going to have to send a text. He shrugged into a shirt, grabbed a tie.

By the time he was snugging up the tie, he was being watched by a pair of bright blue eyes. Tiernan's head was pillowed on his own arm, and with his hair spread out over the pillow he was the best reason to climb back into bed and tell the rest of the world to go blow itself Kevin had ever seen.

"Why am I thinking you're going hunting?" Tiernan's voice was blurry with sleep, for all his eyes were noticing.

"I suppose I am, *lanan*." He crossed to the bedside, bent, placed his hands to either side of the Fae's head, and bent to him for a kiss. "I have to go get the car, and the cell phone I realized I left in the damn car. Then I'm going after the dickhead who's after me." *Because nothing is taking me away from you, lover—not Arthur O'Halloran, not a body in the basement at Purgatory. Nothing.*

Tiernan stifled a yawn. "Shit. I can hardly move." He tried, and groaned softly. "You need me? For anything?"

"That's what a lawyer would call a leading question." Gently, he ran his tongue over the Fae's eyebrow ring, remembering how he'd wanted to do that from the moment he'd seen it, though then he'd had no idea why. "Get some rest, lover. I can handle this. Hell, after what we've just been through, I think I could rip this asshole in half without breaking a sweat."

"This is the one who's blackmailing you?" Tiernan growled softly and made another attempt to get up.

Kevin shook his head and planted a splayed hand on the Fae's chest, gently pinning him to the mattress. "Yes, and you're in no shape to be fighting a lawyer. I don't want to need to get you rabies shots."

Tiernan's snort of laughter was quiet, but genuine. His eyes closed briefly then opened, flashing frustration. "Damn. Still can't Fade."

"You don't have to." Taking his weight on an

elbow, Kevin tangled the fingers of his other hand in his fiancé's hair. "*Lanan,* you saved me once tonight from what I'm guessing is a fate considerably worse than death, and at a cost I can't even begin to imagine."

Tiernan's crystal hand caught at his wrist, and Kevin nodded. "Yeah." He brushed a kiss across Tiernan's lips. "I've got this one."

Another kiss, and he straightened. Tiernan's gaze held his. "Good hunting, *scair-anam,*" Tiernan murmured, with a slight smile, before his eyes drifted closed again.

"Damn straight," Kevin whispered.

***

Kevin moved quickly from the taxi to his Mercedes. There hadn't been any police presence when the cab pulled up, and from what he could tell from the relatively fresh coat of ice and skin of snow from the night before, there hadn't been a lot of motorized or foot traffic around the back entrance—the way you'd expect if a body was being brought out. So maybe their secret was safe a little longer. Either that, or he really sucked as a private eye.

He slipped into the driver's seat and started up the engine, was reaching for the seat belt when a blinking light caught his eye. His phone, plugged into the dash. He detached it from its cradle, woke it with a touch. A text was waiting from David.

My office, 1st thing. Bring yr lawyer if u have 1.

Kevin groaned aloud, his forehead coming to rest on the steering wheel. *What the hell do I do now?*

***

"Good morning, Mr. Almstead."

Somehow, Kevin managed to make himself smile and nod at Francesca. Calm, pleasant, totally professional but with a glint of a wicked sense of humor, she was the ideal receptionist. She was one of the few who hadn't been treating him with condescension since the last meeting of the partnership committee. And she wasn't giving him the Eye of Death now, which might—just might—mean David hadn't said anything to anyone else yet. *Maybe he hopes I'll prove O'Halloran wrong.* Which was the thinnest possible thread to hang a hope on, but he was taking every thread he could get. "Morning, Frannie."

He made his way through the lobby, heading off down the corridor leading to his office, rather than the one that would take him straight to David's office. He could spare a minute to ditch his coat and collect his thoughts before he had to face whatever inquisition was waiting for him. And hopefully somewhere between here and there, lightning would strike, and he'd figure out some way to convince his friend he was being framed.

What in the… His office door was closed, the light on inside. He pushed it open—and stopped dead, a growl rising in his throat at the sight of Arthur O'Halloran, sitting at *his* desk and looking up from *his* computer, a quintessential shit-eating grin on his face. "What the fuck are you doing in here?"

"Just making sure you haven't destroyed evidence." The older man was maddeningly calm, his smile one that begged to be erased with a fist.

"Anything could have happened since I just discovered your duplicity last night."

Quickly, Kevin shoved his hands into his coat pockets, so the clenching of his fists could go unnoticed. His fingertips brushed the flash drive he'd dropped in his pocket the other night, and he dared to feel a little twinge of hope. "It's not going to work, you know."

"Why not?" O'Halloran crossed his arms behind his head and leaned back in the chair, which creaked alarmingly. "All the evidence points to you." He nodded meaningfully at the computer screen, which was showing the damned billing spreadsheet.

"You know and I know I'm not responsible for that. And you're not smart enough to cover your tracks completely." His fingers closed around the flash drive.

O'Halloran shrugged slightly. "Do I have to care? I have that exquisite photograph, which means you're motivated to make a full confession. Which in turn means that no one will be looking closely enough to figure out the billing entries are faked."

Kevin's palms went slick with sweat, but he managed to keep his voice even. "You're assuming I give a damn what you do with that picture." *Hurt my fiancé with it, though, and there won't be enough of your ass left to disbar.*

One silver eyebrow arched. "A bold play, Almstead. And one I wouldn't have expected from you. Even if it is a bit late in the game." O'Halloran sat back up, leaned in, studied the monitor with pretended fascination. "But even assuming you aren't lying through your clenched teeth, you can't argue with what's on the computer. Mondrian certainly didn't, when I sent a copy to him this morning."

"Maybe I can't." A real smile curved one corner of Kevin's mouth up at a sudden thought. "You know Birgitta Olafsen? We consult with her sometimes on securities fraud cases—she's a forensic computer scientist." *Oh, yeah.* Gitta could make a computer roll over, play dead, sit up and beg, cook your dinner, and light your post-coital cigarette. "She'll know whose computer accessed the billing software and made those entries." Maybe he was blowing smoke. He wasn't sure. But even if he was, he was willing to bet O'Halloran wouldn't know.

The other lawyer blanched, but recovered too quickly for Kevin's tastes. "Your use of the word 'forensic' assumes there's been a crime committed. And a forensic examiner is never going to get anywhere near my computer. Even if this does get tracked back to me, none of this will ever show up as anything more than billing errors. And errors the Balfour Trust could easily afford, and accepted, without thinking twice about it." The grin was back, and it turned Kevin's stomach. "A crime with no victims, Almstead."

"Crime? You want to talk about crime?" The memory of a knife poised to plunge into his throat was forcing its way back into his forebrain—no, best not to tell O'Halloran about the corpse, but he'd be damned if he'd let the son of a bitch get away with blackmail, with or without a living accomplice.

"No need, Kevin. I've heard more than enough."

Kevin caught just a glimpse of O'Halloran's normally florid face going dead white before he spun around toward the voice. David Mondrian was coming around the doorjamb, his gaze colder than Kevin had ever seen it.

"How long have you been listening?"

David's gaze flicked briefly to Kevin, before settling on O'Halloran like a pin sinking into a butterfly. Or a cockroach. "Enough to want to ask you a few questions about photography later, Kevin. But at the moment, my questions are all for my 'shocked and appalled' informant."

O'Halloran cleared his throat. Kevin turned back in time to see him wipe with an unsteady hand at a face that had gone an interesting shade of gray. "Dave, I can explain."

"I'm sure you can. The question is, will I listen, or will I—"

The tone of a cell phone ringing cut through the air; O'Halloran twitched, reached into an inner pocket of his suit, and checked the touchscreen, managing to sound calm despite the sweat that still beaded his pale face. "What is it, Frannie?"

Kevin growled under his breath. O'Halloran must have forwarded his office phone, so no one trying to reach him would realize he wasn't in his own office while he rifled Kevin's desk and attempted to rape his computer. From the look of him, David was coming to the same conclusion, and was none too pleased.

"He's what? Why didn't you stop him?" If anything, O'Halloran looked even more alarmed at whatever the receptionist had said than he had when David had appeared in the doorway. "Never mind, I'll take care of it."

He touched the phone off, and got quickly to his feet. "I'll be right back—oh, don't be an idiot," he snapped as Kevin moved to block the path to the door. "My nephew's here, he says it's urgent." He gave Kevin a tight, unreadable little smile. "It's not as if I can go anywhere, for God's sake." And before Kevin could move or say a word, O'Halloran pushed past him and David and headed off down the hall at a speed amazing for a man of his bulk.

His nephew? Kevin stared in the direction he'd gone, stunned. *Can't be. Or he has more than one.* Because there was no way Janek O'Halloran could have survived what Tiernan did to him.

"Son of a bitch," David murmured, rubbing the bridge of his nose as if trying to stave off a headache, releasing it to run his palm up over the balding top of his head before meeting Kevin's eyes. "Damn, Kevin. I'm so sorry."

"There's nothing for you to be sorry for." Kevin shook his head, trying to bring his focus back to the here and now. "Nothing at all."

"Sure there is." David crossed to the office's guest chair and sank into it, watching as Kevin shrugged out of his coat and hung it on the tree beside the door. "I thought there might be something to his allegations. Christ, you must have had a heart attack when you got my text."

Kevin shook his head. He started to go behind the desk, but decided he didn't want to be sitting where O'Halloran's ass had so recently rested, and perched on the edge instead. "It gave me a few bad moments. But he was good, Dave. I don't blame you a bit for buying his bullshit. He really thought he had me, and I'm sure he figured if I caved, none of you would ask any awkward questions."

214

"And he apparently assumed you'd do just that." There was the hint of a smile on the older man's face. "Looks as if he misjudged you."

"Well, he might have been right not all that long ago." Kevin arched a brow. "I seem to recall a certain managing partner telling me I needed to grow a pair."

Mondrian actually blushed. "I never said that."

"No, but it was pretty clearly implied." Kevin laughed softly, and felt some of the tension go out of his shoulders. "Good thing I took your advice."

"What was he holding over your head?" David frowned, shook his head. "Maybe I shouldn't ask. I don't know. But I'm really not in the mood for surprises today."

Kevin took a deep breath, let it out slowly. "He has a picture of... let's call it a point where I let the heat of the moment cloud my judgment." He felt himself blushing, though it was doubtful whether David could see it through his day's growth of beard. "He threatened to send it to my father. If he'd sent it to you, I'm sure you'd have said something to me about it by now."

"All right, that's good enough for me." David glanced at his watch, and pushed himself up out of the chair. "I think he's had about enough time to take care of business—care to come with me to finish holding his feet to the fire?"

"Lead on."

Kevin followed his friend down the narrow corridor that connected the associates' offices, into partner territory with its wider aisles, richer furnishings, quieter voices, muted lighting, closed doors.

And smell of blood.

Oh, shit.

Kevin pushed his way past David, to where the heavy mahogany door to O'Halloran's office stood ajar. He nudged it open with a foot, his heart hammering.

Amazing how much blood there is in a human body, was his first, barely coherent, thought. Arthur O'Halloran's corpse was sprawled across his desk, his throat cut nearly to the spine, his head lolling back at an obscene angle, blood still trickling from the gash. And his blood-smeared cell phone lay on his chest, right next to his severed and still bleeding hand. His left hand.

Behind him, he heard what sounded like David Mondrian retching, and the soft sounds feet made when they ran on thick pile carpeting. Small wonder David was ill, the luxuriously appointed office looked like an abattoir. *It's not possible*. The words echoed around and around his head. *But it is. No wonder it didn't look like they found the body at Purgatory. There wasn't anybody in the storeroom to find.*

The sound of Kevin's cell phone, in the midst of all this, was so incredibly out of place it almost startled a laugh from him. Reflexively, he reached for it to shut it off.

And turned even paler than he was at what was on the screen. A picture. And:

Kevin—what the hell is this?—Dad

CHAPTER TWENTY

Greenwich Village
New York City

Tiernan woke exactly where he had fallen asleep: on Kevin's chest with one of his human's legs loosely wrapped around him. He looked around as best he could without turning his head. His drawings were where he left them nearly a month ago, tacked to the stark white wall, the one of Moriath pierced by the blade he was all but certain was now in the *Marfach*'s hands. Past them, he saw the door to his apartment, triple-locked in the Manhattan way, and magickally warded in a very *un*-Manhattan way. If he turned his head just a little, he could see the bathroom, with two nearly matching Armani suits hanging from the hook in the door.

I'm getting married. This afternoon. He blinked, bemused. They could have been married in D.C., of course, just as easily, but Kevin had confessed to a daydream of a Manhattan wedding. Plus, this apartment made the perfect honeymoon suite, not much to it at all except the bed and that decadent shower.

"Penny for them?" Kevin's voice was its usual early morning rumble, and, as always, the sound and the feel of it beneath him were enough to stir the Fae's cock to life.

"What time is it? I'd look at the clock, but I'd rather not move my head unless it results in making you moan."

His fiancé laughed, a low, delicious sound, dark eyes flicking sideways to take in the travel alarm on the nightstand. "It's a little after nine. Why do you ask?"

"Why do you think?" Easing away from Kevin's body slightly, Tiernan ran a hand down the beautifully cut abs that jumped slightly under his touch, bent his head and flicked his tongue over one hard-puckered nipple.

"Shit." Kevin groaned softly, but the eyes he turned on Tiernan held something other than pleasure. "We're meeting my dad for lunch at Bouley at 11:30, remember?"

"Oh, hell." Tiernan's eyes closed; his caresses went from libidinous to an awkward attempt at comfort as he rested his head on Kevin's shoulder. "I didn't forget. I just shoved it into my fuck-I- don't-want-to-deal-with-this box."

"Which has been a little crowded lately."

Tiernan felt a kiss land in his hair, an arm go around his shoulders, and grimaced at the thought his lover was the one consoling him, when it was the human who had been losing so much sleep over the past two weeks. If Arthur O'Halloran had decided to make sending that text to Thomas Almstead his one last act of malice, then Tiernan wanted the poxy bastard back so he could end him properly. Though the same death his brother Lorcan had received was oddly fitting. And if it had been the *Marfach* who had been responsible for the sending of it, dwelling in the Stone he himself had been stupid enough to fuse to a barely living human body... well, one more reason to show the creature the true meaning of the word 'pain'.

"Quit worrying about me, I'll be fine."

Tiernan snugged his arm tighter around Kevin's chest in response, until he could feel the rise and fall of each breath. "You never did tell me what your father said on the phone when he saw that photo." Kevin had spoken with his father once—at least, once that Tiernan knew about—since the day of O'Halloran's murder. He could have eavesdropped, since his hearing was almost painfully acute. But he'd chosen not to, wanting to leave his partner the privacy to handle the situation in his own way.

A sigh brushed softly against the Fae's shoulder. "He asked if the picture was real. I said it was. He asked me who the other man was. I told him." A deeper sigh. "He asked me if I'd lost my mind. Not quite in those words. I said I hadn't." His fingers worked into Tiernan's hair, tangling themselves. "He asked if I had anything else to say for myself. I told him we were getting married. I suppose I should have led up to that a little more gradually."

Tiernan's mouth twisted in a wry smile. "I'm not sure it would have done any good."

"Probably not. Dad doesn't have much patience for small talk." Kevin pulled Tiernan down, settled his head in the crook of his shoulder. "Anyway... he asked me to repeat myself, and I did. He didn't say anything for a while. I thought maybe he'd hung up. Then he said, 'I need to think.' And that was it."

"Shit." Tiernan's voice was muffled slightly in Kevin's neck. "Did he ever answer the invitation?" Kevin had decided to send his father a written invitation to lunch and to the wedding itself, rather than try the phone again. Awkward as hell, but not inviting him would probably have been worse. Probably.

"He texted. Asked when and where lunch was going to be, nothing more." Kevin's free hand wandered over Tiernan's back, down over the elaborate tattoo on his hip, the Pattern's mark; not erotically, more like he was seeking contact. "He does love his smartphone. He started getting into techno-toys in a big way after Mom died—she could never see any use for them. He retired a first sergeant, but when they were both home, Mom's word was law."

It always surprised Tiernan how much he enjoyed the fragments Kevin offered from his past. Blood was everything to the Fae, yet he had few such tales of his own parents, his father having died in a duel when he was only ten years old, and his mother enjoying the favors of one male or female after another, as any Fae would. Any Fae not Royal. Or, on this side of the Pattern, SoulShared.

"Hey, what happened to your eyebrow ring?" Kevin's fingertips brushed lightly over the spot where the fine gold ring had been.

"It's in on the bathroom sink." Where he'd left it last night, when they'd stumbled back into the apartment after their bacchanal—the party cut short because in this whole teeming city, it turned out that the only decadent pleasure that interested either of them was the other. "I'll put it back in after the wedding."

"After you meet Dad, you mean." Dark eyes narrowed.

"Well…" Tiernan shrugged. "It sounds like you're going to have a hard enough time persuading your father to accept your kinky exhibitionist fiancé without me sparkling when the light hits me."

Kevin snickered, somewhat against his will from the sound of it. "Yeah, he's never been Team Edward, I think it's safe to say." But then the frown came back, kicked up a notch or two. "Don't pretend to be someone you're not, not for my dad. He'd see right through it, for one thing. And I'd hate it." The gentle stroking of Tiernan's back began again. "You're having a hard enough time with the Armani."

"Does it really show that much?" Tiernan made a face. "Maybe I should start thinking of it as a costume I'm required to wear sometimes."

"Your 'Partner's Trophy Husband' attire?" Kevin's voice was gently teasing, but Tiernan knew how the subject embarrassed him. Arthur O'Halloran's partnership interest in the firm had been posthumously stripped from him, and his name removed from the firm's masthead, based on the fraud he'd perpetrated against one of the firm's oldest and best clients, and when David Mondrian proposed making Kevin a partner in his stead, there hadn't been a single 'no' vote. "I have to admit, you make one hell of a trophy."

Tiernan snorted. "Can't wait for the first time you try to show me off, *lanan*."

"I'm looking forward to that, myself." A slight

smile tugged at Kevin's lips. "Now, promise me you'll put the ring back in?"

"Only if I don't have to get up right this minute to do it."

"Deal."

***

"If you pretend you're in leather, will you be able to relax?"

Tiernan, perched uncomfortably on the edge of the seat of the modern, pearl-grey chair, heard Kevin laugh beside him, and snorted. "It's not the suit." He tugged absently at the soft black calfskin glove that covered his left hand. "Well, maybe it's the suit. Kind of." He glanced over at Kevin. The human wasn't precisely relaxed, and given what was about to happen it would have been nothing short of astonishing if he had been, but he was certainly more at ease than Tiernan was. "The suit itself doesn't scare me. You were in Armani the night I met you. But…" He frowned, looking for words. "You were the one who was out of place that night. Off balance. And that suit made you a challenge. But we were on my home ground, and I knew I was going to win." He stared at the glove.

Kevin caught at his gloved hand, held it tightly. "You *did* win. Don't think for a minute the fancy suits and the cars and all the shit the money's going to bring with it matter. They aren't why I wanted to be a partner, they've never been part of it. I wanted it for the chance to do the kind of work that I love to do." He pressed a kiss to the soft leather. "That's unusual,

222

or so I've been told. The partners don't know what to make of me. But you do." Dark brown eyes met his, the hint of a wicked twinkle in their depths. "You know *exactly* what to make of me."

Tiernan's hand tightened around Kevin's. The glove was a pain in the ass, but a necessity in public. No way could a fully functional transparent hand be passed off as a prosthesis. "As often as—"

A throat cleared behind them. "Kevin?"

Tiernan felt the tension shoot through Kevin's body even before he heard the sharp intake of breath. The hand holding his squeezed once more, then released as Kevin got to his feet.

The Fae turned where he sat, and found himself looking up at what his fiancé might look like in another thirty or forty years. Or not, depending on what SoulSharing did to a human lifespan. *Yet another addition to the fuck-I-don't-want-to-deal-with-this* box. Thomas Almstead was a few inches shorter than his son, and a few pounds heavier. Not so heavy that he strained the buttons of his vintage but pristine dark green and khaki uniform, though. Shit, the man had Royal Defense written all over him. Not in the gray hair, or the lines on his face, but in the way he held himself. And in the measuring way he was regarding his son.

"Dad?"

To anyone else, Kevin's voice would have sounded calm and even. To Tiernan, the slight unsteadiness he heard was enough to bring him to his feet in a rush, to turn and stand just close enough to let his partner feel his presence without having to turn his head.

223

Kevin had his father's eyes, and having those eyes rake him up and down and not give him the slightest indication of whether he'd measured up was more than a little disconcerting, no matter whose face they were in. And then they dismissed him entirely, as they returned to Kevin. Slowly, the elder Almstead put out his hand. "Son."

Kevin took the offered hand, the tightness in his face giving way to a relieved smile as the older man pulled him into a quick embrace. "You're looking great, Dad. And you broke out your service Alpha? We're honored."

"Well, dress blues would have been a bit much for lunch, even here." Mr. Almstead looked past his son and one eyebrow went slowly up as he studied the Fae. "And you're Tiernan Guaire." One arm moved slightly, as if he thought about extending a hand. "Old enough to vote yet?"

"For a while now—"

"Mr. Almstead? Is your party complete?"

Conversation more or less ceased until the maître d' escorted them to their table, a waiter had taken their drink orders—Tiernan just barely avoiding asking for a straight shot of black sage honey—and another waiter left them their menus. The vaulted ceilings gave an impression of spaciousness in an enclosed setting, making the most of limited space in a very New York way, and sunlight streamed in the row of windows off Duane Street.

Tiernan glanced at his menu, but didn't really see it. His attention was all on Kevin and his father. And on the silence, giving the lie to the initial camaraderie. It went on, and on; Thomas cleared his throat, pulled reading glasses out of his breast pocket, and made a show of looking at the menu. Kevin rolled the edge of a napkin between his fingertips and glanced at his watch. *Fuck.*

"How long have you known?"

Two heads jerked up, two gazes went to the gimlet-eyed sergeant who regarded Kevin over the tops of his glasses. The tone had been mild, appropriate for a public place, but the older man's face was blank, a careful expressionlessness that made the hair stand up on the back of Tiernan's neck. His jaw clenched hard, his back straightened and stiffened.

Kevin caught his eye, and shook his head almost imperceptibly before turning back to his father. "Known what, Dad? That I loved Tiernan? Since the minute I met him."

As if I deserved that, Ianan. *Or deserve it now, for that matter.*

Gray eyebrows shot up. "No, not that you loved your... partner. That you're gay." Oddly enough, though he'd seemed uncomfortable with the term 'partner', the older man's voice didn't catch on the more loaded word, or for that matter sound any more strained than one might expect from an angry father. "I'm feeling blind-sided here, Kevin. And I don't care for it."

"Oh." The sound was thoughtful. "I guess I didn't... I wasn't expecting you to ask that." His brows drew together. He sat back in the chair, looking to Tiernan, his gaze turning pensively to the nearby fireplace as Tiernan held his breath. Kevin didn't consider himself gay, he knew that much. A late-night Google crawl had yielded the term "pansexual," and it was what his *lanan* felt most comfortable with. Attracted to individuals, not to an entire gender. It was a safe bet, though, that his father wasn't going to be up for wrapping his head around that right now. Later, hopefully. The Fae and his human were going to have more than enough secrets, and there was no sense in adding to the weight of them unnecessarily. But not now.

Kevin rested his elbows on the table, steepled his fingers, and stared past them at his father. "I don't know, Dad. Sucks as an answer but it's the only one I have. Some days, I'd tell you that Tiernan showed me what I am for the first time, others I'd tell you I've probably always known." He shook his head. "I wouldn't have ambushed you with it, if it had been left up to me."

"That was going to be my next question." The elder Almstead was not entirely satisfied with his son's answer, but appeared willing to let it go for now, in pursuit of other game. "What the hell was going on with that picture?"

"Blackmail." Tiernan could keep silent no longer, and the word came out as a growl. "Bastard of a crooked partner at work was hiding his thievery behind your son's good name, and thought the picture would keep Kevin in line once he found out what was going on."

That sharp regard was fully on him and he would have been moderately amused to find himself sweating if this had been anyone other than his *lanan*'s blood kin. "Hiding how, exactly?"

Tiernan opened his mouth to reply, closed it again as Kevin's hand rested lightly on his forearm, and let his lover do the explaining.

"He picked a client so big it never looked at its legal bills. He picked *me* because he figured if anyone figured out the scam, they'd believe an associate twice passed over for partnership would stoop to stealing from a client. And he billed personal expenses and extra hours to the client, under my name."

Thomas' face was slowly turning a very interesting shade of red. His jaw muscles worked in a way that reminded Tiernan of Kevin in a mood.

"I figured out what he was doing when I went to check my billable hours and spotted the extra charges." Kevin picked up a water glass, studied it, sipped. "And he figured out I'd figured it out. So he had... an accomplice... shadow me. The accomplice took the picture, and sent it to him. He showed it to me, told me he'd send it to you if I blew the whistle on him. Then he decided to turn me in anyway, to hide his tracks. But he ran his mouth a little too loudly and was found out. I assume he sent you the picture out of spite."

The elder Almstead's upper lip curled in a snarl. "The cocksucking sonuvabitch."

Kevin choked on his water. Tiernan barely turned what would have been an incredibly inappropriate laugh into a strangled cough. *Of all the epithets...*

"What did I—oh, *Christ*—"

The arrival of their drinks gave the gray-haired sergeant a few minutes to regain his composure. By the time the waiter departed, he was shaking his head slowly, one side of his mouth turned up in a rueful half-grin. "Your mother would have skinned me for that one." Slowly, the smile faded, as Thomas turned his Glenlivet around and around in his hand. "Tell me the bastard's been dealt with."

"He's dead, Dad."

"Unpleasantly. For him," Tiernan was unable to resist putting in.

"But not necessarily for you?" The gaze that met his was utterly level, calm. Tiernan found himself wondering what Thomas had seen, in a brief human lifespan, that allowed him to contemplate the prospect of violent death with that kind of equanimity.

"Not at all." Tiernan smiled faintly. "But your son's not marrying a murderer." *Not in the way you think, anyway.*

"A gold-digger, though?"

"Dad!" A spluttering sound came from Kevin's general direction. "Tiernan isn't—"

"Let the boy answer for himself." Thomas leaned forward slightly, fixing Tiernan with a look that had undoubtedly left human recruits quaking in their boots, if not pissing themselves outright. "If he can't, he's not worth your time."

"*Dad—*"

"He's right, Kevin." Tiernan raised his ungloved hand, motioning an I-got-this at his *lanan*, without taking his eyes off his *lanan*'s father. "I'm not a 'boy,' and I assure you, I am not after your son for his money." A corner of his mouth quirked up, as he remembered his brother weeping diamonds as he begged for his life. "I am after your son because I can't imagine living without him." Ignoring the color he could feel rising in his own cheeks, he put up a pierced eyebrow, returning the sergeant's measuring stare. "And what *I'm* wondering is, why are *you* so calm about *that*?"

"Oh, God," he heard Kevin murmur.

Apparently, Thomas heard it too. He turned for a moment, a faint smile shadowing his eyes and the corners of his mouth, before he returned his attention to Tiernan. "You bite back. Good." The older male sipped his scotch, tapped a finger pensively against the glass. He looked up abruptly, sitting forward in his seat. "It started in Vietnam. Considerably before your time."

Tiernan succeeded in keeping a smile from his face, but only just. He'd known males who had gone off to fight in what had been known in that time and place as the War of Northern Aggression, though of course that was going to be another secret Kevin's father would never hear.

"There was a kid named McAllan. Not much older than me, but he'd gotten in country before I did. We were in the same squad, but he was on a different fire team. Then I was promoted to lead a team and he was reassigned to mine." Thomas rested his elbows on the table, looking from Tiernan to Kevin, and back again. "Mac saved my life. Twice. Lost most of a leg doing it the second time." The older man fixed him with a stare, and Tiernan felt his Stone hand twitch self-consciously. "They were going to discharge him, after that, but Mac wasn't buying it. He fought it, and they finally reassigned him stateside. He ended up at Walter Reed working with amputees."

"You've told me about Mac," Kevin put in quietly. "Quite a few times."

"Never did tell you the whole story, though." Thomas cleared his throat. "Most guys, you lose track of, after a reassignment or a rotation. Mac was different. We stayed in touch, even after the war

229

ended—there were a few of us who kept up with him, not just me. Mostly the ones who decided to stay and make a career of the Corps, like he did. So we heard what happened when he was discharged." The older man's face began to redden again and his grip tightened on his nearly empty glass. "His stateside C.O. found out he was gay. And insisted on an undesirable discharge."

"Dad—"

Thomas waved his son off, his attention fixed on Tiernan. "We did what we could. Two majors and a colonel from 'Nam wrote letters. Major Fielding even went to D.C. to kick some ass in person, but the S.O.B. at Walter Reed had his mind made up. Mac had engaged in 'conduct unbecoming,' and that was the beginning and the end of the story."

Dark eyes bored into Tiernan's blue ones, decades of anger in their depths. "It was wrong, Tiernan. It's been wrong for the last third of a century. That's how long I've had to think about it, and *that's* why I'm not reacting like a complete horse's ass to the news my son is marrying a man. Am I entirely comfortable with it? No. In all honesty, I am not. Not yet. But am I going to reject my only living son, and the man he tells me he loves, because of it? Hell, no."

In the stunned silence that followed, Thomas turned to Kevin. "One other part of the story I never mentioned. That asshole who blackmailed you was fucking with more than one good name. Mac's real name is Kevin Charles McAllan."

The expression of stunned relief on his partner's face left Tiernan feeling dizzy. Kevin hadn't said much on the subject, but the Fae knew how he'd been dreading this conversation. *Maybe you never do know your kin, even the closest.* "Thank you. Sir." He couldn't remember the last time he'd ever called anyone "sir," even in a fuck-you-very-much sort of way, but this once, it felt right.

One gray eyebrow went up. "'Sir'? The respect is appreciated, young man, but don't think for a minute that I won't feed you your balls if you hurt my son."

"Dad!"

Chuckling, Thomas picked up the menu that lay next to his elbow. "What do you say we order? I think you boys have something you need to be doing, before long."

CHAPTER TWENTY-ONE

Kevin stood, hands plunged into the pockets of his suit, staring at the lectern. The justice of the peace was still out in the reception area, gathering and double-checking their paperwork; he turned the rings in his pocket round and round with his fingers, wondering at the way they never warmed to his touch. Good thing he'd noticed the hand-crafted body jewelry in the window of the tattoo and piercing parlor in the ground floor space over Purgatory. The owner of the parlor had referred him to a jeweler who had been able to craft rings out of two of the links of the truesilver chain coiled around the carrying strap of Tiernan's battered duffel bag. *God, I hope this doesn't turn out to be one of those what-the-fuck-were-you-THINKING surprises.*

"Second thoughts, *lanan*?"

Kevin started, turned to see Tiernan at his side. The Fae stood with his back to Thomas, who was studying the abstract picture hung behind the lectern. He smiled, just a slight curve of the lips, and his voice was low, barely more than a whisper.

"Please tell me you're joking." Kevin's hands came out of his pockets and he reached for his partner's ungloved hand. "You don't really think I want to back out of this, do you?"

One eyebrow went up, the gold ring in it catching a hint of the indirect lighting overhead. "I'm hoping you haven't had an attack of sanity since we signed the paperwork." The Fae squeezed Kevin's hand, the quickness and tightness of the grip giving lie to his casual tone.

"Not happening." Kevin held Tiernan's hand firmly, following the direction of the clear blue gaze as it darted around the room. The dark wood lectern was flanked by a long, low sofa, a darker shade of purple than the lavender of the walls. *"Really?"* had been Tiernan's laconic comment when they were first ushered into the west chapel in the old Department of Motor Vehicles building. "You, on the other hand, have the air of a man marking the location of the exits."

"Me? Hell, no. I want to do this." Yet just a touch of white showed all the way around those so-blue irises, and the Fae's tongue darted out to run around lips gone dry. "I think it *is* the damned suit, after all. Makes me twitch."

Kevin looked his partner up and down. The thought of what lay under all that impeccable tailoring was necessitating thoughts of sleet and Polar Bear plunges. Yet now that he looked for it, there was something in the way Tiernan held himself that was decidedly ill at ease. "You're definitely more the denim and leather type." He grinned with a sudden idea. "Give it a little while, maybe a few months, and we'll throw a wedding reception at Purgatory. To make up for you indulging my whim to have the wedding here in New York. We'll hire out the whole place. And then you'll get to dress *me* up."

The slow smile that spread across the Fae's face and lit his eyes told Kevin he'd hit the bull's-eye. "I want a lap dance."

"Name your pleasure, *lanan.*"

The door opened enough to admit the justice of the peace. "Sorry that took so long." The woman smiled at Thomas as she passed him on her way to the lectern, settling the lapels of her simple black robe, then set a manila folder on the pitched surface before coming back to where Kevin and Tiernan waited. "I just wanted to be sure I had the right file—wouldn't do to give you gentlemen the wrong vows."

Thomas coughed, and Kevin wondered how much of their murmured conversation his dad had overheard. "Just get them married, Your Honor." His voice was gruff, but there was a hint of laughter in the lines around his eyes. "Anything with 'I do' in it will probably do in a pinch."

"Dad…"

Kevin couldn't help laughing as the J.P. gave him what looked like a commiserating wink before stepping up behind the lectern. She tapped the small boom mike, leaned into it, puffed a lock of salt-and-pepper hair out of her eyes and pushed the microphone away. "We don't need this, I don't think—you can all hear me, right?"

Kevin nodded, his heart suddenly racing, and out of the corner of his eye saw Tiernan doing the same. "Yes, ma'am," Thomas put in, drawing himself up.

"You're not expecting anyone else?" This to Kevin and Tiernan, somewhat quizzically.

"We have everyone we need." Tiernan's normally silken voice was slightly hoarse, the clear crystalline blue of his eyes touched with sapphire as his gaze locked with Kevin's. "Let's do this."

The justice smiled, and opened the folder, glanced down, adjusted her glasses, and began.

"We are come together at this time and in this place to share in the joy and love of Kevin Almstead and Tiernan Guaire. May the love that has brought them to this day continue to be a blessing to them from this day forward."

Kevin tried to be properly attentive, but the short, slight woman in front of him didn't stand a chance of holding his full attention, not when he could sense his almost-husband at his side. He tried to hold his head still and glance sidewise—but the unguarded expression he saw on Tiernan's face stole his breath. It seemed impossible that such a short time ago a man's eyes had never moved him, a man's hands had never aroused him. Now? Now it was impossible to think about those eyes without wanting that hot blue gaze raking over every inch of him. And the hands? *Forget about the hands, buddy, you have the whole rest of this ceremony to get through…*

"To this moment Kevin and Tiernan bring the fullness of their hearts to share with one another. They bring the dreams which bind them together in spirit; they bring their individuality, which will be preserved, but out of which will emerge their life together."

Quit ogling the Fae, dammit. This time, his gaze turned the other way, toward his father, with a little smile. Thomas stood at parade rest, every inch the soldier. His face was set in lines of concentration, as if he took his duties as witness very seriously. As Kevin watched, those lines softened a little and one end of his mouth curved up in a smile. *God, please, let Dad be okay with this. Let him accept my husband. Please.*

"Kevin?"

From the way the justice was saying his name, Kevin got the impression it wasn't the first time she'd called it, and he blushed. "Sorry."

She chuckled, cleared her throat, and peered over the tops of her glasses. "Kevin, will you have this man to be your husband, to live together with him in the covenant of marriage?"

Oh, God, this is it.

"Will you love him, comfort him, honor and keep him, in sickness and in health, and, forsaking all others, be faithful to him as long as you both shall live?"

Comfort him. In his mind, he was cradling Tiernan to his chest, turning the Fae's head away from the ruined forearm pressed between their bodies, making love to him to draw out the pain left behind by the ley energy. *Hells to the yeah.* "I will."

Tiernan, the justice, and his father were all looking at him, and Tiernan at least seemed on the verge of laughter. *Shit, did I say the other part out loud too?*

"Tiernan?" The justice turned to the Fae, a previously invisible dimple coming out in her cheek, confirming Kevin's suspicions.

"Yes, your Honor?" Tiernan's voice was dry, amused, his face a careful study in nonchalance.

"Enough already," Kevin muttered under his breath, his own laughter under precarious control.

The justice cleared her throat, her eyes twinkling. "Tiernan, will you have this man to be your husband, to live together with him in the covenant of marriage? Will you love him, comfort him, honor and keep him, in sickness and in health, and, forsaking all others, be faithful to him as long as you both shall live?"

The silence stretched out. Tiernan's eyes continued to hold Kevin's, but the laughter faded from his piercing blue gaze. Tiernan reached out and caught Kevin's hand in his gloved one. The simple touch, and the hand he used, were more eloquent than any words. "I will."

Don't try to find me.

I can't love you.

What part of that don't you fucking get?

He could hear the words as clearly as if the male who held his hand was speaking them. And yet Tiernan's hand was in his. He'd said *I will*. And he'd meant it.

The gloved fingers tightened around his, and Kevin swallowed a sudden, painful lump in his throat. *A Fae. Magick. Willingly mine. Damn.*

"Kevin?" The justice of the peace—hell, he hadn't even asked her name—eyed him with arched brows, questioning. And he nodded. *Let's do this.*

She smiled. "I, Kevin, take you, Tiernan…"

"I, Kevin, take you, Tiernan…" He still held the Fae's hand, and now he held it tighter.

"To be my husband…"

"To be my husband."

Thomas leaned in, just a little. Bearing witness.

"To have and to hold, from this day forward."

Kevin repeated her words, slowly, clearly.

Though he wondered, as he spoke, what 'holding' might mean, when the one held was other than human, and untameable at heart. And the light in Tiernan's eyes, was that a challenge? Or delight?

"For better or worse, for richer or poorer, in sickness and in health..."

None of which seem to adequately cover being eaten alive by slugs with the tails of scorpions.

"...to love and to cherish, until we are parted by death. This is my solemn vow."

Kevin barely heard the J.P., over the resonance of her words in his own mind. Especially *until we are parted by death.* How close had they come to that already? Or, looking at it another way, was that even possible any more? They'd talked about that, well into the night, on several occasions. There was so much Tiernan's people didn't know about SoulSharing, simply no way to know what it did to a human to become *scair-anam.* Could he die? No way to know. Did it matter to him? Fuck, no.

"To love and to cherish." He drew a deep breath. "Until we are parted by death. This is my solemn vow."

Behind him, he heard his father cough, a gruff, almost apologetic sound, and he smiled. A smile Tiernan mirrored, glancing past him at the sergeant before turning to the justice. "Is it my turn yet?"

The justice laughed, obviously charmed by the Fae's smile, the soft music of his accent. "It certainly is, Mr. Guaire. I, Tiernan, take you, Kevin, to be my husband..."

That music flowed around him, and through him, as his *lanan* repeated the marriage vows in his turn, summing up everything strange and wonderful and unsettling about Tiernan Guaire. Not long ago, Kevin would have sworn he had never been—could never be—the kind of man to fall hard for sensual eyes, a provocative touch, the caresses of a voice that hinted at magick and offered glimpses of a time and place lost to all but memory. And the fact his lover could mesmerize him at will, with any or all of those, said as much about the man Kevin had become as it did about the male he was in the process of marrying.

"*…tseo mo mhinn ollúnta*," Tiernan murmured, in response to the justice's final prompting. "My solemn oath."

The justice shook herself a little, as if she was trying to bring herself back from someplace she hadn't been expecting to go. "Let us… er, let us listen to the words that Kevin and Tiernan have chosen to speak to each other on this joyous occasion. Kevin?"

Kevin studied his shoes for a minute; glanced back at his father; turned to Tiernan. "Four years ago, I was searching for a poem to read at Tanner's funeral, and in the process of looking, I found another one. When I read it, I remember thinking that the beginning… was me. And the end was everything I hoped for. 'Sonnets from the Portuguese,' Elizabeth Barrett Browning, Sonnet 26." *Damn the lawyer, has to cite chapter and verse…*

"I lived with visions for my company

Instead of men and women, years ago,

And found them gentle mates, nor thought to know

A sweeter music than they played to me.

But soon their trailing purple was not free
Of this world's dust, their lutes did silent grow,
And I myself grew faint and blind below
Their vanishing eyes. Then thou didst come—to be,
Beloved, what they seemed. Their shining fronts,
Their songs, their splendours, (better, yet the same,
As river-water hallowed into fonts)
Met in thee, and from out thee overcame
My soul with satisfaction of all wants:
Because God's gifts put man's best dreams to shame."

Tiernan's eyes never left his, all through the recitation. Now, slowly, the Fae reached for Kevin's other hand, and held both. "I didn't prepare anything." His voice was calm, but Kevin could read his partner well enough to know that the calm was a mask. "Because I knew you would give me the words. The same way you've given me everything else I have that's worth having."

"Tiernan…"

The Fae shook his head, with a little smile. "Truth. And your poem brought this one to mind. My apologies for the translation, it's very old and some of the words don't have an exact modern equivalent." He closed his eyes, and when he opened them, the expression was so clear, so unguarded it robbed Kevin of breath.

"You are the song I sing
You are the voice that gives it life

You are the heart it touches.

Before you all was dust

Without you all would be ashes

To lose you would leave my soul empty for a silent eternity.

You gave me your love

You gave me the very love with which I love you

You gave me the soul which loves and is loved."

Oh, damn. Kevin blinked, as the soft leather of Tiernan's glove touched his cheek and came away damp. "*Lanan*," he whispered, not even bothering to try to speak. There was no point.

The justice of the peace cleared her throat, pushing her glasses up to blot under her eyes. "I'm... not usually the one who needs the tissues. Thank you," she added to Thomas, as he tucked the little packet into an inside pocket.

"My pleasure, ma'am." The sergeant nodded to the justice, but his eyes never left Tiernan, the *I'll feed you your balls if you hurt my son* in that gaze beginning to yield to something like *you might work out*.

"The rings?"

Kevin blinked once more, hard, clearing away the last of the tears as his hand went into his pocket and closed around the two circles of metal. Slowly, he withdrew his hand and opened his palm, revealing the gleaming bands the jeweler assumed were platinum. He heard Tiernan's breath catch sharply. The ripples-in-water pattern of the forging was distinctive, and had survived the jeweler's ministrations intact.

The Fae picked up one of the rings. He studied it

closely, in silence, turning it over several times.

"Is it—all right?" Kevin blurted at last. *Fuck, if I blew this…*

Piercing blue eyes met his, touched with the hint of a smile.

"Hells to the yeah."

As Kevin grinned, Tiernan turned to the J.P., who flashed him a smile of her own before looking down at her notes again.

"Each of you brings now a symbol of your love for each other. These rings shall forevermore be a symbol of the love you have declared and the vows you have exchanged. The unbroken circles of these rings represent the special faithfulness you have pledged to each other."

The justice looked up, at Tiernan. When he nodded, she gestured to him and he took Kevin's left hand, speaking carefully and clearly after her:

"Kevin, I give you this ring as a symbol of my vow, and with all that I am, and all that I have, I honor you."

The ring slipped cool around Kevin's finger, a perfect fit. His eyes opened wide as the band immediately warmed. *What the hell? It's never done that before!*

"Truesilver," Tiernan murmured, so softly Kevin had to strain to hear it. "It knows its purpose."

Kevin nodded, and reached for Tiernan's right hand. Holding it in his, he looked to the justice.

"Do you have to use the right hand?" The woman frowned, going up slightly on tiptoe to look over the lectern at their hands.

"My left is disfigured, Your Honor." Tiernan's

voice was smooth, but the tic of a muscle in his jaw hinted at rougher emotion as he held up his gloved hand. "I don't take the glove off in public."

"We won't look."

The warmth in her voice brought three heads around to look at her. She blushed slightly, but her smile never wavered. "If you can wear a ring on that hand, and if you want to be traditional…"

"I… would like that. Very much." The Fae's voice was silk, but silk caught on steel hooks. "Thank you."

I had no idea this meant so much to him. Kevin's fingers tightened around Tiernan's hand. The two of them had talked a little before sleep last night about the wedding service, with Kevin expressing doubt that any ceremony could add any meaning to a bond already outside anything in human experience.

Tiernan's response had been simple. *You need it. Which means we need it*.

The justice's gaze caught Thomas'. She waited for his nod. "Just say when you're ready." With that, she turned her back, and the sergeant did the same, his back proud and ramrod-straight, his hands clasped behind his back at parade rest.

Tiernan was already tugging the glove off as Kevin turned back to him. The crystal of the living Stone caught the light, bent it. A shiver ran through Kevin, one he recognized. This was a totally private sight. It was as if the Fae had stripped himself bare before him. He took the gemlike hand in his own, startled all over again by its warmth. "Ready, Your Honor."

"Then repeat after me."

243

And now it was his turn. "Tiernan, I give you this ring as a symbol of my vow, and with all that I am, and all that I have, I honor you." He slid the band carefully around the transparent fourth finger and gasped softly as the ring took on the same glass-like sheen as the hand itself. Without thinking, he raised the hand to his lips and placed a kiss over the ring.

Tiernan's fingers tightened around his for an instant. Then the grip loosened, and the Fae began to put the glove back on. "The sooner we finish this, the sooner I get you home, *m'lanan*." The voice was light, meant for the listeners, but the look in those eyes went to the backs of Kevin's knees like a blow from a sapper's hammer.

The onlookers turned back as Tiernan finished settling the glove into place. The justice of the peace laughed. "I can take a hint, gentlemen." Waiting for Kevin and Tiernan to turn to face her, she looked from them to Thomas, who was smiling more broadly by the moment. "Now that Tiernan and Kevin have given themselves to each other by solemn vows, with the joining of hands and the giving and receiving of rings, and with you as witness, by the authority vested in me by the State and City of New York, I pronounce that they are husband and husband. You may now—"

"With all due respect, Your Honor," Tiernan cut in with a wicked grin, "I don't need permission."

And Kevin's laugh was cut off by a searing, highly inappropriate—and completely fucking perfect—kiss.

***

Kevin was out of his suit jacket and tie even before Tiernan had the apartment door open, and by the time the Fae finished with the last lock on the front door, he had thrown his coat over a chair and was hanging the suit jacket in the tiny closet. "Are all three of those really necessary? After that last dance at the G Lounge, I'm a little impatient." Small wonder, after what his *lanan* had murmured into his ear as they ground heatedly against one another on the dance floor. *Some of your human legends are true, you know. Dance with a Fae, and you're his, body and soul, until he sets you free.* And all he'd been able to manage was a breathless *Don't you fucking dare*.

"I plan on being just a little too distracted in a few minutes to ward the place magically." Tiernan laughed, a sound that trickled down Kevin's spine and pooled at the base of it in exactly the same way as the pleasure that preceded orgasm.

In fact, come to think of it… "Do tell. In great detail, if you please." He toed off his shoes and started unbuttoning his shirt, then stopped as a shirtless Tiernan crossed to him and took him by the upper arms. *Damn, he's fast*.

"I am so going to enjoy this." The Fae's voice was low, his breath warm in Kevin's ear as he leaned in to tease it with his tongue. "There's a ley line running under this building. I can't tap it directly from here, like I can when we're in the basement at Purgatory, but I guarantee I'm going to fucking rock your world."

"A ley line? Here?"

Tiernan grunted, his mouth wandering greedily down Kevin's throat. "You're overdressed."

"I was trying to do something about that when someone distracted me."

"Lawyers. All talk, no action." Tiernan caught at the front of Kevin's shirt and yanked; buttons flew, and the shirt fell open. The Fae fisted the t-shirt beneath with a soft growl. "Damn. You'd better be commando under those trousers."

Kevin laughed a little breathlessly. "Find out."

Tiernan pulled back, eyeing him narrowly, the lock of hair that had been falling in his eyes all night shadowing his gaze. "Sounds like a challenge." Slowly, deliberately, he stripped Kevin of the shirt, letting it fall to the floor and kicking it away. The T-shirt followed, flung God knew where. Then went Tiernan's glove, peeled away to reveal the breathtaking crystal hand with its gleaming truesilver band. With his right hand, the Fae gripped one of Kevin's nipples tightly between the knuckles of two fingers, twisting until he gasped. And all Kevin could do was stare as the hand of living Stone yanked his belt and trousers open, slid inside, and encircled his engorged cock.

"I damn near did this to you on the dance floor." Tiernan's breath was hot and urgent in his ear, keeping ragged time with the strokes of his hand. "All that don't-touch-me out there on display, begging to be fucked with."

"Do it now." Kevin's hips moved of themselves, thrusting into Tiernan's hand. The suit trousers slid down his thighs, fell to pool around his ankles. He stepped out of them and kicked them away—carefully, so as not to interrupt what Tiernan's hand was doing.

"You'd better believe I'm going to, *lanan*. I have

plans." Tiernan nipped sharply at Kevin's earlobe, then stepped back to unfasten his own trousers. "On your back, if you please." He nodded toward the bed. "And lose the damn socks."

As aroused as he was, Kevin still couldn't keep back a chuckle as he complied, hooking a finger in one sock, and then in the other, dropping them to the floor before crawling to the center of the huge bed. "Remind me to add black dress socks to my list of things that turn you off."

"That has to be the shortest list known to Fae or man." Tiernan was naked now, gloriously so. He stood beside the bed, looking down at Kevin, stroking himself, base to tip as he toyed with his own nipple ring, twisting it between crystal fingertips.

Kevin's hand found his own cock, gripped, wrung it not quite gently. A shudder ran through him as Tiernan's eyes darkened and clear fluid trickled from the slit of his swollen shaft. "You have plans?" His voice came out hoarse, dark.

Without a word, Tiernan crawled into the bed, moving to kneel between Kevin's legs, sitting back on his heels, his cock jutting up and out at a proud angle. Following the urging of his lover's hands, Kevin shifted his weight until his hips rested on Tiernan's thighs, his legs curled loosely around the Fae's waist.

He braced himself to sit up, but Tiernan shook his head. "No. You need to lie back for this to work. But you might want to prop your head with a couple of pillows, 'cause this is going to be hotter than hell to watch."

The wickedness of the Fae's smile told Kevin exactly how he knew how hot it was going to be. And it didn't matter. He didn't give a damn where his husband had learned whatever it was he was about to do, or when—whether sometime in the last hundred and fifty years or in the unmeasured time preceding his arrival in the human realm. As far as he was concerned, he was the fortunate beneficiary and focus of at least a couple of centuries of dedicated research. He grabbed as many pillows as he could reach and shoved them under his head, groaning softly as Tiernan raised his hips and parted his ass cheeks, teasing at his tight entrance with a fingertip.

"Raise up, *lanan*, I need both hands here."

Obediently, if a little awkwardly, Kevin braced his heels and raised his hips. With one hand, Tiernan forced his clenched cheeks apart. With the other, he gripped his own spectacularly hard cock and guided it to Kevin's entrance. He eased the head in slowly, eyes half closing in pleasure as he breached the tight ring of muscle, then held Kevin's hips tightly and started tunneling his way in. "Relax, damn it. Shit, you're just as tight as you were the first time."

Pleasure shimmered up and down Kevin's spine, pooled hot and heavy in his sac. "This is—oh, *fuck*." The sensation when Tiernan reached his prostate was beyond words. His eyes threatened to roll back in his head, and it was only with tremendous effort he was able to keep watching.

"Haven't gotten to the best part yet." Sweat was beginning to bead on Tiernan's brow, to film his chest, and when his cock was fully seated, the spasm of pure pleasure that flitted across his chiseled features made Kevin's shaft jerk and spatter clear liquid across his abs.

"Better than this may kill me."

Tiernan's eyes gleamed. "I'll do my best not to allow that to happen, *lanan*. But here's where I stop talking, for the duration. And there's only one thing you have to do." The crystal hand smoothed over Kevin's chest, warm, soft, caressing. "Lie back and let me pleasure you. I mean it," he added, a touch sharply, as Kevin opened his mouth to protest. "This is for you. Don't worry, I'll enjoy the hell out of it too." The Fae's cock throbbed deep within him, as if in agreement. "But let me do the driving."

Kevin sighed. "If you insist—oh, sweet bleeding *Christ*…"

His voice failed him completely as Tiernan bent to him, and the head of his cock disappeared into the Fae's hot, hungry mouth. Long waves of hair fell forward, but though they kissed his hard and heaving abdominal muscles with silk, they didn't obscure the mind-blowing sight of his *lanan* sucking and fucking him at the same time. He felt soft laughter around his rigid shaft. Then all he could feel was pleasure, dizzying, blinding, deafening. And he wasn't even coming yet. *Damn*.

When Tiernan started moving, what couldn't possibly get better, got better. The Fae couldn't stroke deep, not bent the way he was, but as he rose up to thrust, he let Kevin slip almost all the way out of his mouth, barely keeping his lips sealed around the head. Then, as he settled back, he took Kevin's aching, rigid organ deeper, swirling his tongue over the sweet spot under the head until Kevin was fairly sure he was going to black out. Again the thrust and release, and again the subsiding and swallowing; and again,

Tiernan's hand encircling the base of his shaft on the upstroke this time.

Kevin whispered a stream of curses through clenched teeth, and was rewarded with the slow wringing he craved. And there was something else. Something racing through blood, bone and nerve like wildfire, making his whole body ring like struck crystal. Tiernan drove harder into him, now, each stroke heightening both the pleasure and the ringing. His sac tightened, drew up, and he could feel himself beginning to curve hard. "Tiernan... stop... going to come... want to wait for you—"

The Fae's response was to grip Kevin's hips and drive them down, impaling himself deep in Kevin's ass, jetting thick glassy heat into his clenching hold. Moans around Kevin's cock alternated with deep, hungry suckling, until Kevin too exploded, shot after shot of thick cream going straight down the Fae's throat, no need for him to swallow. Kevin screamed, or thought he did. All he could hear was the roar of his heartbeat in his ears, and Tiernan's choked gasps. His body twisted into a shape of pure ecstasy, the caress of the ley energy coaxing him to a height of pleasure beyond anything he'd ever known.

The tears streaking his face, though, those were pure joy, the bliss of the SoulShare bond. *Mine*, was his only coherent thought. *Mine always*.

By the time he was aware of something outside himself again, Tiernan was lying beside him, wrapping an arm and a leg around him, gently kissing where the tears had passed. "I am the luckiest son of a bitch in two realms." The Fae laughed softly. "And I am definitely keeping this apartment. This is too good to give up."

"You are going to kill me." Kevin grinned, tucking a lock of hair behind Tiernan's ear; leaning in, he traced the tip of his tongue along his husband's eyebrow, teasing at the gold ring. "I wouldn't mind giving you another shot at it later, in fact, but I think I need a little while to get my breath back."

Tiernan's answering laughter was low, and rich, and totally sinful. The lights dimmed, and went out Fae style. Tiernan rolled to let Kevin pillow his head on his breast, worked his fingers into his hair, and held him there. "Rest, then. As long as I feel like letting you."

Kevin closed his eyes with a long, slow sigh. Tiernan's free hand moved slowly, soothingly over his back, simultaneously gentling and teasing. Amazing, how much the world could change in a month. A day. A minute…

"*Lanan?*"

"Hm?" Kevin didn't bother opening his eyes, just smiled against Tiernan's chest.

"What was the other poem?"

"Huh?" Now he did open his eyes, just so he could blink properly in puzzlement.

"You said you found the sonnet you gave me at the wedding while you were looking for another poem, one for your brother's funeral." He felt Tiernan shrug slightly. "I wondered at the time, but I had a few other things on my mind."

"Oh." Kevin laughed quietly. "I took a course on 19th century English poets in college—thought it would help make a writer of me, or at least impress a certain English major—and I remembered a set of sonnets on the death of Robert Browning, so that's what I was looking for. I found the Elizabeth Barrett Browning sonnets more or less by accident—turns out the ones I was looking for were actually by Swinburne."

"What did you recite? Do you remember?" A kiss fell in Kevin's hair. "Knowing I share a soul with someone who loved his brother the way you did, it's good for me."

Kevin's breath caught hard at Tiernan's words, and again when he brought the verse to mind he'd recited for Tanner. "Oh, God…"

"What?" The voice in the darkness was suddenly anxious. "You don't have to—"

"No, no. It's just…" Kevin cleared his throat, took a deep, unsteady breath. "It's the SoulShare," he whispered, then recited,

"He held no dream worth waking: so he said,
He who stands now on death's triumphal steep,
Awakened out of life wherein we sleep
And dream of what he knows and sees, being dead.
But never death for him was dark or dread:
"Look forth," he bade the soul, and fear not. Weep,
All ye that trust not in his truth, and keep
Vain memory's vision of a vanished head
As all that lives of all that once was he
Save that which lightens from his word: but we,
Who, seeing the sunset-coloured waters roll,
Yet know the sun subdued not of the sea,
Nor weep nor doubt that still the spirit is whole,
And life and death but shadows of the soul."

EPILOGUE

Tiernan frowned, wondering what was making him uneasy as he looked around Purgatory. The dance floor was a little emptier than normal for a Friday night, but that made it easier to see the pole dancers, who were in fine form. The bar was crowded, the champagne flowing more than any other drink—which made sense, since it was free. The lap dancers were likewise doing a brisk business down in the cock pit. Tiernan smirked and adjusted his jeans, just the memory of his own private lap dance before the doors opened was enough to put a bulge in the front of them. Damn, his husband was hot.

"What's the matter, *lanan*?"

Tiernan grinned as Kevin slipped an arm around his waist. His human had been true to his promise, and had allowed Tiernan to choose his attire for the wedding reception. Tiernan dressed him in his black leather duster, tight black leather trousers, a pair of black horn-rimmed reading glasses—not that he needed them, but fuck if his lawyer didn't look hot in them—and nothing else. "I have to figure out how to keep it in my jeans for another couple of hours. You're not making it easy."

Kevin's laughter was beautiful. It was the only word for it. "What did I do now?"

"Don't pretend you don't know. If this lawyer thing ever stops working out, you have one hell of a second act as a dancer waiting for you."

Kevin shook his head. "Nah, I always need you for inspiration." He nodded toward the dance floor, where a couple of the house dancers were defying gravity to a pulsing dubstep beat. "I'll leave the show to the pros."

Tiernan followed the direction of his nod—and his eyebrow went up as he finally realized what had been bothering him. The house lights were up. And the last time he'd seen that had been the afternoon he came in to confirm his suspicions about the ley lines. When he'd woken up on a sofa in the cock pit to find the apparently not entirely late Janek O'Halloran looking over his fried and twitching body. "Just as well, I don't feel like sharing," he murmured. "Something really has to be done about the security here."

"You lost me." Kevin's voice was low. He moved closer, though it was unlikely anyone would overhear their conversation given the pounding beat from the dance floor and the low roar of other conversations. The "public" part of the reception, the part Kevin's more open-minded friends and business associates had been invited to, had ended almost an hour ago, and Purgatory was now full of its regulars in a celebratory mood and primed with free champagne. "Did you see something?"

"Not really. I was just remembering the younger O'Halloran. And how easy it was for me to get in here when I wanted to scope out the nexus." Tiernan grimaced. "What if the *Marfach* wants to get back to the nexus?" The only way the former bouncer could have survived what Tiernan had done to him, and walked out of that basement to murder Arthur O'Halloran, was if something else was animating him. The *Marfach* was the only candidate to be that "something else," and there was probably enough pure living magick in the Stone in the asshole's head to sustain the creature. For a while.

"That would be a serious buzz-kill, if I weren't one step ahead of you." Strangely, Kevin's smile had returned. He took a slim, black leather portfolio out from under his arm, handed it to Tiernan. "I did say you had one more wedding present coming."

Tiernan frowned as he took the leather case. "And I told you, it wasn't necessary." But the grin on his husband's face made him look about six years old, and the Fae's frown fled. "What's this?... oh, shit."

The magnetic fastening had fallen apart, revealing a sheaf of densely printed paper. And the top sheet... well, he was no lawyer, but even Tiernan recognized a deed when he saw one. The deed to Purgatory. And his name on it. "Fuck me blind."

"That'll have to wait a few more hours, unless you want to turn down the house lights early." Kevin raked a hand through his hair. "You've mentioned the security issue before. This doesn't solve the problem, but at least it puts the problem into the hands of someone who understands what the issues are." He laughed softly. "Plus, I could be wrong, but I get the distinct impression that you like the place."

"It's made me a few happy memories." Tiernan leafed through the papers in the case, shaking his head slowly. "This has to have cost you a fucking fortune, *m'lanan*. You didn't have to—"

Kevin hooked two fingers through one of Tiernan's belt loops. "Usually when you make partner, you have to buy your shares in the firm. I'd been saving for mine since the day I joined. But they offered me some of O'Halloran's shares after his were taken away. So…" He shrugged. "I had the money."

"But—"

"But nothing. It's yours, lover." Kevin put a finger under Tiernan's chin, drew him forward, and kissed him soundly.

Tiernan opened his eyes at the sound of a chuckle, and turned his head just enough to see a man he thought he recognized grinning at them. Thick brown hair, one pierced ear, a ready grin, and a truly impressive tat sleeve and a half, with a tight-fitting muscle tee hinting at more ink beneath. "Can I help you?"

The newcomer's grin widened. "Possibly. Just wanted a look at the rings."

Before Tiernan could react, Kevin was holding out his left hand for inspection, with a wink to the Fae. "Tiernan, this is Josh—he put me on to the jeweler who made our rings."

"Josh LaFontaine." After a quick look at the truesilver band, the newcomer put out a hand to Tiernan. "I own Raging Art-On, the tattoo and piercing parlor upstairs."

"Ah, that's where I've seen you." Tiernan took the offered hand. "It's good to finally meet." Up close, the man's arm tattoos were even more impressive, vibrant and intricate. "Do you do your own ink?"

"Most of it. I get a little help from a friend for the hard-to-reach spots."

"Tiernan's your new landlord, Josh," Kevin put in with a smile.

"He's—?"

"I'm—?"

"Oh, my God," Kevin murmured. Suddenly he was looking past both men, toward the dance floor. "You don't suppose…" He shook himself. "Excuse me, won't you? I need to go talk to someone."

Puzzled, Tiernan watched him walk away. His husband was heading for the outskirts of a group of onlookers watching one of the pole dancers. One couple stood hand in hand, gently teasing each other as they watched the dancer's gyrations, one bald and heavily muscled, the other with short gray hair and an athletic build. Both wore shorts, a nod to the unseasonable May heat, and the gray-haired man's gleaming prosthetic leg caught the flashing lights from the dance floor. Kevin approached them hesitantly, touched the gray-haired man's shoulder to get his attention.

"Landlord?"

Tiernan's attention snapped back to the man standing beside him. "It looks that way." He looked down at the leather case he still held balanced in one hand. "Yeah, this looks like the deed to the whole building. Shit." He shook his head. It made sense. If security was a concern -- and it sure as hell was -- then best to be able to lock down and ward the whole place. But, *hell*…

"Glad I made the time to come down here, then." Josh glanced at his watch. "But I have a client coming in for a piercing in five. Stop by when you get a chance, I'll show you my setup. And congratulations to you both. I thought Kevin was hot on his own, but damn, you two make a stunning couple." He laughed and clapped Tiernan on the arm, then turned and headed quickly up the stairs, taking them two at a time.

Tiernan turned back to the dance floor, but the crowd had shifted. Both Kevin and the other man were lost to view.

"G'féalaidh tú i do cónaí fada le céle, gan a marú a céle." May you live long together, and not kill one another.

The Fae's hand flashed to the knife he wasn't wearing, as he stepped back and turned toward the source of the words. "Fuck." His gaze went from wary to hostile in an instant. His hands clenched into fists. *This is impossible…*

"You're only taking congratulations from the humans?" Lips that seemed shaped into a permanent sensual pout curled up in a smirk. Pale green eyes laughed through a tangle of sandy curls. "Or was it the wish itself that offended you, your Grace?"

"You have ten seconds to tell me who you are and what the hell you're doing here." He had seen this face, this male, before, over one hundred and fifty years ago, flanking the Prince Royal as that worthy had stood over Tiernan's prone and chained body. He had been wearing the uniform of the Royal Defense then, of a rank low enough it had seemed odd to see him in Royal company. Now he wore a black spiked collar, black leather trousers, and the same fucking smirk. "After ten, you get to find out how good I've gotten at making bodies disappear."

The other male held up a hand. "*S'ocan.*" *Peace. Yeah, like hell.*

"I'm on your side, Noble. Name's Cuinn." Slowly, he lowered the hand, palm out and open.

"I have a side of one. Two, now." Tiernan's hand remained curled where his knife would have hung at his belt had he still been in the Realm. He glanced around, cautious of the small island of quiet around himself and the other Fae. "You aren't the other one, in case you're wondering."

Cuinn laughed. "You have no clue. But I can hardly fault you, as you weren't meant to have one." He hooked his thumbs in the waistband of his trousers, rocked back on his heels. "You also have no clue what a relief it is to see this shit finally starting to work out."

"Weren't meant? Meant by who? You still haven't told me what you're doing here, and you're considerably past ten."

The laugh was starting to grate on Tiernan's nerves. "The answers are the same, your Grace, at least in part. I'm Cuinn an Dearmad. Wisdom of the Forgotten, last of the Loremasters. And if there was any meaning done, we were and are the ones doing it."

"Wisdom, my ass." Tiernan snorted. "And the Loremasters all died in the Sundering."

"I could wish I had your ass." Cuinn shook his head. "But that's beside the point, and I'm spending magick like water here." The other Fae looked around the room, a long, slow, measuring look. "Just let me say this, your Grace. Guard this place well. You and your *scair-anam* are the first, but there are more coming, and they need this sanctuary."

"We're the *first*? What do you…"

"And on your life, don't let an unShared Fae touch the nexus. There aren't so many of our kind on this side that we can afford to lose even one."

Tiernan crossed his arms. "You *still* haven't told me—"

"Enough." The unnerving green eyes closed briefly, and suddenly activity surged around them again. Cuinn's gaze fixed on Tiernan's. "You'll see me again. When you need to. Which won't be when you want to."

"If I wanted an oracle, I'd buy a fucking Ouija board."

"You want an oracle?" Cuinn shrugged. "Your nephew Maelduin heads House Guaire. Moriath died birthing her brother's child."

Tiernan stared. "You can't know that. No one can cross back over the Pattern."

Cuinn rolled his eyes. "So I'm a good guesser. Or not. Your call." He made as if to turn away, then looked back. "The blessings of the Loremasters on you and your *scair-anam*, your Grace. Such as they are, and whether you want them or not. Because you're sure as hell going to need them."

And between one breath and the next, he was gone.

Dead birthing the child Lorcan put in her… my oath kept. And I avenged her death, while she still lived. He blinked. *Assuming I believe any of that.*

"Who was that?"

Tiernan twitched, startled, as Kevin spoke from beside him. His arm went out blindly, encircled his husband's waist, pulled him in. He closed his eyes, breathing in the scent of leather, Acqua di Gio, and his male. Everything that was good about his new life.

With his old one hot on its heels.

"News from home." He opened his eyes, letting himself get lost in his *lanan*'s dark ones. "Company's coming.

Following is the first chapter of Gale Force,
Book Two in the SoulShares Series
Gale Force

Chapter One

The Realm
June 24, 2012 (human reckoning)

Surely there was a way to explain this. *"Your Grace, I have certain moral objections to ending the world as our race knows it"*? Well, no… nice drama, but not strictly true, and it was those little inconsistencies that ended up coming back to bite you in the ass. "Yes, I could. No, I won't."

Liadan had begun to smile with Conall's first pronouncement, but her smile quickly faded. Liadan Mavelle was evidently not a Fae accustomed to hearing the word 'no.' Most Nobles weren't. When one could channel the element of one's Demesne, one got used to everyone—well, everyone who wasn't a Royal—dancing to one's tune. "Somehow, I don't think I heard that correctly."

Of course, if there was one thing a Noble of Air could be sure of doing, it was hearing correctly. Even a commoner such as himself could hardly claim to have missed anything the air might have brought to him. "Then allow me to repeat myself, your Grace." He bowed slightly, letting his mildness carry the weight of his sarcasm. "No."

"Perhaps you misunderstand. This is not a request."

Conall closed his eyes. Maybe the Noble would mistake it for a commoner's subservience. But it actually was discovering there was a point at which inane clichés gave him a headache. "I understand perfectly. But no vendetta is worth the cost of what you're asking me to do."

The Noble lady scoffed. "Cost? To the most powerful mage since the Loremasters? Don't make me laugh."

""I wouldn't dream of it." *Because it might break your face. And come to think of it... No, Conall. Don't go there. Bad Fae.* "Not to me, your Grace. To the Realm." Was it even worthwhile to try to make her understand? He'd given up hope of driving away the greedy, the righteous, and the merely curious; it was almost as if Fae were willfully blind to what the unchecked use of magick did to the world around them. Especially *his* magick.

But maybe this time... "Magick isn't infinite, your Grace.

Whether you channel the elements, as you and your fellow Nobles do, or play with the raw stuff of magick itself, after the manner of us common folk—"

Liadan snorted, a very unladylike sound. "There's nothing at all common about what you do, Conall Dary."

Conall plowed a hand through his hair, until the copper mane stuck out every which way. Maybe if he just looked a little more imposing, a little more impressive, his words and his observations would carry some weight. It didn't help that he'd stopped aging, physically, somewhere short of the mid—to late twenties, the norm for a Fae. He just didn't *look* like what he was, and even a people accustomed to looking youthful for centuries seemed disinclined to listen to him. Even when they could see perfectly well what he was capable of doing.

"Look, your Grace." He glanced around, then up; an apple tree shaded them from the late afternoon sun, blossoms and fruit of every color apples knew hanging just over their heads. He reached up and plucked a perfect golden orb from a low-hanging branch and held it out on his palm. "It's in the prime of life, wouldn't you say? And yet, in the course of things, it ages. Unlike, say, the luckless female who has her eye on your *bragan a lae*." Liadan's intense green eyes narrowed—well, perhaps 'toy of the day' hadn't been the best choice of words. "Your pardon, her eye on Lord Declan. Yet watch what happens, when I age this fruit, the way you ask me to age her."

Conall closed his eyes, cupping the apple in his palms. The barriers he had to keep between himself and his magick were formidable, in necessary proportion to his gift, and taking them down even for so small a thing as this was not something he did lightly, or easily. But if it worked, if he could make her understand, it would be worth it. He sighed, and breathed deeply, and reached within.

And the magick leaped up, as it always did. Swirled within and around him, ecstatically. It gloried in freedom, the way a caged bird did, once released. One of the definitions of magick—one of the best— was that it was the essence of wildness, of untameability. And though it lay quietly enough, stored in every living thing in the Realm, it was never meant to *remain* quiet. It was meant to be set free, channeled, by one with Conall Dary's gift.

Set free. And spent. Irrevocably. He focused, turning his will to the apple in his hand. He filled it with the torrent that poured through him, and shaped it with a whispered word, Air, sculpting power. Pictured the fruit softening, withering. Beginning to die.

"Yes." The Noble lady's voice was a hushed whisper, almost reverent. "Exactly that."

Conall's eyes snapped open. The apple was what he had expected, a mouldering heap of skin and slime that made his skin crawl. Dead petals brushed his skin as they fell from the branch over his head; he looked up and shuddered at the sight of the dull wood of the branch, the mottled fruit, the leaves hanging limply. This was what the branch looked like, with most of the magick sustaining it drawn from it by the demands of his channeling.

"Perfect." Liadan smiled, a very cat-in-cream expression. More a bird-in-cat, actually, anticipatorily sated. "Why would you be unable to do the same to a Fae?"

For a moment, all Conall could do was stare. "Don't you *see*?" He gestured sharply upward with a curt nod.

The female shrugged lazily. "It's a branch. It will recover eventually."

Conall's jaw muscles worked as his teeth ground together. "That's not the damned *point*." If he watched carefully, he might be able to see the power gradually suffusing the branch again, the leaves trembling as if in a breeze, the colors gradually intensifying, the apples filling out, flowers budding once again. But recovery would take time, and the branch would never be exactly as it had been. Everything in the Realm was formed of magick, and every use of magick drained it. Usually the drain was barely perceptible, even to the exquisitely honed senses of a Fae. But Conall Dary, the greatest mage since the Loremasters, left a swath of destruction in his wake every time he tapped his powers. Which left him with no choice but to lock them away, as often and as securely as he could.

"A fruit is meant to age and die. A Fae is not." He fought the urge to speak more slowly, more loudly; to act as if an Air Fae was unable to understand you was the worst insult imaginable. And he had a feeling he was going to need some insults left to fall back on, no sense wasting them all now. "As much power as it took to do this, it would take a thousand times more to age an immortal Fae."

"And you lack the power?" The Lady Liadan pouted, with all the sullen charm of a thwarted toddler. "I wouldn't have thought so, after all the tales I've heard about you. Do you save your powers for those who bed you, so they'll spread nothing but glowing reports?"

Conall's lip curled in a snarl. "Some of us have no need to enhance our abilities, your Grace." There was no way, of course, he was going to tell this supercilious twat he had never dared risk the magical power surge that overwhelmed every Fae during sex. Never dared so much as friendship, not since just after he came into his birthright of power, and learned in the hardest way possible the only thing anyone ever wanted from him was that power. Present company included. "And provoke me as much as you like, I'm not going to damage the very fabric of the Realm so you can have the satisfaction of the shrieks of a wrinkled, toothless courtesan!"

Liadan's hands balled into fists, catching up the pale blue silk of her gown. But her voice was calm, even cool. "You will do as I command, because I command it. You need no other reason, and you will not speculate as to mine." Her dark hair stirred in a wind that seemed to cling to her. "And you will not speak to me in this way."

"I will not waste my breath speaking to you at all." Conall turned on his heel. "As well speak to a stone, it has better chance of understanding."

Conall stopped short, without time for so much as a cry, as the air became solid in his lungs. Caught by surprise, choking, he clutched at his throat, struggled in vain to draw breath. His vision went white around the edges, and began to dance, stars exploding all around him. His chest heaved, without result; he fell to his knees. And in his panic, he reached within for magick. But he stopped. *No—not even to save my life, no—*

—something struck the back of his head, hard, and white went black.

***

There was something warm and wet under Conall's cheek. He looked up, and was seized with a wave of dizziness and nausea so severe that his head hit the floor hard. When it did, the warm wetness splashed; drops fell within his line of sight, and he saw that it was blood. His own, presumably.

What the hell...? He pushed himself up. Well, no, he didn't. His hands were chained behind his back, and the chains were burning him. He sucked in a breath, and damped down his magickal abilities with everything in him. The searing heat told him he was bound with truesilver; truesilver burned at the touch of magick, and chains forged from it burned more fiercely with every use of magickal power by or near the one chained. Unfortunately for him, unless he kept his own abilities under rigid control, he channeled enough magickal energy as a matter of course to burn his hands off at the wrists. Even the small trickle of magick it had taken, and was still taking, to heal the wound that had only just stopped trickling red down the back of his neck was raising blisters. Throw in the way his gut roiled every time he even thought about actively using magick, and no, he was most definitely disincentivized to use any kind of magick.

Where the hell was he? He managed to turn his head a little, and saw a curved gray stone wall limned in moonlight. A bare room, with a polished floor that reflected the moonlight like a flawless mirror.

No, not quite flawless. There was light within it, the faintest traces of it. Points, slivers, arcs. His vision blurred the traces at first; they almost seemed to dance, to shift. But slowly, as he focused, it came clear. Light, like the finest wire imaginable, set in a floor of midnight black, in a pattern of...

Bile rose in Conall's throat, burned at the back of his throat. Not *a* pattern. *The* Pattern. The bitch had stopped the air in his lungs, bashed him over the head with something—probably the tree branch he had so thoughtfully killed for her—and then, somehow, had

269

him truechained and dragged to the Pattern's portal, here to await the proper alignment of the moon to trigger its magick. Disposing of a witness? Or simply mortally offended by his refusal to tear a hole in the magickal essence of the Realm for the sake of her jealousy? If he had to guess, he'd go with the latter; the Lady Liadan didn't seem bright enough to be worrying about the former.

No amount of blithering was helping him ignore the deadly danger just below his face, or doing anything to relieve his growing panic. Gathering all his strength, he pushed against the floor with his legs, and rolled onto his back, away from the lethal gleaming black surface beneath him. Once his head stopped spinning, though, he saw the last confirmation of his suspicions, the round window set into the wall, the circle of the full moon nearly filling it. And when the window was full…

As he watched, shivering, a black shape passed between him and the moon's disk, wheeled, and passed again. A hunting night-hawk, by the look of it, and a *savac-dui*, a black-hooded hawk, his own House-guardian, by the piercing call carried to him by the wind. An Air Fae could understand any language carried by the air, and legend had it that there was a spark of Fae soul in every bird. They understood. Especially the predators, closest kin to a Fae. In their language that was not a language he heard:

fREE yOURSELF

He shook his head, despairing. Small wonder the hawk saw his predicament; nothing escaped the eyes of the night hunters. But as perceptive as it was, he dared not take its advice.

Not that he couldn't. The portal chamber was warded from within by the mightiest magicks of a score of scores of the ancient Loremasters—he could feel the wards, sense the intricacy and the sheer power of the channelings—but if any Fae since the Sundering had any chance at all to break through those wards, it was he.

But, as he had tried to tell Liadan, the cost was too great. Not to him—although he would surely lose his hands to the truesilver, channeling magick so intense. No, the loss of his hands paled beside the toll that would be taken by the magick itself. Magick strong enough to shatter the wards around this place would leave everything for hectares around blasted and devastated, never to recover. It could damage the Pattern itself—even destroy it.

tOO lATE

As the cry reached Conall's ears, the full moon filled the window. A cold light flooded in, and it was as if the floor fell away beneath him, the smooth, unyielding blackness giving way to the brilliant, cold tracing of the lines of the Pattern. A wind began to swirl around him, fierce, battering, and for one heart-stopping moment it seemed he hovered above the cruel edges. He looked down… down… it went on forever, there was no bottom; he hung suspended over nothing but the glittering wires. Panic was a metallic taste in his mouth, a sick fire in his veins. He *could* be free; the magick was surging in him, itself desperate, trying to get away from the yawning chasm below. All he had to do, it gibbered at him, was close his eyes, block out the stomach-twisting sight, and whisper a word. One word.

"No."

And on the word, all fury broke loose. The wind slammed him against the wall, wrenching his shoulders in their sockets; sucking the very air from his lungs, silencing him utterly. His own element, turned traitor.

And then the wind came for Conall Dary.

GLOSSARY

The following is a glossary of the *Faen* words and phrases found in *Hard as Stone*. The reader should be advised that, as in the Celtic languages descended from it, spelling in *Faen* is as highly eccentric as the one doing the spelling.

(A few quick pronunciation rules—bearing in mind that most Fae detest rules—single vowels are generally 'pure', as in ah, ey, ee, oh, oo for a, e, I o, u. An accent over a vowel means that vowel is held a little longer than its unaccented cousins. "ao" is generally "ee", but otherwise diphthongs are pretty much what you'd expect. Consonants are a pain. "ch" is hard, as in the modern Scottish "loch". "S", if preceded by "I" or "a", is usually "sh". "F" is usually silent, unless it's the first letter in a word, and if the word starts with "fh", then the "f" and the "h" are *both* silent. "Th" is likewise usually silent, as is "dh", although if "dh" is at the beginning of a word, it tries to choke on itself and ends up sounding something like a "strangled" French "r". Oh, and "mh" is "v", "bh" is "w", "c" is always hard, and don't forget to roll your "r"s!)

amad'n: fool, idiot

bodlag: limp dick (much greater insult than a human might suppose) *ceangal:* Royal soul-bonding ceremony in the Realm (common alt. spelling *ceangail*)

céle: general way of referring to two people
le céle: together (see phrases)
a céle: one another, each other (see phrases)

cónai: live (see phrases)

dre'fiur: beloved sister

dre'thair: beloved brother

Faen: the Fae language. *Laurm Faen*—I speak Fae.
as'Faein: in the Fae language. *Laur lom as'Faein*—I speak in the Fae language.

Gan: general negative—no, not, without, less

g'féalaidh: may you (pl.) live (see phrases)

fada: long (can reference time or distance)

lanan: lover. Tiernan's pillow name for Kevin, and vice versa

Marfach, the: the Slow Death. Deadliest foe of the Fae race.

Marú: kill (see phrases)

Minn: oath
mo mhinn: my oath (see phrases)

ollúnta: solemn (see phrases)

scair'anam: SoulShare (pl. *scair-anaim*)

sibh: you (pl.)

s'ocan: peace, be at peace

tseo: this, this is (see phrases)

uiscebai: strong liquor found in the Realm, similar to whiskey

veissin: knockout drug found in the Realm, causes headaches

Useful phrases:

tseo mo mhinn ollúnta.: This is my solemn oath.

G'féalaidh sibh i do cónai fada le céle, gan a marú a céle:
"May you live long together, and not kill one another." A Fae blessing, sometimes bestowed upon those Fae foolhardy enough to undertake some form of exclusive relationship. Definite "uh huh, good luck with that" overtones.

Other Riverdale Avenue Books You May Like:

The Siren and the Sword:
Book One of the Magic University Series
By Cecilia Tan

The Tower and the Tears:
Book Two of the Magic University Series
By Cecilia Tan

The Incubus and the Angel:
Book Three of the Magic University Series
By Cecilia Tan

Mordred and the King
By John Michael Curlovich

Collaring the Saber-Tooth:
Book One of the Masters of Cats Series
By Trinity Blacio

Dee's Hard Limits:
Book Two of the Masters of Cats Series
By Trinity Blacio

Caging the Bengal Tiger:
Book Three of the Masters of Cats Series
By Trinity Blacio

A Christmas Tail:
Book Four of the Masters of the Cats Series
By Trinity Blacio

A Venomoid:
Book One of the Night Code Saga
By J.A. Kossler

Made in the USA
Las Vegas, NV
14 February 2021